RHYTHM, MUSIC AND EDUCATION

BY

EMILE JAQUES-DALCROZE

TRANSLATED FROM THE FRENCH
BY HAROLD F. RUBINSTEIN

WITH AN INTRODUCTION
BY SIR W. H. HADOW
VICE-CHANCELLOR OF THE UNIVERSITY OF SHEFFIELD

LONDON
CHATTO & WINDUS
1921

PRINTED IN ENGLAND BY
WILLIAM CLOWES AND SONS, LIMITED,
LONDON AND BECCLES.

INTRODUCTION

The last twenty years have seen, especially in this country, a great advance in musical education. We have come to realise that music is not an outside accomplishment to be taught as an extra to more or less reluctant pupils, but that it is a real and essential part of our educational life, and that its value is not less than that of the study of literature. The appreciation of great music has an influence on mind and character which it is hardly possible to overestimate, and it is well that our educational systems are beginning to recognise this and to embody it in practice.

One of the most important factors in musical education is the training and development of the sense of Rhythm. There is little doubt that Rhythm is the earliest aspect of music which appeals to children. It is, through the whole of our life, the pulse by which the vitality of music can most readily be measured. In addition to this the practice of the right rhythmic movements has a twofold value in education—the purely physical value of training the muscles and improving the bodily health, and the æsthetic value of teaching self-expression in one of its most beautiful forms. The Greeks were fully aware of this, and in the principles of artistic education they are still our masters. There is no need, therefore, to introduce to English readers this translation of Monsieur Dalcroze's famous book. Every one knows how much he has done for the service of musical education; with what skill, devotion and insight he has laid down the principles of his art, and shown the way of carrying them into practice. He has done more than any man living for the study of rhythmic beauty, and in this work he not only explains his method but shows us how it can be carried on and developed.

W. H. HADOW.

November, 1920.

To my friend
ADOLPHE APPIA.

FOREWORD

TWENTY-FIVE years ago, I made my *début* in pedagogy as
Professor of Harmony at the Conservatoire of Geneva.
After the first few lessons, I noticed that the ears of
my pupils were not able to appreciate the chords which
they had to write, and I concluded that the flaw in the
conventional method of training is that pupils are not
given experience of chords at the beginning of their
studies—when brain and body are developing along parallel
lines, the one constantly communicating its impressions
and sensations to the other—but that this experience
is withheld until the time arrives to express the results
in writing. Accordingly I decided to precede my lessons
in written harmony by special exercises of a physiological
nature, aimed at developing the hearing faculties, and I
was not long in discovering that, while with older students
acoustic sensations were hindered by futile intellectual
preconceptions, children appreciated them quite spontaneously, proceeding in due course quite naturally to
their analysis.

I therefore set about training the ears of my pupils as
early as possible, and discovered thereby not only that the
hearing faculties develop with remarkable ease at a stage
when every new sensation delights the child, and stimulates
in him a joyful curiosity, but, in addition, that once the
ear is trained to the natural sequences of sounds and
chords, the mind no longer experiences the slightest
difficulty in accustoming itself to the various processes of
reading and writing.

Nevertheless, the musical progress of a certain number of pupils, whose ear developed at normal speed, appeared to me to be retarded by an incapacity to estimate with any exactitude variations of time and rhythmic grouping. The mind perceived the variations, but the vocal apparatus was unable to give effect to them. I came to the conclusion that the motive and dynamic element in music depends not only on the hearing, but also on another sense. This I took at first to be the sense of touch, seeing that metrical finger-exercises conduce unmistakably to the pupil's progress. Presently, however, a study of the reactions produced by piano-playing, in parts of the body other than the hands—movements with the feet, oscillations in the trunk and head, a swaying of the whole body, etc.—led me to the discovery that musical sensations of a rhythmic nature call for the muscular and nervous response of the *whole organism*. I set my pupils exercises in stepping and halting, and trained them to react physically to the perception of musical rhythms. That was the origin of my "Eurhythmics," and I was sanguine enough to believe that therewith my experimental labours were at an end, and that I might now proceed to construct a rational and definite system of musical education. I was speedily disillusioned. I soon discovered that, out of ten children, at most two reacted in a normal manner ; that the motor-tactile consciousness, the combination of the senses of space and movement, exist in a pure state as rarely as the perfect sense of hearing that musicians call "absolute pitch." I saw the lack of musical rhythm to be the result of a general "a-rhythm," whose cure appeared to depend on a special training designed to regulate nervous reactions and effect a co-ordination of muscles and nerves ; in short, to harmonise mind and body. And so I came to regard musical perception which is entirely auditive as incomplete, and to seek the connection between instincts for pitch and movement, harmonies of tone and time-periods, time and energy, dynamics and space, music and character, music and temperament, finally the art of music and the art of dancing.

The story of my researches, my gropings and failures, as of my definite achievements, may be found in the various chapters of the present volume. In chronological order, these chapters record my ideas as developed from 1897 to the present day in lectures and articles.* The reader will find in the earlier parts of the book a certain number of contradictions, and, in the latter, some repetition of views expressed previously in a different form ; but it seems to me that this series of transformations and developments out of an original general principle may be of interest to pedagogues and psychologists : that is why I discarded my original intention of recasting all the articles according to a definite plan, and on a principle of unity. It may perhaps be of advantage to educationists to have the opportunity of following my progress through all its stages, of which the few secondary and higher schools, already launched on the voyage, have as yet only traversed the first. They will bear in mind that the idea underlying the conception and construction of my whole system is that the education of to-morrow must, before all else, teach children to know themselves, to measure their intellectual and physical capacities by judicious comparison with the efforts of their predecessors, and to submit them to exercises enabling them to utilise their powers, to attain due balance, and thereby to adapt themselves to the necessities of their individual and collective existence.

It is not enough to give children and young people a

* Certain of the last chapters have not previously appeared in print. The remainder were published (some in part only) in the *Tribune de Genève*, the *Semaine Littéraire*, the *Mercure de France*, the *Monde Musical*, the *Courrier Musical*, the *Ménestrel*, and the *Grande Revue*. Finally, certain of them have appeared, in an abbreviated form, in reports of pedagogic proceedings, such as that issued by the Association of Swiss Musicians on the " Reform of Teaching in Schools."

general tuition founded exclusively on the knowledge of our forbears' activities. Teachers should aim at furnishing them with the means both of living their own lives and of harmonising these with the lives of others. The education of to-morrow must embrace reconstruction, preparation, and adaptation : aiming, on the one hand, at the re-education of the nervous faculties and the attainment of mental calm and concentration, and, on the other, at the equipment for whatever enterprise practical necessity may dictate, and at the power to react without effort ; in short, at the provision of a maximum force with a minimum of strain and resistance.

More than ever in these times of social reconstruction, the human race demands the re-education of the individual. There has been endless discussion as to the inevitable effects on the social and artistic atmosphere of the future of the present unsettled state, in which it is impossible to look ahead and prescribe the necessary measures for the safeguarding of our civilisation and our culture. In my judgment, all our efforts should be directed to training our children to become conscious of their personalities, to develop their temperaments, and to liberate their particular rhythms of individual life from every trammelling influence. More than ever they should be enlightened as to the relations existing between soul and mind, between the conscious and the subconscious, between imagination and the processes of action. Thoughts should be brought into immediate contact with behaviour—the new education aiming at regulating the interaction between our nervous and our intellectual forces. Fresh from the trenches, soldiers should be able to continue the struggle in a new guise ; and in the schools our teachers, likewise, should be on the alert to combat weakness of will and lack of confidence, and to train the fresh generations by every possible means to fight for self-mastery and the power to place themselves, fully equipped, at the service of the human race.

In matters of art, I foresee that individual efforts will
continue to attract a certain public; but I believe that
a new demand for collective unity will drive numerous
persons, formerly estranged from art, into association for
the expression of their common spirit. And from that
a new art will emerge, compound of, a multitude of
aspirations, of different degrees of strength, but unanimous
in the quest of an ideal and common outlet for emotion.
This will lead to the call for a psycho-physical training
based on the cult of natural rhythms, and which, guided
by the collective will—working, maybe, subconsciously—
will fill an increasingly important part in civilised life. In
the theatre we shall be shown dramas, in which the People
will play the principal rôle, emerging as an entity, instead
of a mere conglomeration of supers. We shall then find
that all our current ideas on play-producing have been
formed out of regard for the individual, instead of from
a recognition of the resources of a crowd in action. We
shall feel the need for a new technique in the grouping of
crowds—such as the brilliant efforts of Gémier and
Granville Barker have not completely attained on the
stage. Only an intimate understanding of the synergies
and conflicting forces of our bodies can provide the clue
to this future art of expressing emotion through a crowd ;
while music will achieve the miracle of guiding the latter's
movements—grouping, separating, rousing, depressing, in
short, "orchestrating" it, according to the dictates of
natural eurhythmics. The development of the emotions
will enable it to give collective expression to them, though
at considerable sacrifice to the individual. New forms of
music will come to birth, having the power of animating
masses of people, training them in the many processes
of counterpointing, phrasing, and shading musical rhythms
with a view to their plastic expression. All attempts at
reviving the dance have hitherto proved inadequate. A
new art of dancing will accompany the new music, both
alike inspired by an understanding of the innumerable

resources of the human body, allied to the spiritual essence, idealism, and sense of form that alone can give solidity to any art inspired by the imperative dynamic and agogic demands of the ever-fluctuating human temperament.

I leave for treatment in some of the following chapters my observations on the manifold ways of corporal interpretation of the lines of musical sound. My desire, in this foreword, is to record my deep and fervent conviction that, now the War is over, the coming generation will experience this need of forming groups for the expression of common emotion, and that a new art will be called into being, created spontaneously by all those who regard music as a magnificent and potent agent for the inspiration and refinement of human gesture—and this latter as a pre-eminently "musical" emanation of our desires and aspirations.

E. JAQUES-DALCROZE.

GENEVA,
August, 1919

CHAPTER		PAGE
I.	THE PLACE OF EAR-TRAINING IN MUSICAL EDUCATION (1898)	I
II.	AN ESSAY IN THE REFORM OF MUSIC TEACHING IN SCHOOLS (1905)	8
III.	"THE YOUNG LADY OF THE CONSERVATOIRE AND THE PIANO" (1905)	46
IV.	THE INITIATION INTO RHYTHM (1907)	59
V.	MUSIC AND THE CHILD (1912)	71
VI.	RHYTHMIC MOVEMENT, SOLFÈGE, AND IMPROVISATION (1914)	87
VII.	EURHYTHMICS AND MUSICAL COMPOSITION (1915)	110
VIII.	MUSIC, JOY, AND THE SCHOOL (1915)	125
IX.	RHYTHM AND CREATIVE IMAGINATION (1916)	138
X.	RHYTHM AND GESTURE IN MUSIC DRAMA—AND CRITICISM (1910–1916)	149
XI.	HOW TO REVIVE DANCING (1912)	175
XII.	EURHYTHMICS AND MOVING PLASTIC (1919)	195
XIII.	MUSIC AND THE DANCER (1918)	221
XIV.	RHYTHM, TIME, AND TEMPERAMENT (1919)	236
	MUSICAL SUPPLEMENT	259

NOTE TO THE ENGLISH EDITION

THE duty of arranging for this edition of " Le Rythme la Musique et l'Éducation " fell to me as representing Monsieur Jaques-Dalcroze in this country. It was his desire that I should myself undertake the work, but press of other duties made this impossible. I was, however, happy in securing the services of Mr. Harold Rubinstein.

To make a translation that shall represent the thought of the original accurately and in detail, and yet be free from blemishes of style, is no light task ; the reader who is conversant with the original French will agree that Mr. Rubinstein has been successful to an unusual degree.

Acknowledgment is made to Mr. Ernest Read of the Royal Academy of Music for generous help given me in revising the technical passages of the text, and to him and many colleagues and students who have shared the work of proof-reading.

A word should be said in regard to the illustrations, reproduced from photographs by Monsieur Boissonas of Geneva. They are not in the original, and are not referred to in the text, but are included as being of general interest to the reader.

PERCY B. INGHAM.

THE LONDON SCHOOL OF DALCROZE EURHYTHMICS,
   23 STORE STREET, W.C. 1,

November, 1920.

LIST OF ILLUSTRATIONS

TO FACE PAGE

PORTRAIT OF E. JAQUES-DALCROZE   *Frontispiece*

TWO SCENES FROM *LES SOUVENIRS*   74

CRESCENDO OF MOVEMENT   126

SCÈNE FROM *LES SOUVENIRS* (1)   154

SCENE FROM *LES SOUVENIRS* (2)   170

SCENE FROM *LES SOUVENIRS* (3)   172

A PLASTIC EXERCISE   195

A PLASTIC EXERCISE   198

STUDY IN LEAPING (1)   206

STUDY IN LEAPING (2)   208

GROUP EXERCISES   214

SCENE FROM GENEVA FESTIVAL   219

RHYTHM, MUSIC, AND EDUCATION

I

THE PLACE OF EAR TRAINING IN MUSICAL EDUCATION (1898)

The absurdity of studying harmony without the previous acquirement and practice of inner hearing—Necessity of cultivating hearing faculties of harmony students—Character of exercises designed to educate the ear—Dangers of specialised studies, particularly in pianoforte, not accompanied by general studies—The place of motor-tactile faculties in musical education—Summary of special exercises for the adjustment and development of temperament.

ONE of the favourite precepts of professors of harmony is that you must never make use of the piano to work out or take note of successions of chords. Faithful to tradition, I proceeded to enforce this maxim on my classes, until confronted by a student who naively protested: "But, please, sir, why mayn't I use the piano? How am I to hear anything otherwise?" In that moment light descended on me. I saw that any rule not forged by necessity and from direct observation of nature, must be arbitrary and false, and that the prohibition of the use of the piano was meaningless when addressed to young people lacking the capacity of *inner hearing*. The sense of touch may, to a certain degree and in particular cases, replace that of hearing, and I have known composers with incomplete hearing faculties who have yet contrived to produce interesting

B

work composed, as they say, " at the piano." Obviously their studies of harmony have involved the neglect of its supreme law—it being impossible to conceive a true sequence of chords without an inner ear to realise the sound in anticipation.   One thing or the other : Those who have no ear must compose at the piano, those who have an ear must compose without the piano.   The teacher should, therefore, regard it as his duty, in imposing on his pupils the learning of harmonies without recourse to an instrument, to create in them a sense of musical pitch, and to develop their feeling for melody key, and harmony, by means of special exercises.   Do such exercises exist ?   And, if they do, are they taught in our music-schools ?   These were the questions I put to myself, and sought to answer by researches in public libraries, and a study of the prospectuses and time-tables of the colleges of music.   The reply was forced from me—" *No ; exercises for the development of the aural faculties of musicians do not exist, and no single college of music concerns itself with the part played by these faculties in musical training !* "

Let me make myself quite clear : undoubtedly there exist numbers of books in which may be found exercises in reading, transposition, notation, and even vocal improvisation.   But all these may be achieved without the aid of the ear : reading and improvisation through the muscular, transposition and notation through the visual senses.   None of these exercises aim at training the ear, and yet it is through the latter alone that tonal effects are registered in our minds.   Is it not folly to teach music without paying the slightest attention to the diversification, gradation, and combination, in all their shades, of the gamut of sensations called into play by the consonance of musical feeling ?   How has it been possible to carry on a systematic study of music, while utterly ignoring the principal qualification of the musician ?

I therefore set about devising exercises to enable my pupils to recognise the pitch of sounds, estimate intervals, apprehend harmonies, distinguish the different notes in chords, follow the contrapuntal effects in polyphonic music, distinguish keys, analyse the relations between hearing and vocal sensations, sensitise the ear, and—by means of a new system of gymnastics applied to the nervous system—open up between brain, ear, and larynx the necessary channels to form of the entire organism what one might call the *inner ear*. . . . And I assumed, in my innocence, that, having invented these exercises, nothing remained but to apply them in special classes. . . .

Alas! the difficulties I had met with in devising my scheme for the development of the ear were nothing to those that now faced me in my endeavour to introduce the system. Let me recall the weighty objections marshalled against me. The true musician (it was said) should possess, as it were, instinctively, the necessary qualifications for the practice of his art, and no amount of study could supply gifts that must come naturally or not at all : the student's time being strictly limited, it was undesirable to embarrass him with additional labours tending to distract his absorption in finger exercises : his instrumental studies were already adequate to his musical needs, etc., etc. . . . Some of these arguments are sound enough in their place. It is evident that a person should not attempt the serious study of music without particular gifts for the purpose, including an aptitude for distinguishing sounds, and, needless to say, a certain sensibility of nerves and elevation of feeling, without which no musician can pass muster. Apart from that, however, the fact that instrumental classes are filled with individuals unable either to hear or to listen to music, justifies us in asserting that even the conservatoires admit that it is possible to learn to sing and play the piano without being a born musician. Why, then, confine ourselves to training the fingers of these pupils ? Why not try to cultivate their aural perception ?

As regards naturally-good musicians who devote themselves to the study of composition or orchestral conducting, may one not claim that daily exercises in distinguishing degrees of intensity and pitch of sounds, sense-analyses of tones and their combinations, polyphonies and harmonies, in every key, might conceivably render their ear even *more* sensitive, their musical susceptibilities even *more* delicate ? Apart from that, I maintain that in the study of harmony proper (even in classes such as those of the Paris Conservatoire, where only students possessing absolute pitch are admitted) sufficient attention is not devoted to the determination and analysis of the relations undoubtedly existing between sound and dynamics, between pitch and accentuation, between the varying tempi of musical rhythms and the choice of harmonies. The music courses are too fragmentary and specialised : those relating to the piano are not collated with those in harmony, nor harmony with those treating of the history of music, nor is the history of music duly applied to a study of the general history of peoples and individuals. Syllabuses are profuse in their subject matter, but there is no coherence in the tuition. Each professor is confined to his own narrow domain, having practically no contact with those of his colleagues who specialise in other branches of musical science. And yet, as all music is grounded in human emotion on the one hand, in the æsthetic research after combinations of sound on the other, the study of sound and movement should be collated and harmonised, and no one branch of music should be separable from the others.

Style in music varies according to climate and latitude, and, by corollary, according as temperaments are influenced and modified by social atmosphere and conditions of life. The divergencies of harmony and movement ·

which characterise the music of different peoples spring, then, from the nervous and muscular state of their organisms, apart altogether from their divers hearing faculties. Ought we not therefore to devote more attention, in teaching music, to the motor faculties of the pupils, to that *ensemble* of reactions, impulses, pauses, recoils, and movements, whether spontaneous or deliberate, that constitute temperament ? I have often been struck at observing the difficulty small children have in following, while marching, a very slow movement in music, in halting or stepping out suddenly at command, in relaxing their limbs after an anxious moment, in taking their bearings and following each other's movements on being taught the gestures to accompany a song. What wonder, considering the time that must be lost between the volition and the realisation of their movements, that in practising a song their little larynxes should be unskilled, their vocal chords inflexible and inexact, their breathing ill-regulated, to say nothing of their attempts to punctuate and measure the time, and to emit each note at the right moment ! Not only, then, should the ear and voice of the child receive adequate training, but, in addition, every part of his body which contributes to rhythmic movement, every muscular and nervous element that vibrates, contracts, and relaxes under the pressure of natural impulses. Should it not be possible to create new reflexes, to undertake a systematic education of nerve-centres, to subdue the activities of too excitable temperaments, to regulate and harmonise muscular synergies and conflicts, to establish more direct communications between the feeling and understanding, between sensations which inform the mind and those which re-create sensorial means of expression ? Every thought is the interpretation of an action. If, up to the present, muscular movements of hand and fingers alone have sufficed to create in the spirit a distinct consciousness of rhythm, what far more intense impressions might we not convey were we to make use of the whole organism in producing the effects necessary for the evocation of the motor-tactile consciousness ? I look forward to a system of musical education in which the body itself shall play the rôle of intermediary between sounds and thought, becoming in time the direct medium of our feelings— aural sensations being reinforced by all those called into being by the multiple agents of vibration and resonance lying dormant in our bodies ; the breathing system punctuating the rhythms of words, muscular dynamics interpreting those dictated by musical emotions. The child will thus be taught at school not only to sing, listen carefully, and keep time, but also to *move* and think accurately and rhythmically. One might commence by regulating the mechanism of walking, and from thence proceed to ally vocal movements with the gestures of the whole body. That would constitute at once instruction *in* rhythm, and education *by* rhythm.

Alas ! when I consider the enormous pains I am at to persuade music teachers of the possibility of contriving exercises to enable children to *listen to* sounds before executing or writing them, to evoke the thought of a note before its interpretation, I ask myself whether this training of nerve centres will ever enter the realm of practical politics. People will have nothing to do with new ideas so long as the old contribute to their self-satisfaction, and once they have acquired the habit of accepting them at their face value. Every step towards emancipation to which they have condescended appears to them immutable and definitive, and the truth of to-morrow is denounced as a lie to-day. And yet human thought develops, little by little, despite all resistance ; our ideas clarify, our powers of quick decision strengthen, our means of action increase. Who knows but that a day will dawn when professors the world over will recognise the possibility of adding to the divers modes of stimulating sensibility, by processes of adaptation, variation, and substitution, and music teachers will depend less exclusively on analysis, and more on the awakening of vital emotions and the consciousness of mental states? On that day will emerge on all sides new methods, based on the cultivation of combined hearing and tactile sensations, and mine will be the silent gratification accorded those who, in moments of oppression, have yet been able to murmur the eternal : "*E pur si muove !*"

II

AN ESSAY IN THE REFORM OF MUSIC TEACHING IN SCHOOLS (1905)

Music regarded in the schools of to-day as of minor importance—Cult of singing in the colleges of music of the 16th and 17th centuries—Objections of reactionaries—Music should be taught only by musicians—What must be exacted of students—Futility of a musical education that does not inculcate love of music in children—Necessity of gradually eliminating those who have no musical gifts, and forming special classes for children with inaccurate ears and voices or lacking in adequate rhythmic capacity—Syllabus of courses and classification of capacity in children—How to develop "relative" pitch—Keys and scales—Exercises necessary to develop sense of rhythm—The step and the beat—Musical shading and improvisation.

IT is not enough for a select few of the artists and amateurs of a country to be better instructed than their predecessors for the musical standard of that country to be raised and maintained. If the masses are not capable of following—even at a distance—in the steps of that select few, an impassable barrier will sooner or later be erected between the two elements of a people that in these days must unite if they are to co-exist. If the intellectual aristocracy alone is equipped for progress, the ill-trained masses will be unable to follow ; the leaders of the movement—finding themselves isolated, and needing the co-operation of the main body—will be obliged either to turn back and rejoin them, or, continuing their solitary course, be lost in obscurity. I shall be told that it is the fate of reformers to pursue the path of enlightenment in solitude, and that the masses always overtake them in the end ! . . . The masses will not overtake them unless given the necessary equipment and unless

8

sufficiently keen and courageous to traverse, without relaxing, every step of the course. The educational methods of the last centuries are certainly not calculated to enable our children to comprehend and assimilate modern artistic developments. Our artists have forged new implements of creation ; these implements must be adjusted to the hands of amateurs, who must then be trained to handle them, and finally entrusted with them at an age when they are most ripe for 'prentice work, when their hands are flexible and easily adapted to new methods, before the fire of ambition has been snuffed out by disappointment and world-weariness, or before they have acquired the habit of doing things in the old way and are thus prevented from successfully coping with the new. . . . Obviously, no evolution, no progress can be accomplished without the co-operation of youth. It is in virgin souls that new ideas take firmest root. "Bend the green twig as you will," runs an old Persian proverb, "only fire can straighten it out again ; but you want a mallet to drive a pile." The earlier we instil tastes and convictions in a man, the more sure we may be of their durability and solidity. We should regard the child as the man of to-morrow.

The progress of a people depends on the education given to its children.

If it is desired that musical taste shall not remain the prerogative of the cultured few, but shall penetrate the real heart of the whole people, I repeat that a genuine musical education—like the teaching of science and morals—should be provided at school.

It is evident that religion has ceased to inspire our teachers to preserve for musical studies the place they formerly occupied in the general educational scheme. Many good people find themselves wondering why the schools continue to teach singing at all, since no opportunity is given the children of displaying their attainments either in the churches, on secular holidays, in their recreation, or as a rhythmic assistant and complement to their courses of gymnastics.

These good people, who point out that the teaching of music to-day serves neither a practical nor an ethical aim—but ministers merely to the annual delectation of school inspectors—have every excuse for losing interest in musical studies, and regarding them as of no importance. But if they would take the trouble to reflect upon the matter, they would recognise that these studies could and should be given a very definite, practical, and ethical aim, and thenceforward they would do their utmost to encourage and stimulate their development.

Private music lessons are virtually confined to the children of well-to-do families, whose parents are actuated generally either by snobbishness or by respect for tradition. The music master, for whom such lessons provide a livelihood, can hardly be expected to reject a pupil who shows no aptitude for the work. For the same reason, none of our amateur conservatoires will turn a pupil away, be he deaf or idiot. This has the deplorable result of investing a multitude of musical dunces, steeped in affectation, with a reputation for talent—most people being unfortunately under the impression that they have only to take lessons in order to know something, and that, having "gone in for" a particular subject, they must necessarily understand it. And there is the other side of the picture. While the affluence of some parents enables them to provide a musical education for children utterly unfitted for it—to the serious detriment of the art—poverty alone deters other parents, to its even greater detriment, from making similar provisions for their genuinely talented children. Making music a compulsory school subject is the only sure means of mobilising the vital musical forces of a country. Were it undertaken in the right spirit, efficiently organised, and confided to intelligent and competent teachers, every child would at the end of two or three years be put to the test : those who showed talent being enabled to continue their studies to the point of attaining the maximum development of their faculties, the remainder, those devoid of all musical taste, being relieved from the burden of lessons of no value to them, and thereby conferring an almost equal benefit on the art, in being debarred from meddling with it, and clogging its progress by ridiculous pretensions. The coach, in La Fontaine's fable, would probably never have arrived at its destination had the pretentious fly been joined by others ; a swarm of them, with their buzzing and erratic aerial manœuvres, would have exasperated the coachman and distracted the horses. . . . Heaven preserve us from our musical flies !

"Talent," said Montesquieu, "is a gift confided to us by God in secret, and which we display without knowing it." If every child were compelled by law to pass an examination conducted by artists, and to subject himself for a few years to competent control, no single promising recruit would be allowed to pass into obscurity, neither would the hopelessly unmusical evade detection and its logical consequences.

The classification of capacities and incapacities once established—the former receiving due encouragement, the latter rendered comparatively innocuous—the teaching of music could obviously be practised on a more effectual basis. The results would now depend on two important factors, with which we shall deal presently at greater length : the method of teaching, and the choice of teachers. Once our educational authorities realise their responsibilities and set about providing a sound primary musical grounding for every moderately gifted child, and a more thorough training for every exceptionally talented one, not only will they have introduced into school life a new element of vitality, recreation, joy, and health, not only will they have recruited to the ranks of art a large number of adepts whose later co-operation must prove invaluable (assuring and strengthening the existing choral societies, and encouraging the formation of orchestras composed entirely of local talent), but they will also have assembled for future purposes a host of embryonic teachers, of proved learning and appreciable talents, and—still more important—*au courant* with the latest methods of instruction.

These advantages should satisfy the most sceptical as to the desirability of reforming the system of musical education in vogue to-day, even though our motives have no longer the religious and traditional character that actuated our ancestors in the sixteenth and seventeenth centuries in their zest for musical erudition. In those days music was studied with a view to adequate participation in the musical side of religious ceremonies. The acquirement of musical taste was accordingly a result of studies undertaken for this definite purpose. To-day, when religious ardour has manifestly ceased to inspire all but the most primitive vocal efforts, it behoves us to inquire whether the retention of any form of musical tuition in the curriculum of our schools is not a mere survival of routine, and, if so, whether it is not time we replaced this tradition (now that its original meaning has disappeared) by a more vital incentive to progress. Whether this take the form of a desire to strengthen musical taste and to prepare for the study of classical and modern masterpieces, or for hygienic considerations, is not (for the moment) material. The essential thing is that we should know exactly why we are to retain music in our current curriculum. We can later—assuming we are satisfied as to the public utility of such retention— proceed to inquire as to whether this generation is in advance of the preceding ones. Should it appear that absolutely no progress has been made, it is our business to ascertain the cause of this *status quo*, and thence set about devising means for securing a better record for the coming generation. The progress of the man is

one of the results of his preoccupations as a child.
Sound ideas instilled in the schoolroom are transformed
later into deeds, provided that cognisance of their means
of accomplishment is accompanied by an estimate of the
effort necessary for the purpose, and by a genuine love of
the art, in whose cause the effort is to be made. By this
means alone can we make sure of our country keeping
pace with the times, of our choral societies facing the
future instead of burrowing in the traditions of the past,
and of virtuosity becoming a mere means of expression,
instead of the whole end of musical training. By this
means alone can we tempt beauty to our firesides and
fill the void caused by the decline of religion. Our pro-
fessionals, better supported and understood by amateurs,
will no longer seek conquests in other lands, preferring
to remain in the country which they best understand,
and of which consequently they can best sing the
beauties.

The time will return when the People will express in
melody its simple joys and griefs. Children, having
re-learnt to sing in unison the old songs that charmed
their forefathers, will feel inspired to create new ones,
and we shall see the end of that lamentable division
of singing at our music competitions into two parts :
folk-songs and artistic songs.

* * * * *

It goes without saying that, if, after due reflection,
the principle of teaching music in schools at all is con-
demned, a consideration of the suggestions that follow
will be so much waste of time. If, on the other hand,
the necessity of music study is granted. . . . But
there ! . . . At this very moment, as I prepare to
marshal my facts and extract the logical conclusions,
a sense of disquiet steals over me, forcing me to ask
whether it is, after all, worth while to affirm and reaffirm
what is, only to be faced with the imperative and urgent
task, alike of musicians and patriots, of clamouring in

season and out of season for what *ought to be*, demanding as of right, a thorough overhauling of our educational system and resolved, in its cause, to devote whatever necessary time . . . But at these words I seem to see emerging from their tombs the grinning skulls of a myriad reformers of the past. "The necessary time," repeat their mocking voices out of graves where lie buried so many old bodies with so many young hopes : "Have you any idea, poor mortal, of the incalculable hours, days, years involved in your 'necessary time'? The time occupied by countless authorities in 'giving the matter their attention,' by committees in discussing it, by fools in failing to understand it, by fanatics in opposing it, by *arrivistes* in making promises, by the same worthies, *after* arrival, in forgetting them ! Your 'necessary time' will extend far beyond the remaining years of your life, and, at your death, be sure all your fine schemes for reform will be buried with you, as were ours with us ! Cut your coat according to your cloth ; nobody will ever obtain a really radical reform. Limit your demands to a minimum : possibly this 'minimum' will be accorded after a long and persistent campaign— but don't make the mistake of asking for too much, or you will get nothing at all. . . . Only discouragement and disappointment lie in wait for those who seek the good of other people at the expense of the smug self-satisfaction of the Powers That Be. Live happy, thinking only of yourself, and satisfied with things as they are, since the rest of the world accepts them ! "

But—strange phenomenon—these words, instead of damping our ardour, only reawaken and renew it ! Is it so certain that *every* new idea is received with this universal indifference ? Is not such an idea well within the realm of practical politics, provided it arrives at the right moment ? And is not this moment, in our case, actually imminent, now when so many artists, hitherto isolated, are coming together in response to a yearning for mutual love and understanding, for *esprit de corps*, in the common cause of progress and the pursuit of beauty ? Yes, the hour has struck when, by the coalescence of individual efforts, the ideals of our reformers the world over will be attained. And as for the "necessary time" for their attainment, we will face it with unabated confidence, marching ever forward side by side, our eyes fixed on one goal, our hearts beating with a common fervour.*

* * * * *

The teaching of music in our schools fails to produce anything like adequate results, because our educational authorities leave the whole control of the tuition in the hands of stereotyped inspectors. As these are nominated by pure routine, and no attention or encouragement is given to the initiative of any official who may feel tempted to deviate from the beaten track, the consequence is that no innovation of principle or practice has found its way into the curriculum from time immemorial. The theories of Pestalozzi and Froebel on the musical training of young children have been adopted only by private schools. The highly original educational experiments of Kaubert, about the year 1850, received absolutely no recognition in high quarters. The value of Swedish drill was only appreciated after a campaign extending over fifteen years. The brilliant system of analysing and explaining musical rhythm and expression advocated by Mathis Lussy, our compatriot, and one of the greatest of modern theorists, has not up to the present attracted the attention of our educational authorities. Not that this is so remarkable, seeing that, so far as I am aware (I can only pray that I am not mistaken !) music is absolutely unrepresented on our public bodies,

* The Board of Education of the canton of Geneva has just introduced eurhythmics as an experiment in three classes of primary schools, and, as an optional course, in two classes of the Girls' High School (1919).

nor have these latter ever manifested the slightest disposition to confer with professional musicians.* I say I can only pray that I am not mistaken, and that by some chance some stray musician has not, in this or that canton, been summoned to take an active or consultative part in the official school-board proceedings, for we should have to conclude, from the actual condition of things, that his influence had been absolutely *nil!* It is preferable to believe that the failure of our public bodies to assure a development of musical studies compatible with the means and powers at their disposal, is not deliberate. "Not deliberate"—that is to say, the result merely of taking no interest in the question, and of never suspecting its importance.

Music, outside of genuine artistic circles, is held in very light repute not only by our educational authorities, but even by painters, sculptors, and men of letters; and it is by no means unusual to find journalists, otherwise full of zeal for the artistic development of their country, treating music as a negligible quantity, and greeting musical events, either with the smiling indulgence of the condescending patron, or with an equally insufferable affectation of superiority, explicable only in the light of their abysmal ignorance of the art. One would have thought that this same neglect and disdain was hardly likely to be met with in France, where at least a smattering of music forms part of the indispensable equipment of the *littérateur*; but, alas, this smattering usually remains a smattering And if, to her credit, we can record with envy the introduction into French schools of the highly interesting collection of chansons of Maurice Bouchor, we cannot lose sight of the fact that the system of musical education generally in vogue with our Gallic neighbours

* The Board of Education for the cantons of Geneva and Vaud have recently appointed a commission of musicians to reorganise musical instruction in our schools. On their proceedings depend all our hopes of a real reform (1919).

is even more rudimentary than our own, as witness—among other things—the lamentable decline of part-singing in France, the shameful dearth of musical societies, the popularity of the gutter songs of the café-chantant, and the extinction of the oratorio. In German schools the reign of pedantry is everywhere in full force, and the suggestive counsels of eminent specialists like Karl Storck have not yet attracted the notice of scholastic authorities. What is worse, the Froebel schools have fallen into a state of decay. Only Belgium and Holland appear fully to appreciate the importance of a sound and well-organised pedagogic system.

And yet our country is among those whose scholastic institutions command almost universal admiration, thanks to their excellent organisation generally, and to the enterprise and enlightenment of most of our boards of education. How, then, does it come about that only the teaching of music—and of artistic matters in general—should be neglected and abandoned to routine ? The answer is that our scholastic authorities have no understanding of music, and no ambition to acquire one. I shall be told that it is manifestly unnecessary for a geographical expert to be represented on a school board to secure an adequate teaching of geography. Granted ; but only because no member of such a board would be found incapable of realising the value of geography and the importance of obtaining competent instructors in the science. For this purpose he only requires to have received himself a general all-round education, to have a sound judgment, good hearing, and . . . to be able to read. The same applies to other subjects of special training, such as gymnastics. . . . There again, it is not necessary to be an expert to recognise its utility and advocate its extension. Indeed, the arguments in favour of the training and hygiene of the body are furnished by the body itself. And the practical means of developing the flexibility, and securing the balance, of limbs are easy enough to grasp; for that, again, it is sufficient to be able to read intelligently. But music is another matter altogether. Those who have gone through life with an untrained ear cannot be expected to appreciate the necessity of furnishing others with an ear attuned to fine perceptions by the diligent practice of special exercises. Those who themselves cannot distinguish either melodies or harmonies are hardly the best advocates of a system designed to secure these accomplishments for others. And, while they may accept it out of respect for tradition, they will be unable either to select the best method for training the ear, and rendering it capable of analysing the relations and combinations of sounds, or to appreciate the merits of the experts to whom they may delegate the responsibility of selecting such a method. The spirit of music expresses itself in a language of its own, which our scholastic authorities are unable to read. And, unfortunately, they will not allow others to read for them. And yet with them rests the exclusive right of nominating teachers and deciding on methods. . . . That is why music has no share in the general prosperity of our educational system. That is why children learn neither to read, phrase, record, or emit sounds in our schools. That is why our sons and daughters grow up dumb.

"But look here," protests Mr. So-and-So (a familiar and ubiquitous type), "there is surely no need to have a competent general direction to make the teaching effective. At that rate, you would want singing lessons given in our schools by specialists. And yet, as things are, quite ordinary masters produce the happiest results."

. "I am not denying, Mr. So-and-So, that there *are* good masters in our schools; but there are also bad ones, and this would not be the case—or it would hardly ever be—if we had a competent and well-informed direction, and if the training of teachers were more complete so far as music is concerned. Bad teachers must produce bad pupils. If you take the average of those who are successful at examinations, you may be sure that it is far smaller than it would have been if all the teachers had been well chosen. And that, bear in mind, is the principal count in my indictment. I contend that, on leaving school, the greatest possible number of pupils should have received a musical education adequate for the artistic requirements of modern life, and for the application of natural faculties normally and logically developed. These capable masters you speak of—Can't you see what different results they would obtain if their own education had been properly conducted? I am not here going to analyse their methods in detail—indeed, they vary according to the country—but I think I may assert, without fear of contradiction, that one and all are based on theory instead of on sensorial experiment. No art is nearer life itself than music. No art has developed and is still developing more rapidly, no art has inspired so many ingenious theorists or so many systems of teaching, growing ever more simple—proof positive of their pedagogic value. To choose between these systems is admittedly difficult, and we are not reproving the authorities with having chosen wrongly. Our grievance is that *they have neglected to choose* at all, that they have preferred in every case—without a single exception—to retain the methods of the past. What is the infallible criterion of the worth of a system of instruction? Surely the practical results of the system, the technical accomplishments of the pupils who have followed it. Let us for a moment consider those accomplishments.

After their fourth or fifth year of musical tuition in our primary schools, are 50 per cent. of the pupils capable :

1. Of beating time to a tune played *rubato* by the master ?

2. Of reading at sight accurately and in time either the first or second part of a folk-song *with words ?*

3. Of discerning whether a melody sung to them is

in C, F, G, or B flat ? Whether it is in 2, 3, or 4 time ? Whether it is in a major or minor key ?

And that, I submit, is not asking much. One would exact much more of students of a foreign language, who would be expected, on examination, to read and write with tolerable accuracy. And remember that I am only referring to 50 per cent. of the pupils. . . .

After five or six years of study in secondary and higher grade schools, are the pupils capable :

1. Of achieving what we have asked of the pupils of primary schools ?

Are 50 per cent. of them capable :

2. Of writing a simple melody heard for the first time, and a more difficult melody that they know by heart, but have never seen written ?

3. Of recognising whether a piece played to them is a gavotte, a minuet, a march, or a mazurka ?

4. Of improvising four bars in any key ?

5. Of appreciating a modulation ?

6. Of appreciating at a first hearing a change of time ?

7. Of explaining clearly, and illustrating, a single rule of musical prosody, and of " setting " two lines of verse ?

8. Of quoting and illustrating a single rule of phrasing or shading ?

9. Of quoting the names of three celebrated com- posers with their most important works ?

10. Of giving a summary statement of the difference between a ballad, a sonata, and a symphony ?

Questions 1, 2, and 3 correspond to the sort of tests one might apply to a sixth-year student of English or German in writing an English or German phrase to dictation, or replying in English or German to a question put in the same language.

" But wait a minute," will exclaim our Mr. So-and- So, " I don't follow you. Do you really expect school- children to know all those things ? "

"Why not, sir?"

"Why not, indeed! Ask a child just leaving school to beat a *rubato* in time, to guess the key in which a folk-song is written. . . . To expect the students in the higher schools to be able to improvise and modulate and understand musical prosody and goodness knows what not! The mere idea of bothering these unfortunate children, who've already more than enough to do, with the names of the classical composers and their works!"

"What are they to be taught, then!"

"The notes, rests—— "

"Rests with a vengeance!"

"The notes, sharps, flats, symbols . . . all that sort of thing : in short, *music!*"

"Are not the questions I have suggested putting to pupils related to music?"

"Yes, but—— "

"But what?"

"But they are too difficult."

"Not a bit, my dear sir, not in the least. They are of a most elementary nature. One and all relate to solfège, not to harmony, and the last two do not require any theoretical training at all—any more than a good Swiss requires to study history for six years to be able to speak of William Tell, or Winkelried, or General Dufour!"

"Still, our children are not taught that sort of thing."

"Then their education is incomplete."

"Do you expect every child in a class to have a good voice and a good ear?"

"Those who have not should be removed from the class, as we would exclude a blind man from a musketry course, or a legless man from gymnastics."

"That's not the same thing."

"It is precisely the same thing, I assure you."

"But how on earth can you expect children to assimilate that store of knowledge on a single hour's lesson a week?"

"If an hour is not enough, they must be given two, or any number, . . . any number, that is, that may be required to make the lessons profitable. But don't be alarmed, Mr. So-and-So, one hour will be quite sufficient once children are brought up to *sing outside school hours, and music is made to play a part in their everyday life.* One thing or the other: either music lessons should be organised in such a way as to make children musical—that is to say, to bring out their temperament and hearing faculties—or they should be excluded altogether from the school curriculum, and the task of initiating our youth into the beauties of music relegated to private institutions. . . . But what's the matter, Mr. So-and-So ? Did I hear you mutter that a good third of the certificated students of our conservatoires are unable either to improvise or to modulate ? That they would be found incapable of satisfactorily answering any of the questions I have enumerated ? . . . That, sir, is a serious statement to make. Would you be prepared to subscribe to it in the columns of the *Journal de Genève* or the *Basler Nachrichten* ? "

"I would subscribe to it with the deepest regret, but I would subscribe to it."

"The deuce you would ! Well, we shall have to reform the system of training in our conservatoires as well."

*   *   *   *   *

It is the deplorable fact, as we have already stated, that singing and music are regarded at schools as subjects outside the essentials of education. It gratifies a certain number of parents to be able to say that their children can sing, and so the schools provide a superficial training calculated to give them the *appearance* of having studied music. It never—unless by chance—awakens in their senses and heart a real love for music ; it never makes music live for them. They are trained merely in its external side, and its emotional and really educative qualities remain hidden from them. They are not even taught to listen to music. The only music they hear is that which they are set to execute. And on what principle are they taught the art of singing ? It is a matter simply and solely of imitation. One wonders when our authorities will abandon this system of parrot-training; when they will begin to recognise the importance of making singing lessons an integral element in the life of the school, permeating with music every side of its activities ; tending to poetise them with its melodious charms, to vitalise, brace, and strengthen them with its rhythm ; when they will initiate pupils, boys and girls, into the wonders to be attained by an adequate study of part-singing, creating in them, on leaving school—where they will thereby have become accustomed to singing with and understanding one another—the desire to join choral societies. By so doing they will establish a point of contact between the music lessons of the schools and the "conservatorial" studies, where at present these pull in opposite directions, without the slightest attempt at a *rapprochement*—though, indeed, as things are, this would be somewhat in the nature of an alliance between the blind and the paralysed. . . . And in public performances, they will have school choirs accompanied by orchestral societies, drawn from the conservatoires, with a consequent valuable exchange of tastes for these branches of musical activity.

*　　*　　*　　*　　*

The rub will come in the selection of teachers. A wholesale dismissal of the present staffs will have to be made, to considerable heart-burning, and a clamour of protests. But, indeed, the number of music teachers in primary schools, utterly unfitted for their work, is simply appalling. All of them have spent the requisite time at the correct institutions, but how many have profited by it? In how many cases has not the final "*satisfecit*" in the teaching certificate examinations been accorded a candidate who has established his qualifications in every branch except music, out of reluctance to pluck him on the strength of deficiency in a mere artistic subject of minor importance ! These persons will become proficient teachers in every domain save that of music ; they will train their pupils admirably in geography, arithmetic, literature ; they will teach them to become good and right-thinking citizens, but—being themselves deficient in instinct and taste for music—they will fail to awaken the musical instinct and taste of their pupils. They will thus be responsible for the suppression of these instincts and tastes over three or four generations, and for the lowering of the musical level of an entire district for an indefinite period, thereby restricting the general development of the country as a whole. The influence of these teachers is so pernicious, from our point of view, that we cannot allow sentimental considerations in their favour to stand in the way of the interests of the musical culture of a whole people. The danger of retaining as music teachers pedants without either the ear or the voice for their vocation is so patent that it seems incredible that intelligent and enlightened individuals, as are the majority of administrators, should not long ago have recognised the urgent necessity of putting matters on an entirely new footing. We should not omit to mention that those among the present staffs who are really good musicians, with a genuine love of music and a keen interest in its pursuit (and we know a number of them) would have nothing to fear from the revolution we are advocating ; it would be a public loss to deprive *them* of their posts. Zealous in their devotion to music, they ask no better than to be allowed to assimilate new methods, and to be given the opportunity of completing their training in pedagogy. As regards masters whose musical incapacities would bring them under the ban of the new order, we can hardly think that they would care to complain. To give lessons in a subject in which one is neither learned nor interested must be a severe trial for a man of any sensitiveness ; nothing is more unpleasant than to know oneself incapable of doing what it is one's business to teach others to do. For this, among many other reasons, it is of the first importance that the musical education in primary schools—as well as in the higher schools—should be in the hands of musicians. On the musical talents of the master depend the whole progress of the pupils, and, indeed, any interest in their lessons can only be roused by a corresponding keenness displayed by the master giving them.

With all due respect to certain theorists to whom the vibrations produced by the scratching of a pen on paper are as agreeable to the ear as those produced by the "sweet sounds of music," the hearing is an important element in the pleasure to be derived from music, whether exercised in the analysis or creation of sounds, or in the appreciation of their harmonic combinations and melodic successions. We would go so far as to assert—at the risk of incensing certain critics of our acquaintance—that it is hardly possible to appreciate, to judge, or even to hear music without a good ear. The most desirable method of teaching music is, therefore, in our judgment, one which, while enabling the pupil as speedily as possible to appreciate melodies, rhythms, and harmonies, is most efficacious in the development of the auditive faculties on which musical taste and judgment ultimately depend. From this point of view, collective training in schools offers a distinct advantage over the conservatoire system. Practical considerations obliging pupils to dispense with the aid of instruments, they must fall back on themselves, emitting with their voices the sounds they are required to distinguish ; and there is so intimate a connection between the vocal and the aural processes that the development of the one virtually involves the development of the other. The mechanical production of sounds on an instrument does

not call for any special effort on the part of the ear :
the latter serves merely as an agent of control, and indeed,
failing it, the agency of sight, or of touch, is sufficient for
producing the conventionally rough accuracy.   On the
other hand, the efforts necessary to assure the accuracy
of *vocal* sounds conduce to the steady development of
aural faculties.   In other words, while training with the
aid of an instrument may tend to develop the hearing,
that based on singing is calculated to refine the *listening*
capacities.

   The choice of a teacher is, then, of the highest
importance in the training of the ear.   He must
necessarily possess normal sense of hearing, be a practical
musician, and understand the laws of vocal emission.
He must be versed in singing and in the principles that
regulate breathing and articulation, possessing a special
knowledge of the vocal registers of children.   At the
present day no attempt is made to develop children's
voices at school.   They are given no training in
pulmonary "gymnastics," and are thereby deprived of
an invaluable hygienic expedient.   Their head-notes
go uncultivated, to the irreparable detriment of their
vocal system.   A music teacher should know how to
develop every medium of physical expression in his
pupils.

   He should be, in addition, and no less indispensably,
an artist of taste and talent, and a man of tact and
authority, fond of children and knowing how to handle
them.   "*Non est loquendum, sed gubernandum !* "   If, as will
be admitted, it is not enough for a teacher of practical
subjects, like geography and history, to be well versed
in his facts, in order to obtain satisfactory and lasting
results ; if such results in these subjects depend rather on
the material of general interest the master can extract from
them (such as the application of their moral and social
inferences), by how much more should we insist on other
than technical competence in those who are to be

entrusted with the *artistic* education of our children!
The music teacher should make it his first business to
create a feeling for beauty in the souls of his pupils.
We are in the habit of discoursing to children of beauty
without explaining what it means. It is, however, just
as dangerous to "err in teaching beauty as in teaching
truth." The master should also be careful to reveal
to them the existence of a conventional and false conception of art, in order that they may be on their guard
against it. He should be able to illustrate his precepts
with examples from the great masters, and to demonstrate
how and by whom art has been developed down to the
present day, and in what respects it is capable of further
development. He should arouse in them an enthusiasm
for masterpieces, and an ambition to interpret them according to the intentions of their creators. The greatest of
his attributes should be the power of *suggestion*, and, in
the words of J. F. Amiel (extracted from a comparison
very pertinent to the matter in hand), "he should be able
to read the child's soul like a musical score, and, merely
by transposing the key, adapt the song without sacrificing
any of its charm."

It will be objected that the handling of questions of
taste, and of æsthetics generally, should be left to the
experts of higher schools, and that instruction in
elementary schools should be limited to the study of
technique. On the contrary, we assert, after a careful
survey of the whole problem, that it is at the *commencement*
that initiation into the essence of beauty should be
undertaken in conjunction with technical training. How
is one ever to attain technical proficiency without a love
for the object of its application? The æsthetic sense
should be cultivated contemporaneously with the study
of the elementary laws of the art, and, from the first
lessons, the child should be made to realise that the
training is directed as much to the heart as to the brain,
and that he must try to love as well as to understand.

The only real obstacle in the way of our scheme is the selection of instructors for the first five or six years of its application. Later on, the selection will operate almost mechanically—as we shall see in a minute— among the more talented members of the "finishing" classes ; but pending this solution of the problem, resort will have to be made to the kind offices of "interim" instructors, on whom will rest the heavy responsibility of initiating pupils into future duties of so high importance. The whole artistic future of the country will lie in their hands, dependent on their zeal, conscientiousness, and skilfulness. Stationed in the place of honour, theirs will be the noble mission of arousing a feeling for beauty in the hearts of their young compatriots, and of providing, for future purposes, a school of competent instructors, alive to the practical value of their art and fired with the ambition to propagate it and stimulate love for it.

*   *   *   *   *

If, from the point of view of the artistic development of the people, the compulsory teaching of music in our schools offers the immense advantage of bringing latent talent to light and of assuring to musical temperaments the necessary training from childhood upwards, it would be highly dangerous that this tuition should be the same for highly gifted, less gifted, and ungifted children indiscriminately. We must never forget that we are concerned with the teaching of not a science, but an art. "A child may have a taste for science," says La Rochefoucauld, "but not every science will agree with him." Not every child is born an artist ; and while we may find cases where musical instinct, dormant or otherwise concealed, is brought to light by careful handling, most often training will only avail with children more or less predestined to come under its influence. As Sancho Panza proclaimed : "He who hasn't enough has nothing." In proverbial parlance, the most beautiful girl in the world can only give what she's got ; where there is nothing to give, the Devil loses his rights ; you can't get leaves from a dead tree, or an omelet without eggs ; sauce doesn't make fish ; not every one is fated to go to Corinth ; catch your hare before you jug it ! . . . All of which goes to prove that no manner of means will succeed in making a child musical, if he hasn't the germ of music in him from the first. The moral would seem to be that only the most gifted children should receive a musical training at all. But, as our old friend Sancho Panza concludes, "A single rotten apple will contaminate the whole basketful!" And this proverb, based on the observation of a natural phenomenon of universal application, puts us on the road to an important reform. The complete lack of aptitude of a few pupils in a class will prejudice the progress of the class as a whole. We must, therefore, after a certain period of observation, disqualify from further musical tuition every pupil who lacks a good voice, a good ear, and a sense of time and rhythm.

People will stand aghast at the complications this system of elimination threatens to introduce into the organisation of lessons ; but these are more apparent than real. There are fortunately very few cases—at most five per cent.—of complete musical incapacity, both auditive and rhythmic,* and, by reason of their rarity, they are as easy to recognise and classify as cases of idiocy in general school work, or of criminality in everyday life. After a year of musical training (the results of an entrance examination will not be conclusive, since false voices are curable by practice, while careful exercises will often rectify inactivity of the ear and insensibility to time)—after a year, let us say, of musical training, the teacher will have been able to pick out any members of his class totally incapable of following the course, and will transfer them to special classes. There will always remain the resource, should they still desire

* See Chap. XIV., *infra*, pp. 236 *et seq.*

to study music, of following a course at one or other of the conservatoires.   The first classification, by the elimination of " incurables," will enable the class to proceed to its second year's activity under far more favourable conditions, and will be followed by a series of successive classifications, which we will now proceed summarily to indicate.   By this means the organisation of lessons will be established on a clear and practicable footing.

Let us assume the whole course to occupy six years.

After the first year a few pupils find themselves, on examination, withdrawn from the class.   The same examination will establish that the remaining pupils are gifted in varying degrees in sense of rhythm, vocal accuracy, and hearing capacity.   Some will possess all three qualities, others the first two, others again the latter two.   Those who have a good voice and ear, but are devoid of instinct for rhythm, will be set a double course of a particular rhythmic training, of which we will treat later on, and which is included in the syllabus of the first year. While repeating this special course, they will continue the ordinary studies of the second year.   At the end of this year an examination will enable a fresh classification to be made, which, after definitely eliminating untrainable voices, will divide the remaining pupils into the following categories :—

    (a) Pupils recognised from the first as possessing all three qualities, together with those who at the first examination, showed signs only of two qualities, but have acquired the third in the course of their second year's training.

    (b) Pupils with bad voices, but possessing the other two qualities.

    (c) Pupils with undeveloped hearing faculties, but possessing a sense of rhythm and a capacity, thanks to the flexibility of their vocal apparatus, of singing accurately in association with a choir (a fairly common phenomenon).

(*d*) Pupils with good ears and voices, but lacking in sense of rhythm.

This classification will enable the master to divide the pupils of the third year into parallel sections :—

The first (Section I.) will comprise pupils from classes (*a*) and (*b*). The latter (those with untrainable voices, but with good ear, and rhythmic sense inherent or acquired) will take no part in the singing, but will confine themselves to listening to the singing and beating time.

Section II. will consist of members of class (*c*), who in the course of the third year will endeavour to perfect their hearing faculties, and members of class (*d*), who will continue their training in rhythmic movement.

After the examination at the end of the third year, a penultimate classification will be made. Those members of class (*b*) who may have acquired during the year the qualities in which they were previously deficient, will be transferred to Section I. All those who remain devoid of rhythmic sense will be definitely eliminated.

Section I. will thus comprise all those who possess the three qualities necessary to make the complete musician, as well as those with an instinct for rhythm, a good ear, and a bad voice.

Section II. will be composed of pupils with an instinct for rhythm, but whose ear, while incapable of analysing chords and appreciating musical nuances, is yet sufficiently accurate to control the natural precision of the voice.

These two sections will proceed to train concurrently, during the following two years of the course, at the rate of an hour a week. A final classification will take place at the end of the fifth year, and will yield the following result:

Section I. will be divided into two. Section I. (*a*) will consist of members of Section I. who show particular musical promise. They will be accorded during the sixth year a more complete training. Section I. (*b*) (consisting of those not transferred to Section I. (*a*)) and Section II. will continue their previous course.

Finally, at the end of the sixth year of study, the best pupils in Section I. (*a*) will be admitted, after an examination, to a training college course designed for the training of music masters.

"All that is no doubt very ingenious——"

"Hullo, Mr. So-and-So, you're back again?"

"All that, I say, my dear sir, looks highly ingenious on paper, but is, in my opinion, quite impracticable. (I may tell you that your classifications have made my head ache.) In the first place, some of the classes will require to devote two hours a week to this wonderful course of eurhythmics of which you said you would treat later on——"

"Excuse me, but there would be no question of a supplementary course for the pupils in question. They would simply be asked to attend for the second time the course that first-year pupils would be taking for the first time."

"Very good, then. All the same, once you've split up the class into two sections, you'll require an hour's lesson for each section, which makes two together, if I'm not mistaken."

"Your calculation is correct, Mr. So-and-So. I propose to give the class two hours a week for three years, and even three hours during the third year, when Section I. will be divided into (*a*) and (*b*). But this will not involve a reduction of hours in other branches, the lessons being shared by three sections of the same class."

"And the cost?"

"The increased cost will not be very great, and will be largely compensated by the undeniable advantages of the classification. Incidentally, several Swiss schools already devote two hours a week to music lessons. These will benefit materially from my method, which during the first two years will require only one lesson a week." *

* The last few years' experience has convinced me that two hours a week are absolutely necessary.—E. J. D. (1919.)

"Granted ! I have a more serious objection to raise : your classification will be very difficult to work in practice. How is your jury going to decide that certain pupils are devoid of aural accuracy ? "

"By perceiving that they are unable to recognise and reproduce intervals that will be sung to them."

"And inaccuracy of voice ? "

"By their singing out of tune."

"And sense of rhythm ? "

"By their incapacity to divide time into equal beats or to accentuate strong beats."

"But you were speaking of relative aural accuracy."

"That is possessed by those who can only recognise the notes of a tune by comparison with a given note : while those who can recognise them without reference to a standard possess "absolute pitch," and those who are able to analyse combinations of sound can claim to have the completely musical ear. You yourself shall furnish an example. What is this note ? "

"Yes, yes, another time ! . . . So you expect your examiners to understand these fine shades ? "

"They will be professional musicians."

"Who will never make a mistake in their diagnoses ? "

"Every one is liable to make a mistake. But be sure of this : such mistakes as they may make will not have anything like such serious consequences as the mistake of the present system, in allowing incompetents to clog the progress of classes. Besides, our examiners will only commit errors of detail, and these could easily be rectified by the regular teacher; and if he should share in any serious blunder, pupils could always resort to private tuition."

"Between ourselves (I won't tell any one), isn't this classification of pupils into sections of those possessing the three qualities, those only possessing two, and so on, isn't the whole thing an artistic *chinoiserie* ? Do you seriously believe it to have any practical, sensible, useful object ? "

" Yes, Mr. So-and-So, a highly practical, sensible, and useful object. The object of not exacting from pupils more than they are capable of giving ; of carrying each one as far as he can go ; of not discouraging the less gifted ones by making them associate with those to whom their labours are child's play ; of not exposing born musicians to the temptation to slack, by permitting them to compete with their slower-witted companions. I say again, music is an art rather than a science. To learn music it is not enough to be clever : it is necessary in addition to be something of an artist. To confine school music-teaching to elementary facts is to bring it down to the level of the mediocre, and to impede the free development of the naturally gifted. If you are going to deny these a more complete training, you might as well give them none at all, for schoolchildren—boys especially—have little time for private art studies. Initiate schools into art, but not spurious art. Display all its beauties to those whom a judicious examination has shown to be capable of appreciating them. As for the others, put them in special classes. These children of average capacity so segregated will no longer have their natural instincts of emulation damped by the knowledge that, however well they work, they can never come out top. They will progress according to their powers, and will leave school with a moderate appreciation of music, trained to fill their place in the art world as intelligent amateurs and members of musical societies. As for the talented, they will push forward, freed from their shackles, and giving full rein to their natural instincts. Their goal, further removed and higher, will be more difficult to attain : that will not deter them, once they are able to spread their wings. The teacher will lead them to the point whence they can clearly discern it, and thence, guided by their instinct, by dint of hard work, sustained by faith and courage, they will attain it . . . our artists of to-morrow."

If you ask a teacher which is the best method of tuition, he will not reply point blank, " Mine ! "—modesty being one of the pedagogic virtues. But the chances are that the method he will proceed to recommend will be really his. You will recognise it, incidentally, by analogy with the character of its creator. According as he may be a pedant, a hustler, a fool, or a *poseur*, the method will be artificial, foolish, hustling, or pedantic. What is more, children exposed to this method, unless they possess highly individual temperaments, will turn out pedants, hustlers, fools, or *poseurs*. As surely as men are descended from apes, so surely children, trained on obsolete methods, show a tendency to revert to that status. The true educator's task should be, while guiding the child's will, to bring his individual qualities to light. It is better to provide him with the means of choosing between good and evil, beauty and ugliness, than to show him either only the good and beautiful or only the bad. His spirit should be kindled with a faint glow which increases with its own reflection. In Montaigne's words : " The child's imagination should be stimulated to a frank curiosity as to the things we wish him to learn, and guided, by judiciously whetting his appetite for knowledge." The best method of teaching is that which, from the start, offers the pupil a problem which neither his memory nor his instinct for imitation can help him to solve. After a year of preliminaries, of rhythmic exercises, which at once appease the child's need for movement and recreation, and inaugurate his physical and mental development—after a course of training for the lips and tongue, provided by the study of vowels and consonants—singing lessons proper may safely be embarked upon. At this stage, the commencement of the technical side of the training, the music master's first care should be to make the child appreciate the difference between tones and semitones. So long as he is unable to distinguish these infallibly, whether in singing or listening, any attempt at approaching another stage of the course would be to commit an error analogous to teaching the words of a language before the letters are known. I venture to assert that nine-tenths of singing and instrumental masters set their pupils to learn scales before they have attained anything like proficiency in this elementary course. Under these conditions, how are children ever to learn to recognise keys or acquire a sound comprehension of music ?

Every sound method of teaching music must be based on the hearing, as much as on the emission, of sounds. If the hearing faculties of a pupil are weak, they must be developed before he undertakes the study of theory. The noise of a drum calls for neither analysis nor reflection (that is why the drum is so essentially a military instrument). To many children, all sound is merely a noise, and it would be manifestly absurd to commence their training with a comparative study of noises. Only by the application of thought will they come to recognise the point where sound supersedes noise. Their thought should therefore be stimulated and given a direction : there will be time enough afterwards to start training their memories. "Memory," wrote Diderot, "only preserves traces of sensations and consequent mental processes that have had the degree of force to produce vital impressions."

And here we approach the vexed but important question of absolute pitch, that is, the innate and natural perception of the place of each sound in the whole gamut of sounds, and of the correspondence between the sound and conventional word (or letter) by which it is known. There are children who, as soon as they have learnt the names of the notes, will announce on hearing a sound : "That's an A, an E, an F sharp," without requiring any further thought than if they were to pronounce a tree in spring as being green. Many pedagogues believe absolute pitch to be innate and incapable of acquirement by practice. Well and good; but practice can certainly create "relative" pitch. Once the child is sufficiently advanced to appreciate, without ever making a mistake (specialists will understand the importance of this "ever"), the difference between the tone and the semitone, it is possible, by comparison and suggestion, to establish in his mind an immediate correspondence between a note and its name. This training should set in motion a constant association of sub-conscious ideas. The means of awakening and co-ordinating these ideas forms the natural basis of a sound method of music teaching. Our space here being limited, we must refer readers to special works for further information on this subject. We pause merely to record our firm conviction, based on considerable experience, that relative pitch is capable of being developed, by means of training, in every one possessing a good ear, provided such training be commenced at an early age and precede the study of an instrument.

Absolute pitch, incidentally, is only indispensable to a musician who proposes to teach music, and if I have laboured the need for bringing it out in the child, it is only because—be it remembered—our training is designed to prepare the most talented students for the profession of music teachers.

As soon as pupils can distinguish between tones and semitones, they can commence the comparative study of scales, that is, the succession of tones and semitones which give the character of a key. In this connection, we venture to mention a little plan we ourselves have adopted, as a result of considerable professional experience. Each scale being formed from the same succession of tones and semitones, in unvarying order, the pupil will only be able to distinguish one from another from the position of its tonic. The inter-relations of scales will escape him, since, to his ear, the scale of A flat, for example, would be merely the melody of the scale of C transposed to a minor sixth higher, or a major third lower. But if you make him trace the succession of notes of the scale of A flat commencing from *C*, the tonic of the scale of C (namely, C, D flat, E flat, F, G, A flat, B flat, C), the pupil will see at once. that the melody differs from that of the scale of C. He will notice that the tones and semitones are not in the same positions, and (being familiar with the order of tones and semitones in a scale extending from tonic to tonic) will be able, by remarking the places they occupy in the scale in question, to find the tonic for the scale, and so identify the key. By this means a pupil may learn in a year to distinguish the key. The choice of C as the initial note enables any voice to sing all the scales, identifying them from the variations involved in the order of succession of tones and semitones. In other systems this would be impracticable with children whose voices have not a large compass, or beginners restricted to a small register. Indeed, apart from the compass of the voice, the old systems depend on tedious effects of transposition, and, if they allow the singing of certain scales at their true pitch, they neglect to inculcate the inter-relations of the scales which is practicable only by our method of varying the succession of notes between the tonics of C.

Another advantage of our system is that, before long, it so impresses the C on the memory, that a student is enabled to sing to pitch without resorting to the tuning-fork. It is invaluable from the point of view of music-hearing. The pupil trained by our method has no difficulty in discerning the key of any piece, thanks to the perception of the alterations effected in the tonic scale of C, and, accustomed to sing any interval in any setting (that is, in any key), he will be able to. recognise any note irrespective of the instrument that produces it.

It is, therefore, of the highest importance that the teacher should engrave the fundamental C on the memories—in the very gullets, we might say—of his pupils.* He should also, in furtherance of his main object, impose, as a set-off to exercises of intonation, what one might call exercises of recognition or appellation, just as in the primary school reading and writing are taught simultaneously. On leaving the solfège course, the student should be able to name the notes in an exercise sung by another, as well as to sing them himself. To achieve this result, the master should accustom him from the first to identify the key in which another student is singing a stock exercise; next, to name or write to dictation the notes of an exercise taken at haphazard; finally, to distinguish any notes in any key. I cannot over-emphasise the importance of this training; it provides, so to speak, a double development of musical faculties.

But whether one adopts my system or another is of little matter. The essential is that the study of keys should be undertaken as conscientiously and as meticulously as possible. The course should extend over two or three years, or even more—long enough, in any case, to enable us to say of the pupil's knowledge of the inter-relations of the keys that, in the phrase of Montaigne: "It is not incorporated in the spirit, but attached to it; for the soul should be widened, not merely soaked in a thing, and if it is not to be enlarged by learning, better leave it alone altogether."

Once the scales are mastered, the remaining musical studies—with the material exception of those of a rhythmic order—will be child's play, the pupil finding an explanation for everything by reference to the scales: intervals will be seen as fragments of scales, with intermediate sounds left out; chords as notes of a scale on top of one another; resolutions as the property given to notes of a scale left suspended to continue their

* Or the A, or any other note; but C has the advantage of being the tonic of the type scale. The sensation of its sound is impressed by the cultivation of the muscular sense.

progress; modulation as the linking of one scale with another. . . . Everything relating to melody and harmony is implicit in the comparative study of keys, and becomes thereafter only a question of terminology and classification.

      *   *   *   *   *

There remains the element of rhythm, which is also of the highest importance. Analogous to absolute pitch we may find an instinctive feeling for rhythm, which may be awakened and developed by practice.

The gift of musical rhythm is not a mere mental affair; it is physical in essence. Diderot calls it "the very image of the soul reproduced in the inflexions of the voice, the successive variations of passages of a speech, accelerations, deliberations, sparkles, gulps, punctuated in a hundred different ways." For our part, we regard it as the reflex of instinctive corporal movements, and as dependent on the gait, balance, and general harmony of those movements. If a child, in good health and otherwise without physical defect, shows some irregularity in his gait, this irregularity will correspond in music to an irregular manner of measuring time. If, through lack of balance in his movements, he finds difficulty, according as he starts with the left or right foot, in accentuating by a stamp each first step of an alternating series in 2, 3, or 4 time, he will have the same difficulty in accentuating musically the first beats in bars of 2/4, 3/4, or 4/4. If, in making four steps, he has a tendency to make the fourth shorter than the first, or *vice versa*, just the same awkwardness will be reflected in his musical execution. . . . A regular step is the natural apportioner of time into equal fractions, and is the model of what we call measure. The emphasis of one step in two, in three, or in four respectively creates metrical accentuation. And where, in the course of a series of equal steps, a movement of the hand emphasises now one step, now another, the gesture at once creates pathetic rhythmic accentuation. Set a child to sing while in motion; if his steps do not coincide with the beat of the time he is singing, or which others may be singing, he is lacking in a natural sense of time-measure. If he is unable at will to accentuate one or another of the steps, he is lacking in a natural sense of rhythm. And just as one may teach a deaf-mute to speak by means of lip-movements, which have no correspondence, in his mind, to the idea of hearing, so, by accustoming the body to regular symmetrical movements under the control of eye and muscular senses, a feeling for musical rhythm may be produced in an a-rhythmic pupil. For, as La Rochefoucauld puts it, "We are more disposed to indolence in our minds than in our bodies, and good physical habits conduce to good mental ones."

Repeated "squad" drill produces regularity of step in our soldiers. If we could train them to co-ordinate this regularity with that demanded by musical measure they would soon learn to sing in time. In respect of accentuation, on the other hand, military training has a bad effect on the body, as on the mind. It vitiates natural balance by concentrating on the left foot and the right arm. With its invariable "*left*, right," it tends to inhibit the sense of rhythmic co-ordination. If only military instructors would train their men to start off alternately with the left and right foot, to "change arms" more frequently, to accentuate their march to 3, 4, 5, and 6 time, in various *tempi*, and sometimes alternating the time-beat, they would see how far less mechanical, and consequently less fatiguing, marching would become, and what far more flexible and quick-witted men they would turn out. They would further demonstrate that rhythmic-*musical*, were developed along with rhythmic-*physical*, capacities, and so help to procure the introduction of these preliminary exercises into our schools.

We should likewise enlist the support of mothers, if they could only realise how their daughters, by means of these exercises, would lose their inveterate awkwardness and stiffness, and acquire that unaffected grace produced by harmony of movements, and which is no more than complete self-expression.

Once regularity of gait and correct accentuation are developed, it will only remain to enlighten pupils as to the relations between them and the division of time in music into equal parts, accentuated according to certain rules. The analogy will quickly establish itself. We emphatically recommend any method, tending to the study of rhythm, by means of exercises in cadenced marching. These could quite well be taught in kinder-gartens, independently of music, in the form of gymnastics. The child could be trained in a whole series of combina-tions of steps, without being made aware that they were based on combinations of musical time-values. When one came later to teach him the value of notes, and to recognise their formations, one would have merely to remind him of his old marching exercises to provide him with a metrical model as natural as it was easy to follow— just as there are dancers to whom the musical phrases of a ballet are only recalled by thinking of the steps by which they have learnt to represent them. . . . Is it generally realised that a child who can dance the polka has plumbed the mysteries of a 2/4 measure, consisting of two quavers followed by a crotchet, and that an oarsman has similarly mastered 3/4 time composed of a minim and a crotchet ? Let us advance on empiric principles, in the light of these admittedly healthy activities. The child delights in all manner of games in which his body may participate. Gratify this instinct, and apply it to our scheme for the education of the future. There is nothing to be ashamed of in it. Let us be children with children ; it will be time enough to replace our spectacles when we come to discuss music with adult amateurs.

*　　　*　　　*　　　*　　　*

Finally, phrasing and shading must be learnt ; and this part of the training will produce positive enthusiasm, relieving the monotony of certain exercises with a wealth of poesy and beauty. Oh, the old-school *nuances* of musical interpretation! The *crescendos*, the *ff*'s, the *pp*'s executed to order, without a pupil knowing why, or feeling the slightest need for them ; when the whole art of phrasing and shading is so easy to explain, so natural, so attractive, so susceptible of immediate response from the child the least versed in questions of technique! It should appeal especially to us Swiss, compatriots of that marvellous theorist, Mathis Lussy,* who has codified the laws of expression into a unique book,† a monument of wisdom and artistic penetration! I do not suggest that this book should be placed in the hands of the children themselves, who could hardly be expected to grasp its infinite subtleties, but, in Heaven's name, let us introduce it into the colleges, and set every music master to study it and assimilate its smallest details! They will there learn how everything in music can be related to fundamental physiological laws ; how each *nuance*, each accent, has its *raison a'être* ; how, finally, a melodic phrase, with its expressive and rhythmic interpretation, forms an organic entity, and how intimately it is related to its harmonisation. They will be shown how melody is constructed on the model of the spoken word, and how, like the latter, it can be punctuated by commas, full stops, and new paragraphs. And, thus familiarised with the laws of musical prosody, so wonderfully expounded by Mathis Lussy, they will assist this reformer in purging our collections of national songs of the numerous faults that disfigure them, and will learn themselves to compose choral works and ballads in which poesy and music go hand in hand, complementing and vitalising each other.

* We had the misfortune to lose this man of genius in 1909. The *Association des Musiciens Suisses* commissioned M. Monod to write a study of his work, and published it in 1912.

† "Musical Expression." London : Novello & Co.

Once they commence teaching their pupils the real elements of shading and phrasing, they will be astounded and delighted to observe the interest they evoke and the joy with which they are applied. We are too apt to appeal to the child's instinct for imitation, to the detriment of his sense of analysis and his inventive faculties. In Pascal's words, "It is dangerous to let the child see how like an animal he is, without also showing him the grandeur and nobility that is in him." The child loves nothing so much as to construct and embellish, according to his fancy, things that appeal to him. Similarly, he wants lessons which give scope for individuality. Once he has learnt the primary rules of shading, he will never want to sing a tune without being allowed to embellish it with its natural complements—rhythmic and emotional expression and accentuation. Reading will be mere drudgery to him. But you will have only to say: "Now sing that with expression," and his eyes will gleam, his face light up with joy. The tune will at once appeal to him, because he is to be allowed to give something of himself to it. He will sing it with all his soul, only concerned to add to its charm and life. And when he has come to an end, and you ask him, "What mistakes have you made?" how shrewdly he will know and tell you of the false or omitted *nuances* ! With what conviction he will cry, "My rhythm was all wrong ; I sang too loud, I forgot to slow down !" And how he will love to try again, to embellish it, to communicate his vitality to it, to permeate it with his spirit ! All children feel a craving to create, and the teacher should lose no opportunity of turning this disposition to account. He should set them, from their earliest lessons, to improvise short phrases of two bars, then four, then eight, or to replace a bar of a melody by one of their own composition. He will find them revel in such exercises, and make rapid progress in improvising. Let him further appoint different pupils to judge their comrades' efforts, and he will note that their instinct for criticism and analysis is as strong as that for creation, and that, with practice, children can speedily acquire a really subtle and discriminating judgment—assuming, of course, that they are provided with sound models on which to develop their taste and discernment.

Finally, the choice of songs for purposes of school study is a matter of no less importance. Apart from folk-songs, the interpretation of which should be confined to Section II. (*vide supra*), the repertoire of Section I. should contain more difficult classical pieces, but adapted to the scope of children. We should like, in conclusion, to recommend to educational authorities a liberal programme of performances in public (far from disturbing regular studies, they provide a most wholesome diversion in school life), open-air festivities, and walks to the accompaniment of singing—by this means turning the lessons to practical use, and introducing music into the real life of the school. . . .

Music lessons will never be really satisfactory until they result inevitably in giving the child a genuine taste for singing, both solo and choral, and for listening to good music—the most stimulating and comforting of the arts, the only one that enables us to express the heart of hearts in us, and to sense the emotions common to all creation. . . .

III

"THE YOUNG LADY OF THE CONSERVA-TOIRE AND THE PIANO" (1905)

Colleges of music formerly and to-day—The piano, the ear, and music—What does the piano student learn outside of technique and the interpretation of the score? — Music at home and in the concert-room — Advantages to piano teachers of previous general musical education in the pupil—An appeal to professional pianists.

"WHAT a glow there is about you, Mr. So-and-So ! You've got some big business up your sleeve, I'll be bound ! "

"Not a bit of it, only my daughter Leonora has just passed with honours her pianoforte exam. at the College of Music. I won't deny that I'm somewhat elated by the happy event. It's gratifying to feel one's daughter is such a good musician."

"You regard her progress as a pianist, then, as proof of her musical development ? "

"Well, naturally."

"You are mistaken, Mr. So-and-So. A pianoforte training has not always either the object or the result of cultivating musical capacities. On the contrary, too often it does not go beyond providing a useless musical technique to persons who are not musical.

"Formerly all musicians, without exception, were versed in every side of musical technique : to-day this all-round education is only given to composers. The schools of music are filled with young men and women possessing good fingers, lungs, vocal chords, and wrists, but lacking alike a good ear, intelligence, and " soul."

These young people imagine that they have only to learn to play an instrument to become master-musicians ; and the public, for the most part, is incapable of distinguishing between an artist and a virtuoso. In the old days, the latter had to be an artist ; to-day he is often nothing more than an artisan : just as in former times cabinetmakers and glass-blowers were at once creators and workmen, themselves devising the models they executed, while, nowadays, they are content to imitate the old models, or to execute the artistic conceptions of paid designers. There you have an example of artistic decline to which too little attention is given—but to the matter in hand.

"Three-quarters of the students who enter schools of music are not born musicians. Before embarking on lessons suitable for students with good ear, exceptional sensibilities, and fine taste, less accomplished students should receive a preparatory training in ear, sensibility, and taste. Without that they can derive no real benefit from music lessons—they will become mere parrots or apes instead of musicians and men."

"Do you really believe that training can make a bad ear good ? "

"The ear can most certainly be trained."

" Or that it can give a person musical understanding ? "

" It will develop such, if it is susceptible of development."

"That it can create musical taste ? "

"It will awaken and mould it, if the germ exists."

" Aha ! your reply satisfies me that your famous special training will have no effect on persons devoid of musical aptitude."

"The conventional system can't make a musician of a deaf man : the trouble is that it makes a *pianist* of him ! And therein lies the whole folly of the business. In amateurs possessing the rudiments of taste, and a moderate ear, neither is developed, but only *fingers*. Those without any capacity whatever are taught the use of the pedal! And all these four-handed creatures dare to criticise music and musicians on the strength of knowing the ABC of pianoforte technique! Ah, Mr. So-and-So, the piano is the modern Golden Calf!"

"Don't excite yourself, my good sir. You artists can never keep your tempers."

"Nor you amateurs your *tempi*."

"Come, come! Let us discuss the matter calmly and rationally. You tell me that children should not be taught the piano?"

"I didn't say that. I merely contend that an amateur should learn music before he touches the piano."

"But the piano is music!"

"The barrel-organ is also music, but people are not taught it. However, we will discuss the matter calmly and rationally, as you propose. Do you know what an amateur is?"

"An amateur of music—derived from the Latin *amator*, from the verb *amare*—is, my dear friend, a person who loves music."

"Very good. And now tell me this, my friend: Do you love your wife?"

"Do I——? What a question!"

"Of course you love her, I know; she has told me so herself. . . . And do you know her?"

"Do I——? What are you taking about?"

"One moment! You know the colour of her eyes, her hair, her complexion? You know her preferences, her tastes, her aptitudes? You know, so to speak, your way about both her mind and heart?"

"Of course I do!"

"I admit my question was absurd. You love your wife and you know her. You love her because you know her, and if you didn't know her you wouldn't love her. Well, let me tell you, there are amateur pianists who love the piano without knowing anything of music, but simply out of a desire to imitate people who love the piano because they know it. Now I contend that one can only really love and continue to love someone or something, music or woman (the two things are of the same essence), provided one *knows* that someone or something. And that, accordingly, before everything else, our future amateur musicians should be brought to *know* this music that they love, perhaps instinctively, but which they can never truly love until they know it properly."

" Well, and the piano——— ? "

" The piano represents music in the same way as the photograph of Madame So-and-So represents your wife. The photograph recalls to you the features of a lady with whose moral and intellectual qualities you are intimately acquainted. The piano recalls to your ear thoughts whose depth, charm, and poetry you should likewise be in a position to appreciate. The basis of the training to be given amateurs should be the study not of the mechanical means of expression, but of the thoughts that are to be expressed. Once a child can sing correctly, assimilate melodies, analyse chords and melodic successions, distinguish rhythms, phrase infallibly, appreciate forms, produce vocal shadings and accentuations with taste— well, then, you may justifiably sit him down before a piano. After four years of apprenticeship at the instrument, he'll know more than he'd have learnt in six years without having first studied aural training, and, what's more important, he'll know it better."

" Well, well, well ! If you insist, we'll grant you your solfège ; all the same, fingers are an important element in pianoforte playing, and solfège alone won't make them flexible."

" Your point is a sound one. The fingers of the pianist of the future will necessarily be submitted to a special gymnastic course conducive to flexibility. But this course will be independent of the study of the piano, and will not be of a specially musical character."

"In that case the fingers will play incorrectly the moment they're put to the piano, despite all your solfège."

"Perhaps; but the ear, as a result of the thorough training accorded it, will at once correct the mistakes of the fingers, and control the latter. Thus, from the first lesson, the fingers will be subservient to musical taste, whereas, under the present system, finger exercises *form* the taste."

"The cart before the horse?"

"Exactly! I take off my hat to you. Not only have you come round to my way of thinking, but you take the words out of my mouth."

"You were speaking of piano lessons to commence after four years of solfège. How are you going to conduct these lessons?"

"With a view to the attainment of their aim. . . . Tell me, what is your daughter Leonora learning at the moment, after—is it not?—twelve years at the Conservatoire?"

"Eleven and a half only, my friend! Leonora is at present studying Liszt's Second Rhapsody, a pretty hard piece, I can tell you!"

"Splendid! And how long has your daughter been on the Rhapsody?"

"Only two months. But she's got it at her finger-ends at last."

"Splendid! And having it at her finger-ends, she has it in her head as well, I suppose? She understands the structure—— ?"

"Seeing that she knows it by heart!"

"She can follow the modulations?"

"Of course!"

"She told you so?"

"I never asked her."

"Her master asked her, I expect?"

"No doubt."

"Splendid! And what was Miss Leonora playing before the Rhapsody?"

"Beethoven's Sonata, 'Les Adieux.'"

"Does she still play it?"

"Not exactly. You know these very difficult pieces require the deuce of a lot of keeping up."

"But . . . she knows Beethoven?"

"What a question—such a well-known composer!"

"I mean she knows other works of his besides that sonata?"

"She has played also the Concerto in E flat and the 'Ruins of Athens.'"

"And what about the pieces she hasn't played?"

"If you imagine she has time to learn pieces she can't play!"

"She could learn the principal *motifs* of other famous sonatas, of the Quartets, of the Nine Symphonies."

"Well, I confess—— "

"And to come back to the Concerto, does she know that it was written with orchestral accompaniment?"

"Of course! It's written on the score."

"She knows what an orchestra is?"

"Who doesn't?"

"She can distinguish a bassoon from a clarinet?"

"I should hope so."

"An oboe from a flute?"

"Pooh! the oboes are held vertically, the flutes horizontally."

"But I was speaking of their sounds."

"Oh, *that*! . . ."

"Does she know an English horn?"

"Who doesn't ken John Peel? 'Oh, the sound of his horn brought me from my bed!'"

"I see. And so an English horn is just a horn?"

"Made in England."

"Delightful! . . . Now tell me, Mr. So-and-So, if you'll forgive my indiscretion. I take it your daughter, in the bosom of her family, of an evening, will run through the most exquisite passages of the classical and modern composers ? "

"Not very often. In the first place—to be quite honest—her time's not all that it should be. . . . Besides, she has so little leisure for playing. . . . She's always working at her latest piece."

"Quite. And this latest piece, what is her object in learning it ? "

"To train her fingers."

"And her object in training her fingers ? "

"To be able to play her piece ? "

"Hm ! And where will she play it ? "

"At her college exam."

"Is that all ? "

"Possibly at a students' concert."

"What for ? "

"To show the progress she's made, and accustom herself to playing in public."

"Does she intend to become a virtuoso ? "

"Oh no, but——"

"Before whom will she play at this concert ? "

"Before a gathering of friends."

"Will the Press be represented ? "

"Naturally."

"And the papers will mention your daughter ? "

"I should think so. They've already cracked her up."

"They've mentioned her name, *your* name ? "

"They have indeed ! And I was really rather proud, I can tell you. You should have heard my friends at the café ! . . . All, except Dr. Thingummybob, whose daughter has never been chosen to play at a concert. He looked rather glum. . . ."

"Well, I congratulate you. But will you bear with me a little further ? "

"Go ahead ! "

" Does Miss Leonora take part in *ensemble* playing ? "

" Once a week at the College."

" Not in her home ? "

" My dear sir, unfortunately, neither her mother nor I play a note ! "

" But at the College she has her comrades—her pianist and violinist friends ? Possibly she has made the acquaintance of a handsome young 'cellist ? "

" What an idea ! "

" I only thought. . . . A college, congenial surroundings, a sincere desire to make music, reading interesting new works . . . and duet-playing is so delightful ! . . . However ! And no doubt your daughter studies singing ? "

" Of course ! "

" How splendid for you ! How you must revel in the exquisite ballads of Schubert, Schumann, Fauré, Wolff, Cornelius, Robert Franz, Max Reger, Grieg, Sibelius, Chausson, Ropartz, d'Indy, Debussy, de Bréville ! . . . What a treat for you ! "

" Hm ! Leonora doesn't go in for ballads so much. The opera's more her line."

" Oh ! Does she intend to make it her career ? "

" Good Lord, no ! She sings excerpts from operas because they give them to her to sing ! "

" All the same, she must, as a singer, be well up in the classical and contemporary masters of song ? "

" Not particularly. She knows a little Schubert and Schumann, I believe, . . . the best known."

" But the others, the numerous others ? "

" She hasn't time."

" Of course. I was forgetting. . . . Another question. When your daughter calls on one of her friends, and is asked to try the piano, is she able to improvise a few chords ? "

" No ; but she always has a piece in reserve for these occasions."

"But *can* she improvise ?   It's so useful, after finishing one piece, to be able to lead up to the next by a few modulations."

"She doesn't require to ; she's never asked for more than one piece."

"But for her own purposes ?"

"Oh, she doesn't bother about leading up to another piece when she's by herself."

"She can accompany songs, I suppose ?"

"She's tried her hand at it ; but, you know, singers are so difficult to follow. . . ."

"Can she transpose accompaniments higher or lower at request ?"

"Not herself.   She gets them written out for her."

"If you recall a tune of your youth, can she play it by ear ?"

"You're joking ! She's only an amateur, not a real musician."

"Still, I suppose she can rattle off, for the benefit of her young brothers and sisters, folk-tunes which she doesn't happen to possess in print ?"

"Oh, we've always the means of buying them."

"At your family parties, she can oblige with a little dance music, I presume ?"

"Sometimes ; but, you know, we don't like her to play dance music. . . . It requires such a lot of practice to keep time properly."

"I agree, it requires practice.   And in twelve years—I beg your pardon, eleven and a half—it is evident that—— But tell me frankly, do you not sometimes regret that your daughter isn't able to play dance music in rhythm and with the right verve ?"

"I won't conceal it from you, I *do* regret it."

"And the rest—do you regret that too ?"

"The rest ?"

"Yes, the rest : those lost evenings at the fireside with your daughter reeling off beautiful melodies while

her mother sews and you smoke your pipe; those
missing accompaniments from ear to the tunes of your
youth; that knack, as her hands wander over the keys,
of refreshing heart and ear by some impromptu strains—
to give form to her thoughts, her dreams, her little joys
and sorrows? . . . The rest? All the other things I
enumerated, and which look so easy, and which your
daughter can't do, though she can execute so admirably
that difficult Rhapsody of Liszt that you are so fond of
hearing—and that, I'll bet, you've heard often enough?"

" Well, the piano is in the drawing-room, next to my
study. . . ."

" That's nice for you, isn't it?"

" No, it isn't nice for me, I can tell you! And
if it weren't for her concerts and the papers and
Dr. Thingummybob—— But you're leading me on to
make such confessions, . . . you mocker!"

" Say rather, comforter. The story of Miss Leonora
is the story of nearly every young girl who spends twelve
years of her life—— "

" Eleven and a half!"

" Who spends eleven and a half years of her life in
practising scales to enable her to play Liszt's Second
Rhapsody—which a pianola, without any practice, can
play far better—and who, a fortnight after the exam. or
concert, won't be able to play eight bars of it without
breaking down! She devotes eleven and a half years of
her life to studying the piano without giving a moment's
thought to music, without knowing anything of the great
composers and their styles and their works; without
being able to express her own thoughts by a few simple
chords; without knowing how to accompany or transpose,
or play chamber music; without even being able to
provide dance music for her friends; without giving
her father and mother a little satisfaction, which isn't just
pride, . . . for I'll bet Miss Leonora declines to play her
grand Rhapsody in her own family circle?"

" Resolutely ! "

" She declines because she's always between two difficult pieces : one of which she is learning, the other forgetting ; the result being that she can only play one or the other at a given hour, a given minute. She and her numerous comrades have neither understanding nor love for music. For proof, you have only to wait till they marry, when they give it up without a pang. Your regrets, Mr. So-and-So, which are shared by all fathers, by all real musicians, satisfy me that I am right in advocating a reform of our system of teaching music. This reform is simple and practicable. It applies not only to the piano, but to every instrument, and to the voice. It consists in including in the curriculum practical exercises for the training of the ear and the taste, and for the awakening of the individuality of the pupil ; in familiarising amateurs with the beautiful, in acquainting them with the styles of the classical masters, in enabling them to compare and analyse them ; in furnishing them with a mechanism adequate for reading fairly difficult pieces without mistakes, and with the technical and æsthetic equipment for interpreting works with feeling, but without sentimentality, with passion, but without hysteria, with rhythm, but without show. Always provided that pupils, gifted with powers of so high an order as to enable them to interpret pieces of extreme virtuosity, instinctively and without the slightest sacrifice of style, be permitted to pursue their technical bent ; but not, in Heaven's name, before the moulding of their spirit and heart to the understanding and love of the art ! . . . We aspire by these means to produce a race of amateurs who will attend concerts no longer out of snobbishness, but from a yearning for beauty, who will appreciate the works they hear, because they have taken the trouble to familiarise themselves with their structure and analyse their content. Pupils destined for an artistic career will no longer have their

progress impeded by the participation in their studies
of budding amateurs. They will strive incessantly to
overcome the technical difficulties that are daily intensify-
ing; and will take up the study of philosophy, ethics,
and æsthetics, indispensable to the artist of to-day. As
to those pianoforte teachers—and they are many—who,
victims of circumstances, are obliged to inculcate the
technique of the piano into young people ignorant of the
fundamental laws of music, they will heave a sigh of relief
at finding themselves discharged from their thankless
occupation as teachers of scales and arpeggios, and will be
only too happy and proud to change their vocation to
that of the music-teacher of old—initiators into the cult
of eternal beauty."

"I quite realise the importance of this reform : I
appreciate all its advantages. . . . But the application of
your ideas, the programme to be carried out, the technical
means of accomplishing the artistic results you have in
mind—what a complicated, if not utterly impracticable,
business !"

"On the contrary, nothing will be simpler. We
have first of all to submit our scheme to the professional
musicians of our country ; to put this question to them :
'Is it possible to teach musically-gifted children (1) to
listen to and to hear music ; (2) to read it ; (3) to
phrase and shade without merely imitating models ;
(4) to transpose ; (5) to improvise ; (6) to learn
melodic and harmonic laws ; (7) to possess a general idea
of the progress of music throughout the ages, to know
the great composers and their most important works, and
to be able to quote them, and from them ; and (8) finally
to *understand* and *feel*—that is, to *love*—music ? '

"There will be nothing further to ask. If our
musicians reply in the affirmative, the reform will be
accomplished, for the means are easy in the extreme. It
is simply a question of teaching what wasn't taught
before."

" And what, in your opinion, will be the reply of the musicians of our country ? "

" The reply will be in the affirmative."

"And what will become of children absolutely antipathetic to music ? "

" Oh, they'll have to be eliminated."

" You are an extremist, my friend ! But having received this reply in the affirmative, how will you next proceed ? "

" We will approach the adherents of the old system, and we will say to them : 'Gentlemen, you have devoted time enough to the musical development of our people. We recognise and thank you for your per-severance, your zeal, your noble and artistic intentions, but we are persuaded that you are working on wrong lines. We want you to make our children musicians, and not mere virtuosos. The new methods are quite practicable. We will answer for them, if you will come into line, thereby rendering the highest service both to art and to your country.' . . . And what do you think the really intelligent and musical spirits among them will reply to that ? "

" They will reply in the affirmative."

" And the others—those that don't ? "

" Oh, they'll have to be eliminated."

" You are an extremist now, Mr. So-and-So ! "

To my dear friend
and collaborator,
NINA GORTER.

IV

THE INITIATION INTO RHYTHM (1907)

*Ear, voice, and consciousness of sound—Body and consciousness of rhythm—
Analysis of relations between movements of voice and those of whole muscular system—Movements in time and space—Necessity for developing
vitality of muscular movements to make music alive—Gesture and rhythmic
reactions—Birth of rhythmic thought (rhythmic feeling)—Polyrhythm and
polydynamics—Physical capacity of different races—Necessity for collaboration of parents to establish a composite rhythmic culture.*

To be completely musical, a child should possess an
ensemble of physical and spiritual resources and capacities,
comprising, on the one hand, *ear, voice,* and *consciousness of
sound,* and, on the other, *the whole body* (bone, muscle,
and nervous systems), and the *consciousness of bodily
rhythm.*

The ear enables us to perceive sound and rhythm,
and to control this perception. The voice provides the
means of reproducing sound, enabling us to realise the
idea the ear has formed of a sound.

Consciousness of sound is the faculty of the mind
and whole being to "place," without recourse either to
the voice or to an instrument, any succession or combination of sounds, and to distinguish any melody or
harmony by comparing the sounds of which it is composed. This consciousness is acquired after repeated
experiences of both ear and voice.

By means of movements of the whole *body,* we may
equip ourselves to realise and perceive *rhythms.*

Consciousness of rhythm is the faculty of "placing"

59

every succession and combination of fractions of time in all their gradations of rapidity and strength. This consciousness is acquired by means of muscular contractions and relaxations in every degree of strength and rapidity.

No schoolmaster would set a child to draw something with which he was not familiar, and before he knew how to handle a pencil. Nor would he begin to teach him geography before, having learnt to walk and gesticulate, he had acquired an elementary sense of space ; nor direct him to draw a map until he could not only handle a pencil and trace lines, but had also acquired both a sense of space and an idea of the lie of country. No one can exercise several faculties at the same time before he has acquired, however crudely, at least one faculty.

Consciousness of sound can only be acquired by reiterated experiences of the ear and voice ; consciousness of rhythm by reiterated experiences of movements of the whole body. Since the practice of music demands the simultaneous co-operation of ear, voice, and muscular system—and it is obviously impossible, in the early stages of music study, to train all these musical media at the same time—the question arises as to which of them should be attended to first.

The movements that produce the voice in all its shades of pitch and loudness are of a secondary order, depending on the elementary rhythm of breathing. We are therefore left to choose between the *muscular system* and the *ear*, confining ourselves to the capacity of each of these—not of forming sound, since this depends on the special muscular activity of breathing, but of executing and perceiving *rhythms*.

The muscular system perceives rhythms. By means of repeated daily exercises, *muscular memory* may be acquired, conducing to a clear and regular representation of rhythm.

The ear perceives rhythms. By means of repeated daily exercises, *sound memory* may be acquired, sharpening and stimulating the critical faculties. This will enable the student to compare the perception of sound rhythms with their representation.

If, at this stage—working on the principle that execution should precede perception and criticism—we compare the functions of the ear with those of the muscular system, we arrive at the conclusion that the first place in the order of elementary music training should be accorded the *muscular system*.

It may be objected that the perception of rhythm by a child does not necessitate its execution on the part of the child himself, the rhythmic and metrical movements effected by an object or by other individuals being equally capable of awakening in his body and mind the perception of those movements ; and that, on the other hand, only the memory of rhythms perceived *outside of himself* will enable him to realise them in his own person. . . . However logical this argument may sound, I adhere to my opinion, founded on the observation that a child's body possesses instinctively the essential element of rhythm which is *sense of time*. Thus :—

(1) The beats of the heart, by their regularity, convey a clear idea of time, but they are a matter of unconscious activity, independent of the will, and therefore valueless for the purposes of execution and perception of rhythm. (2) The action of breathing provides a regular division of time, and is thus a model of measure. The respiratory muscles being subject to the will, in however qualified a degree, we are able to operate them rhythmically, that is to say, to divide the time and accentuate each division by a stronger muscular tension. (3) A regular gait furnishes us with a perfect model of measure and the division of time into equal portions.

Now the locomotor muscles are *conscious* muscles, subject to absolute control by the will. We therefore find in *walking* the natural starting-point in the child's initiation into rhythm.

But walking is only the starting-point, for the feet and legs are not the only limbs set in motion by conscious muscles, and so available for the awakening and development of the consciousness of rhythm. This consciousness demands the co-operation of all conscious muscles, and thus a training of the whole body is required to create rhythmic feeling. We may remark, in passing, that herein lies the complete condemnation of the present method of musical tuition, which consists in teaching a child an instrument before his organism has a clear and distinct consciousness of measured and rhythmic muscular movements.

Muscles were made for movement, and rhythm *is* movement. It is impossible to conceive a rhythm without thinking of a body in motion. To move, a body requires a quantum of space and a quantum of time. The beginning and end of the movement determine the amount of time and space involved. Each depends on the gravity, that is to say (in relation to the limbs set in motion by the muscles), on the elasticity and muscular force of the body.

If we assign in advance the ratio between the muscular energy to be deployed and the quantum of space to be traversed, we determine thereby also the quantum of time.

If we assign in advance the ratio between the muscular force and the quantum of time, we thereby determine the quantum of space. In other words, the finished movement is the product of the combination of muscular energy and the space and time involved in its formation.

If we assign in advance the amounts of space and time it is indispensable, in order to effect a movement in harmony, that we should have mastered our bodily mechanism : a lack of control would cause us either to exceed the space or curtail the time, while, on the other hand, a too long retention would result in either leaving a portion of the space uncovered or in exceeding the time.   Neither weakness, stiffness, nor inattention should be permitted to modify the formation of a movement, and a properly executed rhythm requires, as a preliminary condition, complete mastery of movements in relation to energy, space, and time.

To summarise the preceding observations, we may establish the following conclusions :—

1. Rhythm is movement.

2. Rhythm is essentially physical.

3. Every movement involves time and space.

4. Musical consciousness is the result of physical experience.

5. The perfecting of physical resources results in clarity of perception.

6. The perfecting of movements in time assures consciousness of musical rhythm.

7. The perfecting of movements in space assures consciousness of plastic rhythm.

8. The perfecting of movements in time and space can only be accomplished by exercises in rhythmic movement.

*　　　*　　　*　　　*　　　*

As trainers of body and ear, we are faced with two important questions :

1. Should we exercise the limbs of a child ?

Certainly we should.   Music requires finger exercises, and hygiene demands the training of the rest of the body, without music.   No harm is done in training the fingers of a pianist without reference to sound.   Indeed, we have found numerous people, of good musical ear, so captivated by sound that they lose all sense of time, duration, and accentuation, and thus accustom themselves to ignore it or treat it as of secondary importance.   (*Vide* the so-called "*à la* Chopin" school of pianoforte playing.) If at the commencement of a lesson sound is eliminated, rhythm attracts the whole attention of the pupil.

Rhythm is the basis of all art. But in gymnastics, of the hygienic and athletic orders, the body is exercised without reference to rhythm; and the smattering of regularity and symmetry with which the bodily movements of the class are invested, to facilitate the supervision of the simultaneous movements of its members, serves neither to awaken nor to produce rhythmic consciousness. To develop the sense of rhythm in a child it is not enough to set him to execute regular and simultaneous movements: he must be accustomed to movements of divers intensity, producing divisions of time whose different durations are in a musical rhythmic relation.

2. Should limbs other than fingers be trained with a view to the appreciation of rhythm?

Every conscientious observer will reply with an emphatic affirmative, for he will have noticed that defects in musical rhythmic expression are invariably results of *physical* defects in the musician. Moreover, while the most difficult exercises in complex movement are achieved with the greatest ease by pupils endowed with a sense of musical rhythm, however defective their physique, the simplest exercises present enormous difficulties to those who lack that sense, be they never so well proportioned. A person of rhythmic propensities always presents a certain harmony, an effect of perfect corporal balance; and physical grace can only be acquired or developed in children in corresponding degree to their instinct for rhythm.

It may be noted that there is an intimate connection between rhythm, in all its shades, and gesture. A complete musician, to mark a sharp, vigorous accentuation, will shoot out his clenched fist; his thumb and first finger will unite to describe a fine, acute touch; his hands will sway apart to indicate an effect of delicacy and softness. . . . His body is an involuntary medium for the expression of thought. But there are incomplete musicians in whom this capacity for corporal expression requires developing with as much care as would be devoted to the exercising of weak fingers or rigid joints in a piano student.

——When a pupil at the piano commits an error in rhythm, the limbs of his teacher involuntarily seek to rectify it, not merely by beating the time (that is a conscious gesture, with a definite pedagogic aim), but by a spontaneous effort of the whole body to put the accent in the right place. Not merely one of his limbs, but all his limbs simultaneously stiffen, infusing energy into his muscles and conveying to the pupil the image of what he should himself have sensed in committing the error. For he himself should have been guided by the representation of rhythm, reflected in all the muscles of his body. The consciousness of rhythm once attained, thanks to the necessary exercises, produces a constant reciprocal influence of the rhythmic action in its representation, and vice versa. The teacher, in expounding rhythm by gesture, transposes into movement the representation of his own consciousness, and involuntarily seeks, by this manifestation, to awaken its representation in the pupil, in order that the latter may forthwith transpose it into the form of movement appropriate to him. The representation of rhythm, the reflex of a rhythmic action, is potential in all our muscles. Inversely, rhythmic movement is the visible manifestation of rhythmic consciousness. The one follows the other in uninterrupted. sequence. They are indissolubly linked together.

Observe the movements by which a conductor of an orchestra, endowed with temperament, represents and transmits rhythm. Does he confine himself to movements of the arm alone in seeking to convey to the instrumentalists the image of the rhythm they are to create ? By no means. His knees will stiffen, his foot will press against the platform, his back will straighten, his finger and wrist movements harden. His whole body will be seen to co-operate in his representation of

F

the rhythm : each articulation, each muscle, contributing to render the rhythmic impression more intense ; the aspect of his whole person becoming, in short, the reflected image of the movement of the music, and animating the executants—his own representation of the rhythm being transmuted to them.

Another example. After my little (or big) pupils have practised eurhythmics for a certain time, I give them " exercises in interrupted marching." They will execute a few bars of a rhythmic march, then halt for a bar (later, for several bars) in the position of the last executed bar. The duration of the interruption, the pause, must be estimated and accentuated only in thought ; it being strictly forbidden to count out loud or under the breath, or to move any limb. Yet what do I find ? Those who have not yet attained confidence in the faculty they are on the way to acquire (that of *thinking* in rhythm) seek to deceive me (and themselves too, perhaps) in employing muscles other than those of the leg to execute the rhythm. I catch movements of an eyelid, a nostril, a toe, even an ear, and I have had expressly to prohibit the beating of time with the tongue (while scarcely in a position to control it !). . . . And every musician, by experimenting on himself, will find that, after counting one or two bars mentally, he will feel resonating in his whole organism, so to speak, the *echo* of the time-value, and that, while he appears to be immobile, his muscles are invisibly collaborating with his mental process.

, Man instinctively feels rhythmic vibrations in all his conscious muscles ; that is why it behoves a teacher of rhythm to train through · and in rhythm the *whole* muscular system, so that every muscle may contribute its share in awakening, clarifying, moulding, and perfecting rhythmic consciousness.

The training of the physical will, or the disciplining of the nerve-centres, consists not only in developing the necessary activity of the muscles, but also in learning to reduce these to inaction in cases where their intervention is not required. This training has no place in the regular courses either of music or of gymnastics, yet it is of the highest importance. Every piano-teacher will have noticed that pupils, on being initiated into the use of the pedal, find it much more difficult to remove their foot than to place it there, and more difficult to place it on a weak than on a strong beat. Repeated practice will overcome this inability of the foot to isolate itself from the influence of the hand ; indeed, this special faculty comes naturally to gifted pupils. But is it wise to confide to Mother Nature the tuition of the less gifted ? And would not even born eurhythmists arrive far earlier at their goal if they were subjected to muscular training before attempting instrumental studies ? It is the same with students of the violin, where bow-hand is so difficult to free from the influence of the left hand, and it is also much more difficult to withdraw the fingers from the strings than to place them there. The explanation is that a decrescendo of muscular innervation is much more difficult to accomplish than a crescendo, just as the gradual acceleration is easier than the abatement of a movement.

There is another important reason why, for the rhythmic training of man, it is necessary to exercise all his limbs, and that is—that a child is rarely born poly-rhythmic. To create in him the sense of simultaneous rhythms, it is indispensable that he should be made to execute, by means of different limbs, movements repre-senting different durations of time. These exercises will enable him to subdivide bars into ever shorter intervals of time. One limb, for example, may execute the quarter-values of the time, another the eighths, a third the sixteenths—or, by way of variation, one the quarter-values, another the same in syncopation—and by this means he will attain the necessary facility in dissociating movements to enable him to practise and observe polyrhythm,

While precise relations of time, space, and energy determine the form of the movement, rhythm demands different forms of movement for different accentuations (in other words, different degrees of muscular energy). Accordingly, the study of polyrhythm involves that of polydynamics.

Let us return to the conductor, who will express violence with one hand and tenderness with the other, and at the same time signalises rhythms of different durations, and we have a perfect illustration of the combination of polyrhythm with polydynamics. It is essential that the rhythmician should possess absolute freedom of limb.

To sum up : music is composed of sound and movement. Sound is a form of movement of a secondary, rhythm of a primary, order. Musical studies should therefore be preceded by exercises in movement. Every limb—first separately, then simultaneously, finally the whole body—should be set in rhythmic motion ; the resulting formations, *i.e.* the relations between the energy, space, and time involved, being carefully collated and regulated.

The mastery of muscular energy being essential for the perfect realisation of rhythm, the muscles should be subjected separately and simultaneously to *dynamic* exercises, involving gradations of force, successive transitions, and sudden contrasts—likewise contrasting simultaneous contrasts.

The child should also be trained to introduce intervals of time between the movements to be set to rhythm or measure, so as to become conscious of his capacity for representing rhythm and acquire the mental perception of movement. He should then be taught to distinguish the movement from the sound in musical rhythms, and to transpose them corporally and plastically. Thereby his perceptions will be sharpened, his experience enlarged, his judgment moulded, and his ear habituated to discern rhythmic values without the aid of his eyes, and—once pitch is acquired—he will be able to hear sound without the aid of his physical ear.

By these divers methods of forming rhythmic consciousness, the pupil will come to appreciate time-values and their notation ; his respiratory muscles, fully trained, will be entirely under his control, and he will be ready to undertake, without risk to his voice, the study of tonality. When the tonal sense in its turn has been formed by daily exercises of the ear and voice, then will be the time, and not before, to resort to instrumental studies. The pupil, who will have acquired a perfect confidence in his consciousness of rhythm and sound, with a rich experience of forms of movement and perfect mastery of a well-trained muscular system to draw on, may henceforth devote his whole attention to his instrument, practice at which will have become no longer a torture, but a delight.

I have often noticed, in hearing my children's songs executed in different countries, that the children of southern climes have a natural aptitude for the accomplishment of supple and graceful movement, but lack precision and force in executing energetic and emphatic gestures ; while children of northern countries possess the faculty of effectively punctuating rhythms by means of gesture, but not that of balancing and shading successions of rounded movements. We may conclude from this that the rhythmic character of the music of a country will conform to the physical aptitudes of its inhabitants, for, as is well known, grace and flexibility (in conjunction with lack of continuous accentuation) are the distinctive features of the spirit of " Mediterranean " music ; while the Teutonic musical characteristics are vigour and force of accentuation, allied to a too sudden and rapid opposition of forte and piano—that is, lack of flexibility in shading. I claim that special courses of training will furnish the Southern child with the faculty of accentuation, the Northern with the desired flexibility, thus affecting positively, on the one hand, and negatively on the other, deep-lying tendencies.

All these principles sound extremely simple, and it is probably owing to that simplicity that they are nowhere practised. It would seem (to adopt somebody's analogy) that music is regarded as a fortress that has to be assailed on all sides at once. Those in possession extol its magnificence, splendour, and immensity ; they insist on the number of wings and annexes that belong to it, and then are surprised to find people fight shy of it, though they themselves have pronounced it accessible only to a highly select few. And yet it is open to every one, provided the proper equipment is secured in advance.

Undoubtedly there are impediments to the realisation of our ideals. One of them is the prejudice of parents on the subject of the corporal education of their children. They manifest an extraordinary jealousy on the subject, as though they regarded physical culture as their exclusive province. They raise no objection to other people filling their children's heads with ideas quite foreign to their own, but they will not have their bodies tampered with, they will not allow you to give them balance, to render them vigorous and supple, and to bring out their natural grace. . . . " Grace," they tell you, " develops coquetry," but without adding that "intellectual grace" necessarily involves coquetry of the mind ! . . . " Render the mind flexible—by all means. But hands off the body ! " . . . The amazing inconsistency of it ! . . . Once this prejudice has been obliterated from the mentalities of parents and head masters of schools, musical progress will begin to be realised. The first task of educational reformers should be the education of parents. And yet there must be many among them who share the ideals and aspirations of these reformers, and would willingly collaborate with them and dream the same dream of the future. . . .

But, alas, so many men do not dream, and are content to sleep !

V

MUSIC AND THE CHILD (1912)

The fundamental qualities of the born musician—Divers functions of the ear—Musical education from an early age—Influence of environment—Nuances of rhythm—A-rhythm and its cure—Education and Sensibility—When should instrumental lessons be commenced?—Study of composition—Emotion and Thought—Pianoforte and Singing at school—Children should be taught not only to interpret music, but, before everything, to hear and absorb it—Children's concerts—Influence of school music lessons on musical progress of society—New educational ideas.

THERE are many more musical children in the world than parents believe. A small child may take no interest in music, not care for singing, march out of time in following a military band, and absolutely refuse to take piano lessons, and yet be not wholly lacking in musical feeling. Musical aptitudes are often deeply latent in the individual, and, from one cause or another, may fail to find the means of manifesting themselves—just as certain springs flow underground, and are only brought to the surface after a stubborn pickaxe has opened up the way. One of the functions of education should be to develop the musical instinct of children. But how is this to be awakened at an early age? And what are its external signs?

To be a complete musician, one requires a good ear, imagination, intelligence, and temperament—that is, the faculty of experiencing and communicating artistic emotion. As regards the hearing, we cannot do better than adopt Lionel Dauriac's definition in his " *Essai sur l'esprit musical,*" where he describes a musical ear as

71

"a faculty of the soul." Certainly the mere recognition and apprehension of sounds does not entitle a person to claim the possession of a good musical ear. External aural sensations should, in addition, create an internal consciousness and state of emotion. There are musicians of marvellously trained ear who do not love and respond emotionally to music; others, imperfectly developed aurally, who are yet real artists, capable both of interpreting and creating.

Many parents imagine that the mere possession of a clear and accurate voice implies musical talent. This is far from being the case. As everyone knows, it is rhythm that gives meaning and form to juxtapositions of sounds. A child who can improvise, in a charming voice, successions of notes, without order or measure, may be a far inferior musician to one who has no voice, but can improvise satisfactory march-rhythms on a drum.

It is generally supposed that the mere distinguishing of the names and relations of notes heard constitutes a good ear. Now this is a mistake, for the varying pitch of notes is only one of the qualities of sound. The ear should be able to distinguish the different degrees of tonal intensity, of dynamics, of the rapidity or the slowness of successions of sound, of *timbre*, of all that expressive quality of sound we designate as musical colour. It is the possession of this quality, in my opinion, that augurs best for the musical future of a child. There is no need to despair of a child of six who may find a difficulty in reproducing melodies vocally or on the piano, so long as he is capable of distinguishing melodies, and of responding to gradations of sound, contrasts of *forte* and *piano*, variations of speed—in other words, to musical *nuances*.

Parents often say: "It's no good giving our child music lessons; he's got no voice." Yet, on examination, an expert might find that the child in question was very far from having no voice, but that he was merely incapable of co-ordinating his vocal system with the sounds he was asked to imitate. The fault may lie with his ear, which may be quite sound but is unpractised.

What is involved in making a mistake at the piano ? Merely the playing of notes not indicated in the score. Yet musicians with a fine ear may—like Rubinstein— constantly play wrong notes ; and they remain far better musicians than the numerous pianists in whom ear and temperament conflict, although their fingers never fail them. If a child has no intuition of the conventional accuracy of harmony he will usually be incapable of judging whether his mother is playing right or wrong chords on the piano. But he should be taught to appreciate the *nuances* of music, and to judge whether she is playing softly, loudly, in treble or bass, quickly or slowly, near or far from him, *legato* or *staccato ;* and she can show him the difference between a *crescendo* and a *diminuendo* by placing him behind a door, to be gently opened or closed while the music is in progress. And when he listens to a military band, she can point out to him that each instrument has a different voice, that the big trombone has a deep intonation like papa, and that the clarinet speaks like mamma, while the flute squeaks like Aunt Matilda.

What an obvious opportunity is missed by parents, who must know how children love stories, in not attempting to rouse their interest in music by playing little pieces of a realistic order, illustrative of a story whose characters consist of personages lending themselves to musical treatment, such as galloping horses, little mice with their short, quick movements, chiming bells, etc., etc. ! I have found children follow with intense interest the little descriptive pieces of Schumann, Reinecke, Burgmein, Ingelbrecht, Déodat de Séverac, Fibich, and the like. Long before he knows how to produce the sounds himself, the child may thus be taught to listen to music.

And this is perhaps the best way in which a mother, so long as she is careful not to overdo things—to stop at the first yawn—may arouse in her child not only an interest, but the indispensable *love*, for music. The important thing, as one cannot repeat too often, is that the child should learn to feel music, to absorb it, to give his body and soul to it ; to listen to it not merely with his ear, but with his whole being. Aural sensations require to be completed by muscular sensations—phenomena of a physiological order produced by the permeating influence of sound vibrations. There are persons, deaf from birth, who can yet appreciate and distinguish pieces of music of different styles, by means of sensations of a tactile nature, by the kinds of internal resonance, which, according to the rhythms of the music, vary in intensity and form. The ear is closely related to the larynx, and there is undoubtedly a reciprocal influence between the hearing and the vocal system.

I have known many young people who, on hearing a sound, have experienced a sensation at the back of the throat. The cultivation of the voice will help to develop the ear, provided, of course, the pupil is made aware of the connection between the sounds he hears and the resulting pressure in the larynx. The mere *thinking of* a tune arouses in the throat the muscular movements necessary for its vocal emission. It is therefore desirable, in order to develop the child's ear, to cultivate also his voice.

Environment is another considerable influence. We know how quickly children can pick up accents. I knew an English child in London, who spoke both French and English with a Vaudois accent, his nurse having come from Vaudois. A governess with a harsh voice may have a very bad influence on the child's ear. One cannot be too careful in seeing that, from the tenderest age, the child hears only good music. "A man's education commences at his birth," as Rousseau observed.

Two Scenes from *Les Souvenirs*. Geneva, 1918

"Earliest habits are the strongest," wrote Fénelon. Rollin relates that Roman children, from their birth, were disciplined in the purity of their mother tongue. As Montaigne expressed it : " Our worst vices date from our infancy, and our strongest influence throughout life is our nurse."

In his interesting book, entitled " L'Education musicale," * Albert Lavignac asserts his conviction that " many children fail to become musical through their parents allowing their musical instincts to die of neglect. A father who desired his daughter to become a dancer would carefully watch from her first steps to see that her legs were straight. Similarly we should be on the look-out for deformities or deficiencies in the aural system."

It would be so easy to devote a few minutes a day to setting the child to imitate a note played on the piano, or to sound the A on a pitch-pipe or tuning-fork, and ask him to find the note of the same sound on the piano. There are numerous similar experiments to which one can and should subject children of an early age. We cannot repeat too often that musical instinct does not always emerge of itself, but requires to be brought out by a training in association of ideas. Twenty years ago I wrote some little songs, and set children to punctuate them with bodily movements. I frequently noticed that children who did not care for music, and detested singing, came to love the songs, through love of the movements. The two essential elements in music are rhythm and sound. Often a taste for rhythmic movement will lead a child, possessing only slight auditive faculties, to appreciate music.

*   *   *   *   *

Sensibility is closely allied to sensation. To be a sensitive musician, it is necessary to appreciate the nuance not only of pitch, but of the dynamic energy and the varying rapidity of the movements. These

* Published by Delagrave, 15 rue Soufflot, Paris.

nuances must be appreciated not only by the ear but also by the muscular sense.

Berlioz devotes an interesting chapter to the need for studying rhythm as part of one's musical education. He was preaching in the wilderness—more's the pity ! The study of rhythm conduces to develop not only the instincts for time, symmetry, and balance, but also—thanks to the training of the nervous system involved—the sensibilities. However gifted a child may be, in respect of his aural faculties, he will only become a good musician if he possesses temperament. In the words of the proverb, "We may be armed at all points like a battle-ship, but we cannot progress without a boiler."

What makes music expressive ? What gives life to successions of musical sounds ? Movement, rhythm. The nuances of rhythm are perceptible simultaneously by the aural and muscular senses. In the conventional music lesson an attempt is made, *via* the memory, to give the child a feeling for movement ; never an understanding of movement. This latter should be inculcated by observation and exercise of the instinct for comparison. A feeling for movement can only be acquired (if it is not possessed instinctively) by means of physical exercises. How many people notice the ungainly movements of their friends, while they themselves are unable to move gracefully—though they are quite unaware of the fact ! It is not that their muscles are necessarily intractable ; frequently their nervous system is disordered. The nervous system is an accumulator of energy that can be trained to expend and recuperate its potentialities, on normal lines, and thereby assure the flexibility and force necessary for musical purposes.

A-rhythm is a malady usually caused by the inability of a man to control himself, from a predominance of intellect over nervous functioning. "Will not followed by execution is useless. Will is not enough ; *power* is the essential." In Ribot's phrase, "The aim of education

is to transmute the conscious into the unconscious, and to
establish harmony between these two states." The
senses are not adequately provided for in our schools ;
that is why so few of our people are artistic. Art is not
a domain accessible only to an *élite*. " It is within reach
of all those who are capable of co-ordinating their senses,
by reference to an ideal of beauty and harmony."

Georges Delbrück * most rightly insists on the vitalising effect of training the senses, and on its influence on
the development of artistic feeling, temperament, and
individuality. Were this training provided by our
schools, our musical standard would, in a very few years,
be considerably elevated. Under present conditions,
children can only learn to love and understand music
outside of school hours. The method of *teaching* it
leaves, in my opinion, much to be desired.

    *   *   *   *   *

Parents are apt to confuse music with the piano.
One is only a *real* musician if one plays the piano ! Ask
a person if he is musical, and he will often reply in
embarrassment : " I wish I were. If only my parents
had made me learn the piano ! But I love music, and
never miss a concert ! " And yet these persons may be
far better musicians than many reputed pianists ; † for,
while some of these may be consummate artists, there are
others who do not really care for, or who care for only
their own, music : who, at a concert, can appreciate only
"stunts," have no discrimination for style or construction,
and are neither stirred nor interested by the most
moving works. If the training of their sensibilities had
been undertaken before they commenced their pianoforte
studies, their appreciation, taste, and temperament would
probably have been far more developed. Similarly, if

---

  * Georges Delbruck, " *L'Éducation de la démocratie* " (*La Renaissance
Contemporaine*, 10 rue Oudinot, Paris).
  † *Vide* Chapter III., " The Young Lady of the Conservatoire and the
Piano," *supra*, pp. 46 *et seq.*

young men and women, after studying the piano without appreciable result, were to leave it alone for a time, and cultivate general musical capacities, they would probably acquire the incentive to continue their pianoforte studies with advantage. But the dear mammas, with their naïve candour, are convinced that musical development depends exclusively on learning the piano. What a mistake! Pianoforte lessons, unless preceded by training of the ear and by rhythmic movement, frequently damage the aural and rhythmic faculties. The sense of touch develops, to the detriment of the hearing. The following experiment was made by a friend of mine, director of a conservatoire in a highly musical city. Twelve children of the same age, never having studied music, and selected from a large number, as presenting equal and average musical qualifications and similar hearing faculties, were divided into two groups of six. One of these groups confined itself to studying solfège, the other commenced pianoforte lessons. After a year an examination was held, which established the fact that the faculty of distinguishing sounds had sensibly deteriorated in the second group. The solfège students were then initiated into the study of the piano. After a single year's work, they had overtaken their comrades, who had by then devoted two years to it. This experiment proves that the study of solfège, prior to commencing pianoforte lessons, is not a waste of time for the pupil. Quite the contrary.

It is nothing less than lunacy to set a child to study an instrument before he has been trained to appreciate rhythm and distinguish sounds. Undoubtedly there are "infant prodigies" to whom this generalisation is not applicable. But, while these may be permitted to strum and improvise *ad libitum*, it is highly inadvisable to give them pieces to learn. Too often, the triple labours of finger exercises, reading, and understanding music produce a nervous fatigue that persists throughout their lives.

And what anomalies in pianoforte lessons proper! Unfortunate girls, without a grain of music in them, will practise three or four hours a day for six to twelve years to achieve a certain finger virtuosity, that is kept up only until their marriage, after which their fingers rapidly resume their pristine stiffness and inflexibility. Lionel Dauriac has well said that "marriage extinguishes the accomplishments of three-quarters of our daughters. Once they no longer have time to devote five or six hours a day to martyrdom at the piano, they renounce music and close their pianos. And they would close their understanding of music as well, if their masters had not forgotten ever to open it!"

As for composition, the pupils of most of our colleges of music are taught the external forms of musical expression before they have experienced any feeling worthy of expression ; they are taught harmonies before they are capable of hearing them inwardly ; they are shown how to write counterpoint in two parts before they are sufficiently developed to compose a single melody at all agreeable to the ear. Most teachers of composition will bear me out when I assert that very few of their pupils, before embarking on their courses, have undergone this preliminary training in regulating excesses and vagaries of temperament, rousing it when inactive, submitting it to analysis when it tends to immoderation, detaching it therefrom as a curb to introspection. Patient and persistent practice in counterpoint is indispensable to a composer, forming the basis of his musical education ; but it should not be undertaken before he is capable of assimilating its substance—that is, before his spirit has been saturated in melody, his natural rhythm has found a medium of expression, and music has become a part of him—his whole organism responding in unison with the impressions and emotions that assail it.

It is only by experience, be it remembered, that the inner ear can be formed and trained. No training can be undertaken before some sort of control has been established. In studying drawing, whether landscape or portrait, the student must be brought into immediate contact with the object he is to reproduce. The same applies to music. The aural sensations conveyed by the instrument serve both to indicate mistakes and to suggest the means of rectifying them. Professors of harmony, who oblige their pupils of inferior hearing capacity to dispense with the piano, thereby destroy their instinct for comparison, and make of them mere mathematicians, intellectuals, who become slaves of automatic thought and construction, and whose inspiration, dependent on the nervous influx produced by sound-sensations, gradually dies out. The fact of the matter, as we see it, is this: Musical thought is the result of a state of emotion, and a musical "score" may record this emotion. But its expression requires from time to time to be controlled by sensations. And it is impossible, in an art so sensuous as music, that the memory of harmonies can as effectively recall the original emotions as the actual experience of the aural sensations. In the same way, a painter, imagining a landscape or portrait, and proceeding to depict it without a model, is far more liable to lose touch with Nature than he who pictorially expresses his emotion while in immediate contact with Nature or a human physiognomy. Did not Courbet declare that, before painting, it was necessary to teach the eye to observe Nature? What a pity that tuition in the colleges of music the world over tends always to produce virtuosos instead of good amateurs! And what a happy idea it was of M. Fernand Bartholini, founder of the Conservatoire of Geneva, to devote that establishment exclusively to the education of amateurs, in order to raise the standard of the public and spread the love and appreciation of music in home and concert-hall! If the child's musical education followed the dictates of common sense, it would no longer be necessary for composers to record on paper all the nuances to be followed in execution. The pianist would shade and phrase the music without the need for indications. Poets do not denote the manner in which their verses should be shaded, and music is only a language. The laws of musical expression originate in the human organism, born of the observation of the natural course of our physiological life. Does this not point to the necessity for " musicalising " the student generally before confining him to instrumental studies ? So musicalised, the student will make far more rapid progress at his instrument. Can we not wait till a child is seven or eight before attempting to teach him the piano or violin ? In that case we might commence his musical training, on simple and natural lines, from the age of five or six.

Far be it from me to set myself against the piano and its tuition. I hold that the piano is the most complete of all instruments, as well as the most useful, since it gives an idea of harmony, of polyphony, and even of orchestral tone. But pianoforte teachers will themselves agree with me that it is too much to expect them to teach simultaneously the technique of the instrument and the first elements of music.* Parents should therefore refuse to entrust their children to them until they have first taken a course in elementary music. And this course, tending by human means to instil a love for music, and at the same time to bring its pursuit within reach, should be provided by our schools.

How are we to convince those who administer our national schools—and when will parents demand of them —that music should form an organic part of school life ? Singing at school should be a form of exultation, as well

* This point of view has already been expressed ; but one must not be afraid of repetitions where it is a case of expounding an idea that is seldom practised, and on the practice of which, nevertheless, depends any real reform in musical education.

as a means of collective discipline, for, as Guizot affirmed, "music cultivates the soul, and thus forms part of the education of a people." And Luther wrote: "One cannot doubt but that music contains the germ of all the virtues, and I can only compare with sticks or stones those whom it leaves cold. Our youth should be reared in the constant practice of this divine art." And Shakespeare exclaimed :

> "The man that hath no music in himself,
>   Nor is not moved with concord of sweet sounds,
>   Is fit for treasons, stratagems, and spoils ;
>   The motions of his spirit are dull as night,
>   And his affections dark as Erebus :
>   Let no such man be trusted ! "

*　　*　　*　　*　　*

Our schools do not give music sufficient prominence or provide adequate time for practice. Those who suggest that a *short* daily singing lesson be included in the curriculum are met with the emphatic reply : "Out of the question ! Every master of a special subject— mathematics, geography, languages—is clamouring for extra time. . . . If one submitted to all their claims, twelve hours a day would not suffice to include all the branches of learning." On the surface this reasoning appears sound, but it is based on a false assumption. Actually, music, like gymnastics, is primarily not a branch of learning, but a branch of education.* The school, before everything else, should aim at moulding the physical and psychic personality of the child ; at preparing him for life. If we postponed the study of Roman history till we had reached twenty, our general development would not be affected. But to commence our gymnastic exercises and music practice at an adult age would be to lose most of the benefits they should

---

* A number of head masters oppose any reform in singing-lessons because they hold singing to be a *secondary* branch. This fallacy should be strenuously combated.

provide. Gymnastics mean health; music means harmony
and joy. Each of them provides a refuge and a reaction
from overwork. To make students sing daily, if only
for a quarter of an hour, would be analogous to setting
them every day, between each lesson even, a few physical
exercises. The singing of ballads and songs would thus
become a natural practice with schoolchildren while
singing and music lessons formed part of the school
curriculum. These should be devoted to the study of
musical science, and should be in proportion to the
other branches of learning. They should inculcate a
knowledge not of singing, but of music and how to
listen to it.

*　　　*　　　*　　　*　　　*

There is something profoundly ludicrous in the fact
that, while musical instinct is based on the experience of
the ear, a child is taught exclusively to play and sing,
never to hear and listen. How strange that a master
should never think of saying, "Now keep quiet and
listen for a minute; I am going to play you a minuet of
Haydn's, or a rondo by Clementi, and you shall tell me.
what you think of it"! To my mind, musical education
should be entirely based on hearing, or, at any rate, on
the perception of musical phenomena : the ear gradually
accustoming itself to grasp the relations between notes,
keys, and chords, and the whole body, by means of
special exercises, initiating itself into the appreciation
of rhythmic, dynamic, and agogic nuances of music.
Think of the poor mites driven on to the platform
the moment they can play a little *berceuse*, to show off
their finger training before an audience of parents and
even, if you please, musical critics ! It does not occur to
anybody that it is these very children who ought to be
listening to music ! Concerts for children, such as are
held in Germany and England, are unknown in Switzerland ; but at least our teachers might make use of the
lessons themselves for providing their pupils with the

pleasure of hearing good music, combined with the opportunity of forming tastes and developing critical faculties.
One of the advantages of singing is that it enables the
child to share with his parents the benefits of school
training. Every song a child brings with him from school
enriches, rejuvenates, ennobles, elevates, brightens, unites,
and vitalises the family life. Just as the circle formed by
a pebble dropped into water widens and spreads by the
elastic action of rhythm, so the folk-song, introduced by
the child into his family circle, extends its influence,
breaking through the portals of the home, and potentially
refining a whole district with the joy of its rhythm and
the lesson of its poesy.

A child who forms a taste for singing and good music
will retain it all his life. Our male choirs for the most
part confine themselves to an inartistic repertoire : too
many of our soldiers are content with comic songs : the
men in our mixed choral societies have great difficulty
in reading music : the singing in certain churches is
deplorably bad : the cantor is out of touch with the
organ—the female voices with the cantor, the male
voices with the female—and the organ, obliged to wait
at the end of a verse for the men to catch it up, in
spite of all its anxiety to lead the singing, begins the
new verse itself behind the rest. Our musicians are
reduced to lamenting that our people have not the
instinct for music ; they will go to a concert only to
hear a popular singer's "top notes," never to an organ
recital, or to hear chamber music. . . . And yet Herbert
Spencer, the pioneer psychologist in education, who, in
1849, complained that English girls received no corporal
training in their schools, achieved such wonders by his
influence that those same girls, twenty years later, had
become the premier sportswomen of the world ! And
he could write in 1860 that a scientific education
might train children not only to appreciate art, but
to feel the need for it, and that it was capable in

fifty years of revolutionising the mentality of a whole people !

Undoubtedly a time will come when the teaching of music will form an organic part of the life of the school. Once the idea is comprehended, its application will remain only a matter of days. And will not the day when all countries lay down their arms provide an occasion for establishing in Geneva—at the Rousseau Institute, for example—a centre of educational experiments from which every country may derive benefit ? Progress is in the air, new ideas fly from country to country. M. Ed. Claparède is inaugurating an ingenious system at once natural and scientific ; schools on new lines are being founded and developed in all parts of Switzerland. Dr. Rollier, Dr. Cramer, and many others, are making a success of the "sun cure." The day is approaching, I am convinced, when the music cure will attain recognition. On that day our children will have acquired a new vital impulse. If our grandparents had received the musical education I am advocating, we ourselves would better love and appreciate music. Let us not deny our descendants these added musical faculties, this more complete artistic joy ! Through innumerable centuries men march in file before time, and the burden of life is passed from hand to hand, from generation to generation ; and the will of each man may decide whether that burden shall become lighter or heavier, and it is the duty of each one of us to see that it becomes lighter. When our mothers realise the part they play, voluntarily or involuntarily, in the evolution of humanity, they will grasp the needs of education and help to emancipate our children from the conventions that restrict their intellectual and physical development.

Parents should never lose sight of the fact that our bodies and souls are the product of fabulous efforts of development and progress through thousands of centuries, and that the future depends on us as we depend on the past. It is their duty to care for the humanity of to-morrow, to prepare the way for future progress, and to assure for their descendants nobler instincts, more elevated aspirations, and a completer happiness : there is no higher duty than to sow the good seed and prepare the harvest of joy for others.

VI

RHYTHMIC MOVEMENT, SOLFÈGE, AND IMPROVISATION (1914)

Sound, rhythm, and dynamics—Harmony of imaginative and practical faculties —Absolute music and corporal experience—The psychic force of rhythm— The study of movement awakens the whole being—The study of solfège awakens the sense of hearing (pitch, realisation of keys, and tone-quality)— The study of improvisation at the piano externalises conceptions of rhythm and solfège, and strengthens the sense of touch—Table of exercises in rhythmic movement—Table of exercises in solfège—Table of exercises in improvisation—Intimate connection between these tables.

EAR-TRAINING alone will not make a child love and appreciate music ; the most potent element in music, and the nearest related to life, is rhythmic movement.

Rhythm, like dynamics, depends entirely on movement, and finds its nearest prototype in our muscular system.* All the nuances of time—*allegro, andante, accelerando, ritenuto*—all the nuances of energy—*forte, piano, crescendo, diminuendo*—can be "realised" by our bodies, and the acuteness of our musical feeling will depend on the acuteness of our bodily sensations.

A special gymnastic system, habituating muscles to contract and relax, and corporal lines to widen and shrink in time and space, should supplement metrical feeling and instinct for rhythm. This system of gymnastics must be adaptable to the most divergent temperaments ; for no two individuals, however well endowed intellectually and physically, will react in quite the same way—one following the instructions more slowly, another more quickly. Some

* See Chapter IV., pp. 59, 60.

succeed in executing a particular exercise in a given time, but fail, on a sudden command, to commence a new exercise, and continue the first in spite of their anxiety to interrupt it.   Others, having made a good beginning, suddenly hesitate, and finish in confusion what was begun with full confidence and clarity.

The fact is, that for the precise physical execution of a rhythm, it is not enough to have grasped it intellectually and to possess a muscular system capable of interpreting it ; in addition, and before all else, *communications* should be established between the mind that conceives and analyses and the body that executes.

These communications depend on the functioning of the nervous system.   It is rare, in these days, to find a person whose mental and bodily processes are perfectly harmonised.   Relations between the imaginative and executive faculties are too often compromised by a lack of freedom in the nerve currents, owing to the resistance of certain muscles, produced by the tardy transmission of mental orders for their contraction or relaxation.   The consciousness of a persistent resistance in the muscular system, or a disorder in the nervous system, produces mental confusion, lack of confidence in one's powers, and general "nervyness."   This condition, in its turn, produces lack of concentration.   The brain finds itself a prey to incessant solicitude, which prevents it from functioning clearly and devoting the necessary time and repose to the control of the whole organism and the analysis of the orders to be issued for execution.

The better our lives are regulated, the freer we become in every way.   The more words included in our vocabulary, the more our thought is enriched.   The more automatism possessed by our body, the more our soul will rise above material things.   Constant concern with our bodies deprives us of a large measure of freedom of spirit.   Are not most men slaves of their corporal functions, prisoners of matter ?   And, contrary to the popular idea, the premature development of intellect, and over-specialised studies, far from clarifying the mind, are apt to disturb and unbalance it. What is known as "absolute" music is music completely dematerialised —not directly addressed to our sensorial faculties, but which seeks to awaken emotion by means of developments and combinations of a metaphysical order. This transcendent form of art can only be appreciated by those who have triumphed over their bodily resistances, and yet this attainment may involve primary physical means. So long as the body has not been perfectly developed, there must be constant friction between sensations and feelings, and this incessant conflict between body and spirit will prohibit the necessary spiritualisation of matter. Music can never be rendered entirely pure until the body has been purified, and this can only be accomplished by seeing oneself clearly and discerning one's impurities.

One of the first results of exercises designed, on the one hand, to create automatisms and to assure the effective working of the muscular system, and, on the other, to establish clear and rapid communication between the two poles of our being and encourage the expansion of our natural rhythms—one of the first results of these exercises is to teach the child to know and control himself, and, as it were, take possession of his personality. Initiated into the marvellous mechanism of this body of ours, provided for consecration as a worthy dwelling-place for the soul —confident of achieving without effort or preoccupation any movement suggested by others or by himself—the child will feel rising and growing in him the will to make full use of the abundant forces in his potential control. His imagination will likewise develop, inasmuch as his spirit, freed from all constraint and physical disquietude, can give free rein to his fantasy.

Functioning develops the organ, and the consciousness of organic functioning develops thought. And as

the child feels himself delivered of all physical embarrassment, and mental obsession of an inferior order, joy will
come to birth in him.   This joy is a new factor in ethical
progress, a new stimulus to will-power.

The aim of all exercises in eurhythmics is to
strengthen the power of concentration, to accustom the
body to hold itself, as it were, at high pressure in readi-
ness to execute orders from the brain, to connect the
conscious with the sub-conscious, and to augment the
sub-conscious faculties with the fruits of a special culture
designed for that purpose.   In addition, these exercises
tend to create more numerous habitual motions and new
reflexes, to obtain the maximum effect by a minimum of
effort, and so to purify the spirit, strengthen the will-
power, and install order and clarity in the organism.

The whole method is based on the principle that
theory should *follow* practice, that children should not be
taught rules until they have had experience of the facts
which have given rise to them, and that the first thing to
be taught a child is the use of all his faculties.   Only
subsequently should he be made acquainted with the
opinions and deductions of others.   Before sowing the
seed, you must prepare your soil.   In respect of music,
especially, the present practice is to put an implement in
the hands of children, who have no idea what to do with
it.   We have frequently deplored the fact that they are
taught the piano before they have shown any musical
propensities,* before they can hear sounds or appreciate
rhythms, before their feeling for sounds and rhythmic
movement is developed—before their whole being
vibrates in response to artistic emotions.

The aim of eurhythmics is to enable pupils, at the
end of their course, to say, not "I know," but "I have
experienced," and so to create in them the desire to
express themselves ; for the deep impression of an
emotion inspires a longing to communicate it, to the

* See Chapter III., p. 46, and Chapter V., p. 71.

extent of one's powers, to others. The more we have of life, the more we are able to diffuse life about us. "Receive and give !" is the golden rule of humanity ; and if the whole system of rhythmic training is based on music, it is because music is a tremendous psychic force : a product of our creative and expressive functions that, by its power of stimulating and disciplining, is able to regulate all our vital functions.

The actual practice of individual rhythms (as also the method adopted for the purpose) is more than a pedagogic system. Rhythm is a force analogous to electricity and the great chemical and physical elements, —an energy, an agent—radio-active, radio-creative— conducing to self-knowledge and to a consciousness not only of our powers, but of those of others, of humanity itself. It directs us to the unplumbed depths of our being. It reveals to us secrets of the eternal mystery that has ruled the lives of men throughout the ages ; it imprints on our minds a primitive religious character that elevates them, and brings before us past, present, and future. Thus it seems to me to be destined—in a far distant future, when sufficient high-minded people can collaborate for the purpose—to create more intimate relations between mental and nervous processes, and to unite all the vital forces of the individual. But confining myself to my rôle of musical pedagogue, I can here only insist on the tremendous part played by rhythm in the formation of *musical* individuality, and indicate the nature and scope of the exercises invented up to the present, and their close connection with those relating to the subjects of elementary musical training next in order of importance, namely, those of the hearing faculties (solfège) and of the capacity of spontaneous creation (improvisation).

*   *   *   *   *

THE STUDY OF RHYTHMIC MOVEMENT AWAKENS THE WHOLE ORGANISM

The study of RHYTHM awakens:

1. Feeling for bodily rhythm—

2. Aural perception of rhythm—

and

(1) develops, by means of a special training of the muscular system and nerve centres, the capacity for perceiving and expressing nuances of force and elasticity in time and space— likewise concentration in the analysis, and spontaneity in the execution, of rhythmic movements, enabling pupils to read, mark, and finally create rhythm (both mentally and physically).

(2) develops, by means of a special system of aural training, the capacity for perceiving and expressing nuances of force and time— duration of sounds, spontaneous and deliberate appreciation of sounds— likewise concentration and spontaneity in their analysis and *vocal* expression, enabling pupils to read, mark, and finally create sound rhythms (both mentally and physically).

*   *   *   ;   *   *

The study of SOLFÈGE awakens:

the sense of pitch and tone-relations and the faculty of distinguishing tone-qualities.

It teaches the pupil to hear, and to reproduce mentally, melodies in all keys (single and simultaneous) and every kind and combination of harmony ; to read and improvise vocally ; to write down and use the material for constructing music himself.

*   *   *   *   *

The study of pianoforte IMPROVISATION

combines the principles of rhythm and soltège, with a view to their musical externalisation, by means of touch ;

awakens the motor-tactile consciousness, and teaches pupils to interpret on the piano musical thoughts of a melodic, harmonic, and rhythmic nature.

*　　　*　　　*　　　*　　　*

The following exercises are designed to train, on these principles, body, ear, and mind.

RHYTHMIC MOVEMENT

1. *Exercises in Muscular Relaxation and Breathing.*—The pupil is trained to reduce to a minimum the muscular activity of each limb, then gradually to apply its powers. Lying on his back, he relaxes his whole body and concentrates his attention on breathing, in all its processes ; then on the contraction of a single limb. He is then taught to contract simultaneously two or more limbs, or to combine the contraction of one limb with the relaxation of another. This enables him to note its muscular resistances, and to eliminate those that serve no purpose. Exercises in breathing may be associated with those of innervation, and applied to all positions.

2. *Metrical Division and Accentuation.*—The pupil is trained to distinguish different times by marching the beats and accentuating the first beat of each bar with a stamp of the foot. Gestures with the arm accompany each step, and emphasise the first beat by means of a complete muscular contraction. On the weak beats, steps and gestures should be executed with a minimum of muscular effort. Then, on a sudden command, at the word "hopp," the pupil must contrive to prevent his arm from contracting or his foot from stamping. Or, again, the word "hopp" may be made to convey the order to stamp suddenly or contract the arm on a different beat, or to substitute a leg movement for an arm movement. It is extremely difficult to separate leg from arm movements, and it is only by dint of repeated exercises that, eventually, distinct automatisms are created.

3. *Metrical Memorisation.*—After "hopps" have indicated various distinct movements, the pupil has to recall these movements; and in the order in which they were executed. These exercises thus constitute a form of analysis, and conscious and deliberate application, of sub-conscious movements. The pupil must have executed each movement before he explains and notes it.

4. *Rapid Conception of Bar-time by the Eye and Ear.* —Once the student can execute movements in a certain order and substitute, at the word "hopp," one movement for another, he becomes capable of dispensing with definite commands. These are replaced by aural and visual symbols, representing their sensations. Series of bars are played to the pupil, whose ear dictates appropriate movements; or, again, the sight of the movements executed by others, or noted on the blackboard, calls for their spontaneous expression by direct imitation.

5. *Conception of Rhythms by Muscular Sense.*—The body possesses a certain number of natural rhythms, which manifest themselves in a definite time and with a certain degree of energy, according to temperament. The perception of the degrees of muscular tension is accompanied by that of the variations of time-duration, and strengthened by the sensation of greater or smaller amplitude of the movement in space. This amplitude depends on the greater or lesser degree of resistance of the conflicting muscles. By means of a whole series of graduated exercises, the pupil is trained to adapt different muscular processes for short and long durations respectively, to estimate durations according to the sensations of tension and extension of muscles, of opening and closing of limbs in space, to co-ordinate the different dynamic forces of the body, and to apply the measure of space to the control of the duration and intensity of muscular contractions. The master should be careful to see that the co-ordination of movements does not rob them of their spontaneity.

6. *Development of Spontaneous Will-power and Faculties of Inhibition.*—Musical rhythm consists of movements and repressions of movements. Musicians with irregular rhythms are those whose muscles are too slow or too quick in responding to mental orders, who lose time in substituting one movement for another, or who cannot check themselves in time, or else check themselves too hastily, ignoring the art of *preparing* repressions of movement. Special exercises will enable the pupil to check movements suddenly or by degrees, to change a forward for a backward or sideward step, and *vice versa* ; or to effect a jump, at command, without breaking the time, and right himself with a minimum of effort, again without breaking the time.

7. *Exercises in Concentration. Creation of Mental Hearing of Rhythms.*—The practice of bodily movements awakens images in the mind. The stronger the muscular sensations, the clearer and more precise the images, and thereby the more metrical and rhythmic feeling is developed ; for feeling is born of sensation. The pupil who is able to march in time, and according to certain rhythms, has only to close his eyes to imagine himself continuing to march metrically and rhythmically. He continues the movement in *thought.* If his movements are slack, his imaginative representations of them will likewise be slack. The precision and regulated dynamic force of muscular automatisms are a guarantee of the precision of thought-automatisms, and the regular development of imaginative faculties.

The study of repressions of steps prepares us for *rests in music.* These, if devoid of movement, are by no means devoid of life. The study of periods intercepted by rests teaches the pupil the laws of *musical phrasing.*

8. *Exercises in Corporal Balance, and to Produce Continuity of Movement.*—Ease of movement depends on balance. The conception of movements extending over long beats is fortified by stability of attitude, and the assurance of continuity in the movements. This continuity should be

capable of operating in all degrees of muscular energy, and of being interrupted at will. The clear perception of continuity and interruption assures that of the balance of rhythmic bars and the conception of their divers processes of construction, all of which relate to the science of opposition and contrast.

9. *Exercises for the Acquisition of Numerous Automatisms, and their Combination and Alternation with Actions of Spontaneous Volition.*—Muscular actions, after constant repetition, pass outside the control of the brain. New reflexes can be created, and the time lost between the conception and realisation of the movement reduced to a strict minimum. The cultivation of automatisms should be effected in all nuances of *tempo*. Conformity with these nuances depends on the perception of the degrees of muscular energy necessary for effecting the movements. Automatisms should be capable of replacement by others without effort; they may be combined and harmonised over different parts of the body. The pupil should also learn to combine automatisms of his limbs with those of speech and song. The laws governing the natural rhythmicisation of verbal rhythms are similar to those relating to the balance of sound rhythms, whether vocal or instrumental.

10. *Realisation of Musical Note-values.*—Notes of long duration are formed by the adding together of notes of short duration : this is the Greek conception of rhythm. The pupil, trained to express a crotchet by means of a step forward, will divide up longer notes by movements made while in that position. A minim will be interpreted by a step forward, followed by a knee-bend, etc., etc. When the pupil has accustomed himself to these various movements indicating divisions, it will suffice for him to execute them mentally and to take his step forward by a movement of uninterrupted progression. This will maintain the exact duration necessary, for he will be mentally making these divisions.

11. *Division of Beats.*—Exercises in the dividing of notes of long duration are resumed, but by an inverted process (the modern conception of duration). Each crotchet should, at command, be subdivided into two (*duolets*), three (*triolets*), or four (*quadriolets*) shorter steps, etc. This division may naturally be facilitated by a mastery of bodily balance and the means of transferring the weight of the body ; by diminution of the activity of constraining muscles, and by the perception of the relations between space and time. For the execution of *syncopation by anticipation*, the step that has to be made at a particular moment and in a certain time is replaced by a shorter step effected in half the time, the second half of the time being occupied by a knee-bend. For the execution of *retarded syncopation* the step is prolonged half the time, and the movement forward replaced by a bending. This is the most difficult exercise of the course. The most musically gifted people can only execute it with ease after some months of practice. Once the student can perform it without trouble, he is recognised as having attained an elementary rhythmic flexibility sufficient for the acquisition of a feeling for expressive accent (*accent pathétique*). Children usually have less trouble in acquiring this flexibility than adults.

12. *Immediate Realisation by the Body of Musical Rhythm.* —This is a question of the spontaneous representation of musical time-values and degrees of force by muscular and respiratory actions, transposing sound-rhythms into plastic rhythms. The exactitude and promptitude of the execution depend on the utilisation of acquired bodily automatisms, and on the development of the faculties of psychic concentration. The mind has no time to record all the elements of the musical rhythms : the body expresses them before the brain has even a clear idea of them. This is a phenomenon identical with that of verbal expression. A word once heard is repeated without analysing its formation. It is only after hearing it

H

in thought that all the letters forming it can be tran-
scribed.

Once the corporal expression of musical rhythms has
become comparatively easy, one may develop the student's
powers of concentration by setting him, while executing
a rhythm already heard, to listen to a second: one automatism being in operation while another is preparing;
the body in the past, the mind intent on the future.

13. *Exercises in the Dissociation of Movements.*—These
are exercises preparatory to the execution of dynamic
nuances. Just as, at the piano, one hand may play *forte* to the
other's *piano,* so the plastic expression of vitalised musical
rhythms demands conflicting nuances of muscular innervation in different limbs. Special exercises enable the
student to contract a certain muscle in one arm, while
the same muscle in the other arm remains decontracted.
Other exercises show him how time may be subdivided
in one way by one limb, in another by a different one
—*e.g.* by the execution in a given time of three equal
movements with the feet and two, four, or five with the
arms. Even more than the others, these exercises contribute to the development of concentration.

14. *Interruptions and Repressions of Movements.*—
Balance and punctuation of bars and phrases of "corporal
speech," according to the laws of musical phrasing—
Antitheses and contrasts—Study of anacrusis—The
different ways of breathing—The different ways of check-
ing and interrupting steps and gestures.

15. *Double and Triple Speed and Slowness of Movements.*—These exercises constitute a bodily preparation
for the musical processes of developing a theme known
as "augmentation" and "diminution." It may be noticed
that, in their fugues, composers usually confine themselves to doubling or quadrupling the speed or slowness
of their theme. A new element in rhythmic development is constituted by trebly augmenting or diminishing
the speed of a binary rhythm.

16 and 17. *Plastic Counterpoint and Polyrhythm.*— These exercises are simple transpositions in the corporal sphere of current exercises of musical technique. The advantage of these transpositions is that they accustom the organism to experience simultaneously impressions of various kinds. One can imagine counterpoints of all kinds. The interesting and useful thing is to experience —*live*—them organically. Polyrhythm is facilitated by the cultivation of automatisms. An arm will execute a rhythm automatically, while the mind regulates the execution of a second rhythm by another limb.

18. *"Pathetic" Accentuation—Dynamic and Agogic Nuances (Musical Expression).*—All the preceding exercises aim at developing feeling for time and rhythm. The following exercises tend to awaken the student's temperament, and to cause his body to vibrate in unison with music. They "place" the different degrees of amplitude of movements, the *crescendi* and *decrescendi* of innervation, teaching the body to pass rapidly from one expressive *nuance* to another, seeking to arouse the personal music of different individualities, and to establish lines of rapid communication between the aural and motor systems by an attempt to perfect the harmonisation of the nervous system, trained to immediate activity or passivity, as occasion demands. In short, they endeavour to co-ordinate external music with that within each of us, and which is only the echo of our individual rhythms, our sorrows and joys, our desires and powers.

19. *Exercises in Notation of Rhythms.*—The student is trained to record a rhythm he hears or sees executed.

20. *Exercises in Improvisation (Cultivation of Imaginative Faculties).*—The student, upon command, has to improvise a series of bars in 2, 3, 4, 5, or 6 time, etc., or to invent rhythms, utilising given elements, with or without anacrusis, with pathetic accentuation, rests, syncopations, etc., in phrases and sentences ; likewise combined rhythms.

21. *Conducting Rhythms (Rapid Communication to Others—Soloists or Groups—of Individual Sensations and Feelings).*—Being given a rhythm that the students know by heart, a student has to conduct a performance of it by indicating in expressive gestures the agogic or dynamic nuances.

22. *Execution of Rhythms by Several Groups of Pupils (Initiation into Musical Phrasing).*—Each rhythm of a musical phrase is expressed by a group of students, the *ensemble* of the groups punctuating the different episodes of the complete work.

* * * * *

It must be understood that these exercises do not profess to constitute the whole artistic training of the student, but they must, in due course, inevitably develop his self-knowledge—revealing to him his numerous motor faculties, and augmenting the sum of his vital sensations. Art cannot dispense with knowledge of life. Only by familiarising the student with life can we develop in him a love for art and the desire to pursue it.

Aural Training (Solfège)

After a year's rhythmic training, the student passes into the solfège class. He will continue the above series of exercises, the master adapting them to the needs of a musical voice and ear. After developing the student's mental hearing and physical expression of *rhythms*, he will proceed to train his power of hearing, realising, and creating musical *sounds in rhythm*.

APPLICATION OF EXERCISES IN RHYTHMIC MOVEMENT TO THE STUDY OF SOLFÈGE

1. *Contraction and Decontraction of the Muscles of the Neck and the Breathing Muscles. Rhythmical Gymnastics for the Lungs.*—The study of different methods of vocal

attack, and the enunciation of consonants. Conflicting movements of arms, shoulders, and diaphragm. Combination of vocal attack with the corresponding attack in beginning to march. Distinguishing divers nuances of intensity of sounds. Connection between breathing and vocal emission. Study of vocal registers.

2. *Metrical Division and Accentuation.*—Differentiation of bars by means of vocal and labial accentuation. Attacking sound at a definite moment at or without the command. Rapid substitution of a corporal movement for an attack of sound—of an attack on a consonant for one on a vowel.

3. *Metrical Memorisation.*—The master signifies by "hopps" a series of attacks of sound regularly measured and accentuated. The student memorises their number and accentuation, and repeats them.

4. *Rapid Conception of Time by the Eye and Ear.*—Study of musical symbols, staves, and clefs. Metrical expression by breathing movements, or vocal sounds, of series of measured notes written on the blackboard or sung by the master.

5. *Perception of the Pitch (of Sounds Sung) by Means of Dynamic Muscular Sense.*—The student learns to differentiate vocal sounds from the sensation produced by the varying degrees of tension of the vocal chords, and according to the localisation of sound vibrations. His hand, laid on his chest, neck, jaw, nose, or brow, enables him, by means of the different forms of resonance of vibrations, to realise the pitch of the notes emitted. Study of the relations between the intensity and pitch of sound. Study of major and minor keys. Recognition and imitation of selected notes in the scale. Divers modes of setting a series of notes to rhythm. Reading melodies.

6. *Application to the Voice of Exercises in Spontaneous Will and Inhibition.*—Substitution, to order, in a melodic rhythm, of the voice for bodily movements, and *vice versa*.

Spontaneous accentuation and punctuation at signs from the master. Sudden checks and resumption of the song at other signs.

7. *Exercises in Concentration. Creation of Mental Hearing of Sounds.*—The student sings a melody or a scale. At the word "hopp," he ceases singing and continues the melody or scale in *thought.* Aural perception of the harmonics of a sound. Distinguishing the tone of a particular voice from a medley of others singing or talking, etc.

8. *Association of Continuous Bodily Movements with Sustained Vocal Sounds. Their Combination with Interrupted Movements.*

9. *Exercises in the Acquisition of Vocal Automatisms, and their Combinations and Alternations with Vocal Expressions of Spontaneous Will.*—The student sings a scale according to a certain rhythm. At the word "hopp," he continues the scale on another rhythm. . . . Or he may, after singing a series of thirds or fourths, etc., sing another interval at command. . . . Or again, while singing the scale, he may have to jump to one or other of the notes at a sign from the master, etc.

10, 11, and 12. *Application of Rhythmic Exercises to Vocal "Realisation."*—Chains of rhythms, *i.e.* imitation in canon, bar by bar, of a melody sung by the master. . . . Study of rests.

13. *Exercise in Dissociation.—*

The student sings *ff* while the body makes movements *pp*

    ,,   ,, *pp* ,,   ,,   ,,   *ff*

    ,,   ,, *ff* while one limb moves $<$ and another $>$

    ,,   ,, *pp*   ,, $>$,, $<$

    ,,   ,, $<>$,,   ,, *ff* ,,   *pp*

    ,,   ,, 3 notes while the arms or feet execute 2, 4, or 5 movements, and *vice versa*, etc.

14. *Study of Rests and Phrasing.*—Anacrusis—Rests occupied by mental singing—Sentences and phrases—Law of contrasts and antitheses—Contrapuntal phrasing.

15. *Double and Triple Speed and Slowness of Movements.*—The student, while singing a melody, must, at the command "hopp," effect the double speed or slowness of a bar or beat. The arms beating the measure continue their movements in the original *tempo.* Combinations and contrasts of double or triple speed, or slowness of sound, with that of limbs.

16 and 17. *Plastic Polyrhythm and Counterpoint.*—The student will sing a rhythm while marching only the second half of each note-value, or *vice versa.* He will learn to sing a melody while executing a different rhythm by means of bodily movements. He may execute a canon : singing the first part, clapping his hands for the second, and marching the third. He will listen to a two-part rhythm in the same time, and proceed to sing first the higher, then the lower part. He will listen to a succession of chords, and reproduce each vocal line one after the other, etc., etc.

18. *Emotional Accentuation—Dynamic and Agogic Nuances (Musical Expression).*—The student is trained to accentuate the important notes of a rhythm, to accelerate or retard, effect *crescendi* or *decrescendi*—first by instinct, then by analysis. Study of the relations between the pitch and accentuation of sounds.*

19. *Exercises in Notation of Melodies, Polyphonies, and Harmonic Successions.*

20. *Exercises of Vocal Improvisation.*—The student sings a melody upon a given rhythm, or improvises rhythms upon successions of notes of equal duration.

21 and 22. *Conducting of Rhythms.*—The student learns a melody by heart, then conducts it before a group of students, who interpret it according to his indications. The same for melodies in several parts.

* * * * *

* See the rules of phrasing and accentuation in the three volumes entitled "*Les Gammes et les Tonalités*" (Jobin & Cie., Publishers, Lausanne).

As will be seen, all these exercises in solfège correspond, number for number, with those in rhythmic movement. The student will also learn to distinguish keys, according to the method described in my "Essay in the Reform of Musical Education" (pp. 8 *et seq.*), and applied in the three volumes on Solfège, already referred to. He may then commence the study of harmony. Control of the progressions is assured by his feeling for movement, faculties of concentration, hearing, and listening (cultivated by his rhythmic training), and sense of muscular force regulating the accuracy of the voice. Before transcribing successions of chords, he will feel them resonate within him. Appreciating the connection between melody and movement, there will remain the co-ordination of movement, melody, and harmony. He will then be in a position to undertake the study of

Pianoforte Improvisation

i.e. rapid and spontaneous instrumental composition.

For this section of musical education, which is the synthesis of all the others, the student will require a special technique for fingers, hand, and arm, etc., facilitated, like that in solfège, by his training in rhythmic movement. The above excercises will therefore have to be adapted to new requirements created by instrumental technique. These will naturally embrace the special and universally known exercises, without which it would be impossible to acquire perfect virtuosity. But we must point out that what pianists call "technique" is too often confused with simple rapidity. Dancers of the old school, though possessing extraordinary velocity, are devoid alike of balance in executing continuous movements and of feeling for correct nuances, phrasing, and successions of harmonised gestures—and yet they pass, with spectators and critics, for past masters in virtuosity, the word virtuosity being, to them, synonymous with velocity ! The same is apt to happen with regard to instrumental virtuosity, which becomes a mere exercise in rapid movements, failing to produce that unity of perceptive and reflective sensorial and analytical activities, which alone can conduce to perfection of style. Every musical manifestation should rest on a joint physical and intellectual basis, demonstrating the inseparability of body from soul. If instrumental technique is to produce a mere mechanical flexibility of fingers, why not replace these by even more efficiently flexible machines ? For our purposes the ideal technique can only be attained by a constant collaboration of fingers and brain, allying muscular sensations with emotional feeling. A musical *virtuoso* requires more than mere agility and physical power, vitality, and instinct and for decorative effects : he requires, in addition, diversity of touch in slow as in quick movements, in runs as well as in melodic phrases ; balance of dynamic effects ; the art of musical " breathing," that is, of establishing regulated contrasts ; and the art of adapting to his particular temperament the individualistic effects of the great composers.* I know few pianists capable of treating a " run " as a simple acceleration of speed in the musical realm of ideas and feelings, and who refrain from isolating the particular line of the run from the *ensemble* of divers opposing or converging lines constituting the architecture of the piece.

Before touching the piano the student should possess the muscular mechanism necessary for its mastery—at least, as regards the practising of preparations and repressions of movements, and combinations of synergic and constraining muscles. He should likewise be

---

* We should mention the remarkable work by Mlle Blanche Selva, on Pianoforte Technique, in which may be found highly interesting observations on the physiology of movements at the piano. The exercises of the Selva method, like a number of the Leschetizky, Philipp, and Matthay methods, are based on direct observation of the natural rhythms of the hand and arm.

familiar with the elements of solfège, and possess the ear to enable him to compare mentally sounds on paper with those he is about to produce on the instrument. The following table of exercises is founded on the preceding two, with which the reader would do well to compare it. It does not include the regular exercises in harmony and counterpoint, which are indispensable for pianoforte improvisation, and which may be practised concurrently with our own.

Application of Exercises in Rhythm and Solfège to Practice of Pianoforte Improvisation

1. *Exercises in Muscular Contraction and Decontraction.*—Study of the different mechanisms of the arm ; attacking sounds by means of different starting-points in the movement of the arm, forearm, and wrist. Study of articulations of the shoulder, forearm, wrist, and fingers, in associated and dissociated movements (isolated and combined articulations) ; divers articulations of the fingers (phalanges, cushions, and tips) ; wrist raised or lowered, etc. Dissociated movements, vertical and horizontal, *legato* and *staccato.* Technique of the pedal.

2. *Metrical Division and Accentuation.*—Study of the scales with regular accentuations and equal time-measures (duolets, triolets, quadriolets, quintolets, etc.) in every tone and tempo. The same with arpeggios and successions of chords. Regular accentuations in unequal beats (alternations of duolets and triolets, quadriolets and sextolets, etc.). Irregular and pathetic accentuations at the word "hopp." Application of all these exercises to different rhythmic formulas.

3. *Metrical Memorisation.*—The student plays scales and successions of chords not specially accentuated. By means of the command "hopp," the master calls for a series of notes, regularly or irregularly barred and

accentuated. The student memorises their number and accentuation, and repeats them (without "hopps").

4. *Rapid Conception of Time by the Eye and Ear.*—The master plays softly, at a second piano, scales in various times or rhythms. The student at once imitates (in syncopation) the rhythms and accentuations, noticing the repetition of accents, which he afterwards reproduces from memory. The same with successions of chords. The student plays chords or melodies upon rhythms indicated on the blackboard.

5. *Study of Rhythms in Space by Means of the Muscular Sense.*—The student, with his eyes closed, directs his arms to different points of the keyboard, and measures the distance between these points, according to the greater or lesser amplitude of the movements, and the difference of the muscular sensations they call forth. While playing a scale, the master's " hopp " instructs him to skip an octave, two octaves, or a third, fifth, etc.

6. *Application of Exercises in spontaneous Will and Inhibition to Piano-playing.*—The master's " hopp " calls for pauses and resumptions of playing, changes of rhythm and tone, chords, transpositions, variations of pace, alternations of nuances, etc.

7. *Exercises in Concentration. Mental Hearing.*—While executing a succession of chords, the student pauses to hear mentally the chord he ought to play. Playing only three parts in a chorale for four voices, and following the fourth part in his mind, etc.

8. *Associations of Arm and Vocal Movements.*—The student sings a continuous melody, which he accompanies by chords or scales, and *vice versa*.

9. *Exercises for the Acquisition of numerous Automatisms, and their Combination and Alternation with Actions of spontaneous Volition.*—The student executes a fixed rhythm, concentrating on its melodisation and harmonisation. At the word " hopp," he must invent a rhythm of a different order. Or, *vice versa*, the " hopp " evokes a modula-

tion simultaneously with a change of rhythm, or a change of rhythm in one only of the hands, etc. The voice follows the melody played on the piano ; at "hopp" it suddenly opposes a different melody or another rhythm —the "hopp" elicits changes of time, suppressions or additions of beats, or fragments of rhythms, etc., etc.

10, 11, and 12. *Application of Rhythmic Exercises to Pianoforte Execution.*—Practice of agogic nuances, calculated *accelerandi* and *ritardandi* ; of syncopations by anticipation and retardation ; of subdivisions of time-durations, etc., etc.

13. *Exercises in Dissociations of Movements.*—The two hands playing with contrast of rhythm, time, nuances, phrasing, tone-quantity or tone-quality.

14. *Study of Rests and Phrasing.*—Sentences and phrases ; different kinds of rests and anacruses. Laws of contrast.

15. *Double and Triple Speed and Slowness of Movements.*—The student plays scales or successions of chords, and, at "hopp," augments or diminishes the pace doubly or trebly. Agogic augmentation and diminution of given rhythms. Combinations of double and half, triple and double speeds, etc.

16 and 17. *Plastic Counterpoint and Polyrhythm.*—The student's left hand plays a note or a chord on the second half of the beat executed by the right hand. And *vice versa.* Counterpoint in duolets, triolets, quadriolets, etc. Different rhythms and beats in either hand, and exercises in canon. Study of various kinds of counterpoint—pianoforte counterpoint to vocal themes, and *vice versa.* Polydynamics.

18. *"Pathetic" Accentuation— Nuances—Laws of Expression.*—Study of relations between harmony and rhythm,* chords and accentuations, agogics and dynamics, touch and hearing. The part played by modulation in

* See fifth part of the Dalcroze method : " *L'Improvisation et l'accompagnement au piano* " (Jobin & Cie., Lausanne). (In preparation.)

the development of musical themes, and in expressions of spontaneous emotion.

19 and 20. *Notation and Improvisation of Rhythms.*— The student improvises a bar at the piano ; then notates it as a figured bass. Pianoforte improvisation of rhythmic accompaniments to vocalised melodies. Invention of rhythmic melodies to accompany barred successions of harmonies.

21. *Conducting Rhythms.*—The student improvises freely at the piano, under the direction of the master or another student, who beats the time and indicates the dynamic and agogic nuances.

22. *Improvisation at Two Pianos (or in Quartet).*—Two students improvise alternate sentences or phrases.

*   *   *   *   *

A comparative study of the above three series of exercises will serve to show the necessity for conscientious research into the elementary relations between the three principal branches of musical education. It is significant that no previous study of harmony or composition has indicated the reciprocal influence of rhythms and dynamics on melodies and harmonies. In fact, musical education hitherto has failed to establish any correlation between the different constituents of music, treating each as isolated and specialised. Our musical mentors of to-morrow will have to work towards the general harmonisation of these elements.

VII

EURHYTHMICS AND MUSICAL COMPOSITION (1915)

Rhythm in nature—Theory of the born musician—Experiments in musical rhythm—Contrasts between movement and its arrests, sounds, and silences —New method of noting time-values—Unequal beats—Analysis of the elements of a rhythm—Rhythmic activity in dissociation and opposition— Musical periods and the art of phrasing—The emotional effects of rests —Agogic nuances—Twice and three times as fast and as slow—Rubato— Observance of the sense of time-duration—New education and methods.

HAVE you ever found yourself on some fine summer's day lying on a grassy slope, watching the trees quivering with life, and above them the clouds ploughing a blue sky, whilst a soft breeze stirs the leaves and branches and causes the cornfields to undulate ? . . . At first you will be conscious only of a vast collective movement, a colossal harmony of sounds and rhythms. . . . Then, little by little, your eye and ear may distinguish details of the symphony, and discern in this harmonious conglomeration a whole polyrhythm of incomparable richness. Each larger rhythm will split into numerous distinct groups of smaller rhythms, and blend or conflict with other movements of a different order, the aspect varying infinitely according to the degree of force of the wind which brings it to birth. Nature, in her eternal movement, vibrates both in time and out of time. The mighty rhythm of the universe is a compound of myriads of synchronising rhythms of infinite diversity, each possessing individual life. One cannot witness this polyrhythm without wondering that such rhythmic profusion

as nature pours forth, whilst providing virtually the
painter's whole inspiration, so seldom appears to move
or inspire the musician. Music is a combination of
rhythm and sound. How comes it that, since Beethoven,
our musicians have sought progress only in harmony
and tone, and have lost the mastery of sound-movements in which the great Flemish composers and
John Sebastian Bach excelled? The ear is capable of
appreciating not only variety of tone-quality, nuances of
intensity, and differences of pitch, but also the infinite
variety of time-values and duration. Primitive peoples
manifest, with regard to polyrhythm, far more ingenuity
and originality than ourselves. Would it not be worth
a musician's while to devote as much care to the study
of agogics and dynamics as to that of melody and
harmony? At least, one would suppose that the
experiments of fellow-musicians, particularly sensitive
to sound-movements, would not be without interest
to him.

But this is apparently not the case, since so many
music professors find our attempts at education "by
rhythm" useless or fantastic. It might be worth our
while to reason with them, in the hope of converting
them; but life is too short, and we prefer creative work
to bandying words. One can understand an inability to
recognise the *equal* importance of rhythm and sound in
music, but I maintain that no true musician, entering a
hall of machinery in full movement, could fail to be
captivated by the whirr of the fabulous symphony produced by the magic of combined and dissociated rhythms,
and to be tempted inevitably to extract the secrets of this
moving and quivering life that animates nature, man and
his work alike.

*   *   *   *   *

There is a theory regarding the "born musician,"
according to which no amount of musical study can have
any influence on temperament. On this is based the

verdict of certain seers that rhythmic movement can be of no direct service to the art of music ; for (they tell you), on the one hand, it has nothing to teach the born musician, and, on the other, a person not born a musician can never be made one ! This theory, which is held by many musicians, will not " hold water." Eurhythmics reveals to the born musician a host of subconscious resources, which he could otherwise acquire only by dint of long years of laborious and repeated personal researches and experiments. On the other hand, alone among all systems of musical education, eurhythmics is capable of awakening dormant or moribund temperament, of provoking in the organism the conflicts necessary for establishing the control and balance of resistances, and of bringing to consciousness, by means of the harmonisation of cerebral and motor centres and the canalisation of nervous forces, undreamt-of sources of creative and artistic vitality.

It is impossible for those specialising in music to judge eurhythmics from a public demonstration. The minute work of analysing and constructing rhythms can only be appreciated in the lessons, and then only by persons who are themselves actually taking part with their whole body and mind, *i.e.* personally experiencing them. A public demonstration can only exhibit the results, conveying no idea of the enormous difficulties body and mind encounter in combating nervous resistances, and in performing their rhythmic functions in calm and concentration.

But, apart from its general bearing on the human organism, eurhythmics exercises a further influence on the art of music itself—an influence that will assume a definite shape only when creative artists of all kinds have thoroughly assimilated its principles, put them into practice, and extended their scope. . . . At the same time, fifteen years of assiduous research have accumulated a sufficient amount of evidence of the potential creative powers (from the strictly musical point of view) of the method to justify the publication of its principles. It would require a whole volume to expound the detailed processes of our experiments, and the concatenation and association of ideas which they have brought to light, and it is to be feared that a summary exposition of certain of our claims will appeal to some minds as mere amiable paradoxes. We are confident, however, that others, better trained, will immediately grasp the essentials of our system, and it is to them that we dedicate these suggestions, which only time can fully justify.

    *   *   *   *   *

In no other system is rhythm treated with the pedagogic care accorded to other branches of musical science. Berlioz, in a too little read chapter, deplores the omission from conservatoire syllabuses of special classes in rhythm, and indicates the numerous researches that might be undertaken, and the profound studies to which a musician should devote himself, in this totally unexplored region of musical movement and dynamics. He, however, neglected to place musical rhythm, and to give a clear idea of the part it plays in musical composition. We can judge a work of architecture only in relation to the space in which it is constructed; and similarly musical rhythms can be appreciated only in relation to the atmosphere and space in which they move. In other words, *musical rhythm can only be appreciated in relation to silence and immobility.* Study the conditions of silence, and you at once create the necessity—from the human as from the æsthetic point of view—of furnishing it with its natural counterpoise—sound—which, in breaking it, sets in relief its enormous recuperative, and, consequently, emotional capacities. Musical rhythmics is the art of establishing due proportion between sound movement and static silence, of opposing them, and of preparing for the one by means of the other, according to the laws of contrast and balance on which all style

I

depends ; according to the nuances of time and dynamics that constitute the individuality, and the nuances of tone, pitch, and intensity of sound which create in music that higher element of a mystical and impersonal nature, that connects the individual with the universe. A rest in music is simply an interruption of the sound, or a transference into the region of internal hearing of phenomena of external hearing.* Unfortunately, the ambition of most of our present-day musicians would seem to be to annihilate silence in sound ; and a regeneration of the art of music will largely depend on the place our future geniuses will assign to "rests" in the architecture of rhythm. The realisation of the possibilities of the infinite variety of time-durations is also in an embryonic stage, and an inexhaustible source of new emotions will enrich the art of musical expression once its scope, at present limited to the employment of harmonic, contrapuntal, and orchestral nuances, is extended to include all the new emotional resources contributed by nuances of sound-duration. All art is based on contrast. An *accelerando* or *ritardando* attains vitality only by contrast with the normal *tempo*. Nuances of time exercise an irresistible and inevitable influence both on melody and harmony ; and the development of the latter will depend not only on the extent to which musicians of the future concern themselves with agogic and dynamic variations, but also on the direct influence of human emotions on durations of sounds, of beats, and of bars—on the reciprocal relations of these, and on their contrasts with the higher and inexorable serenity of silence.

*　　　*　　　*　　　*　　　*

New Notation of Musical Time-values.—Before treating of the relations of time-values, it will be convenient to establish certain new forms of writing these. Long notes in compound time have up to the present been

---

* The rest, while devoid of movement, is by no means devoid of life. (See Chapter VI., p. 95.)

recorded by means of a slur between two or more notes of ordinary duration (*e.g.* 9/8 = 𝅗𝅥.𝅘𝅥., or 15/8 = 𝅝.𝅘𝅥.). In introducing bars of 5, 7, and 8 beats, also unequal beats and rhythms in which agogic nuances of a highly subtle and delicate nature are obtained by successions of different and varied time-values, the necessity arises of amending our system of musical notation with a view to recording no matter what gradations of time, by reference to a single fixed symbol. The following is suggested : as a dot after a note (𝅝.) prolongs the latter by half its value, two dots, one on top of the other (𝅝:) shall be taken to prolong it by a quarter of its value, and three dots (𝅝⋮) by an eighth of its value. (See Appendix, Ex. 1.)

* * * * *

Time Signatures.—We propose a new method of indicating the time of a piece at the beginning, or changes in the course of its development. In many cases the present signatures are neither clear nor consistent. In indicating a 3/4 bar the figure 3 denotes the *number* of beats, and the 4 the *duration* of each beat ; but in writing 6/8 the figure 6, instead of denoting the number of beats, denotes their subdivisions, etc. It would be preferable to utilise the first number to indicate consistently the number of beats, and to denote the duration of each beat by the symbol corresponding to that duration.* (See Appendix, Ex. 2.)

* * * * *

Alternating Bars.—There is no reason to insist upon regular bar-lengths throughout an entire piece. In most folk-songs the melody is subject to irregularities of measure. It is only in the conventional and classical works of the last two or three centuries that we find a systematic division into regular bars. Far be it from us

* This has been the practice of some teachers in England for over thirty years.—*Translator's Note.*

to object to this classical regularity of bar-time, but, seeing that every irregularity in a work of art must be the product of an emotion, we suggest that the question of the employment of irregular bars should be the subject of special analysis on the part of every musician. We have set out briefly the divers causes of an emotional nature that may justify the exceptional use of irregular bars in the most scientifically constructed music. (See Appendix, Ex. 3.)

*   *   *   *   *

The Coincidence of Metre ana Harmony.—Every change of time or rhythm calls for modifications in the harmony. Metre and harmony have a reciprocal influence on each other, and a succession of notes scanned in threes requires a different harmonisation from one scanned in fours. The same sounds may be treated either as integral parts of the harmony or as unessential notes, according to the metre. And the resulting variations of harmonisation, apart from their metrical significance, constitute an excellent exercise for the student of harmony. (See Appendix, Ex. 4.)

*   *   *   *   *

Anacrusis and Phrasing.—The unity of a musical phrase depends not only on the shape of its melody, but also on the logical use of its rhythmic elements. If we closely analyse any classical work, we shall find that the impression of order which it conveys is due to the fact that no element of form alien to the main idea, which is the product of a general emotion, is allowed to enter other than as a contrast to the elementary rhythm, on which the initial theme is based.

Mathis Lussy, one of the pioneers in the study of the physiology of rhythm, has written a book wholly devoted to anacrusis, which every musician has read or should read.* This is not the place to insist on the

---

* "*L'Anacrouse,*" by Mathis Lussy (Heugel, éditeur, 2 bis, rue Vivienne, Paris).

importance of the anacrusis in musical phrasing. An analysis of the elements constituting a very simple rhythm (see Appendix, Ex. 5) will, however, indicate the profound modifications in the plastic aspect of a rhythm, and in its influence on the sound of that rhythm, introduced by an anacrusis.

* * * * *

Contrasts of Activity and Repose.—Having established the relations and manner of combination of the divers elements of a rhythm, we must next show how—by the repetition of rhythms alternating either with rests (contrasts of activity and repose) or with the opposition of different rhythms—one achieves the logical construction of musical phrases.

All art is based on contrasts, on antitheses. Pictorial art depends on contrasts of light and shade, on contrasts and shades of colour. The art of architecture consists of contrasts of lines and plastic material. In music, the simple development of primordial rhythmic elements produces an effect of monotony. After every form of activity, our human nature requires to recuperate by resting or changing the nature of its movement. To study the nature of contrasts—the nuances of activity and of its antitheses, and of their carefully balanced manifestations, and the harmony of opposing movements in the individual under the influence of feelings and sensations —is to surprise the secrets of sentient and sensitive life itself. (See Appendix, Ex. 6.)

* * * * *

We have now shown the fundamental laws according to which balance may be established between the different elements of a rhythm—between a rhythm, its repetition, and contrasts of silence or counter-activity. There remains for us to trace the results of our system in so far as they involve the introduction in logical sequence of the elements of a dynamic and agogic order. These are the direct product of spontaneous emotion, creating individual life in the social order and diversity in unity.

Let us treat first of the irregularity of beats, and endeavour to show how, once the alternation of uneven bars is admitted, we are led, in attempting to combine two such measures so as to form what we may call a compound measure, to originate a new means of expression : *unequal beats.*

Unequal Beats.—Regular compound bars are produced by the grouping at double or triple speed of regular bars. Just as we may vary these by introducing uneven bars, so uneven groupings of notes of short duration may be formed. These will produce at first sight an impression of irregularity. But their conscious and persistent repetition will create a new regularity and symmetry which will prevent their compromising the unity of the metre. Incidentally, this manner of grouping exists in embryo in the alternating accentuations of six quavers in 3/4 and 6/8 times. (See Appendix, Ex. 7.)

* * * * *

Many musicians fear that these disparities and irregularities may prejudice unity of style, by producing abrupt and jerky phrases and rhythms. It is, however, an established fact that every series of uneven time-values repeated at *regular intervals* gives an impression of *regularity*, in the same way that the twelve-foot rhythm of an alexandrine, since Victor Hugo, is retained intact, though those twelve feet, previously severable only into six and eight, may now be split into sections of three fours, four threes, six twos, and even into variations of four and eight, three, five and four, etc. Far from abruptness, the style has thereby acquired a new flexibility. Exactly the same is happening in music. It is necessarily difficult to describe in words the broad value of this new means of musical expression and shading already used by a few musicians like Ravel, Cyril Scott, Stravinsky, etc. Those who are impervious to the psycho-physiological appeal of these emotional irregularities could never be moved to employ them, or, if they were, would not be able to employ them naturally. Education may, however, if undertaken in time, repair all such deficiencies. (See Appendix, Ex. 8.)

*　　*　　*　　*　　*

Changes of Pace.—The subdivision into three shorter notes of an isolated beat in a bar whose regular beats are twofold—or *vice versa*—may be adopted in the succeeding bars as a regular subdivision, and thus initiate a quicker or slower pace, as the case may be. That is the real meaning and purpose of the agogic nuances designated under the approximative indications of *un poco più lento* or *un poco più animato;* it may also help us to appreciate the so-called *rubato* in Hungarian music, which is not a real *rubato,* but whose effects of contrasted movements are produced by the establishment, as time-unit, of neither the crotchet nor the quaver, but the semiquaver. (See Appendix, Ex. 9.)

*　　*　　*　　*　　*

Rests.—The rest in music is the negative equivalent of the sound-duration that it replaces; and, conversely, sound is the positive equivalent of the rest for which it is substituted. The art of music might derive enormous benefit from a new conception of musical sound as contrapuntal to silence (rests), instead of as obliterating the latter, as is the present practice. Actually, the maximum time occupied by rests in the course of a symphony lasting three-quarters of an hour is not more than two or three minutes. We smile at the ineptness of a painter who overloads his canvas with colour, but it nevers occurs to us to question the taste of the composer in according an infinitesimal place to the sole element of contrast that can throw sound-movement into adequate relief—the rest. A rest serves to conceal preparation for succeeding activities. The length of this preparation for future action depends on the course of the preceding arrest of activity.

Movement may be suspended—

(*a*) by sudden exhaustion ;

(*b*) by progressive exhaustion.

The interruption, that is, the *rest*, may be followed—

(*a*) by an immediate resumption of energy and activity ;

(*b*) by a slow recuperation of energy.

In each of these cases the preparation for the rest, and the resumption of movement, are of different nature and speed.

Through rests, music may acquire a third dimension —length, breadth, and *depth* (the rest, like a note value, penetrates, so to speak, the volume of the rhythm). Provision is made for rests in every art save music, which alone pours itself out in a constant flow of nervous energy, in incessant volubility, insufficiently punctuated for breathing purposes. Imagine four persons all talking vigorously at once. . . . According to the classic symphonic procedure, there may be an occasional lull, while one or other of them is silent. But there will always be at least one to continue the discussion. And with what prolixity and self-assurance ! This shows a fundamentally false conception, the complete rest forming one of the most natural elements of contrast.

A rest, while deprived of movement, is by no means deprived of vibration. . . . While the sound is arrested, the external rhythm becomes internal, and continues to vibrate in the hearer's organism. Silence may be more eloquent than speech. Succeeding sound, it perpetuates the latter in the soul of the auditor—whether in music or in conversation. We recall Molière's couplet :

> " A sigh, or a blush, or a look of despair,
> Or even a *silence*, the heart may lay bare."

(See Appendix, Ex. 10.)

*　　　*　　　*　　　*　　　*

Twice and Three times as Quickly and Slowly.—Under the impulse of particular emotions rhythms may quicken or slacken. Musical form, established on sound traditions, admits the possibility of a double or quadruple, half or quarter, speed of binary rhythms ; of triple or sextuple, third or sixth, speed of ternary rhythms. Why not double the speed of ternary, or triple that of binary rhythms— an entirely new development ? Why not halve the speed of quinary rhythms, quintuple the speed of binary rhythms ?

Music is composed, in Schumann's phrase, with our heart's blood. Why be content with such a pedantic circulation of that blood ? The circulation depends on our nervous system, on our general or particular emotional state, or temperament, that modifies from day to day the circumstances of our life, the acuteness of our desires, our prejudices, our revolts, our appeasements and our submissions. Is not variety the essence of art ? And may not variety exist in time-values and their infinite degrees as well as in harmony and tone-colour ? It may be objected that a poet may remain perfectly natural while conforming to the classical exigencies of lyric expression. Granted ; but in poetry it is a question of arranging words rhythmically to express pre-existent thoughts, whereas in music it is the rhythm itself, produced by emotion, that most commonly gives birth and form to the melodic idea.

A musical education should therefore encourage the free development and progress of rhythm. Every augmentation of this faculty, in providing new media of expression, will contribute to the enrichment of music as a whole. (See Appendix, Ex. 11.)

*　　*　　*　　*　　*

The realisation of original, beautiful, and finished inspirations, demands an adequate organism. Unfortunately, too many ideas and visions fail to attain expression through lack of flexibility and mobility in the exponent. A musician, steeped in the classical traditions of rhythm and measure, will never be able to avail himself of the achievements of eurhythmics, until he has assimilated the media of expression produced by the practice of one or other system of education by and in rhythm. Exercise develops our organs. Musical educationalists have only to meet in sympathy, and collaborate, for the cause of eurhythmics to be won. In, twenty years' time, the new methods we are advocating will have become classic. For the time being we are up against not only the indifference, but even the resistance of certain musicians. These negative spirits—who disparage or denounce original works without attempting to understand them—are often mere " grousers," disillusioned alike as to themselves and their calling. Others scorn the new out of veneration for the old. They, at least, may be respected, and even have their uses, acting as signposts on the road of progress, reminding pioneers that their work can live so long only as it constitutes a logical evolution out of past endeavour. Eurhythmics requires for its ideal manifestation the intimate, whole-hearted collaboration of a great pianist, a great singer, a great master of harmony, a great conductor, and several accomplished instrumentalists—one and all devoting heart and soul to their work. Durable artistic works are not created out of mere intuition : they demand a complete mastery of their art by the accumulation of experience on experience. Artists of the present day are manifestly deficient in feeling for simple time-durations and their potential nuances. They are careful to avoid wrong notes and wrong harmonies, but remain blissfully unconscious of correct time-values. Has one ever known a critic protest against mistakes of this sort ? And yet, for musicians who have studied eurhythmics and possess the time-sense, the degrees of time-duration constitute a scale of shades to be as carefully followed as variations of pitch. *Inter alia,* a whole new literature for the organ will be produced once organists have acquired this sense of time—that instrument being deprived of all nuances of a tactile nature.

Obviously, a revolution in style cannot be accomplished in a day. Every style is the product of the ideas and practices of the period. But how are modern ideas ever to take definite shape so long as our musicians refuse to discard the methods of the past, to adopt even the means of attaining progress, while they refuse even to investigate the claims of those whose instinct informs them of possibilities of expression hitherto unthought of? Education by and in rhythm is in effect no more than a collation and development of the ideas that are everywhere in the air. Thus unequal beats, unconsciously employed by a few of our musicians, are in constant use in the East. The whole art of musical expression may be enriched by the new sensibility resulting from the acquisition of a sense of time-duration and all its nuances. In seeking to initiate composers of to-morrow into the logic of unequal bars, unequal beats three times as fast, and other rhythmical devices, our intention is by no means to influence them to compose in a new style, but merely to assure a greater scope for the expression of their genuine emotional impulses. Admittedly, our illustrations are for the most part examples of irregular form; but, on the one hand, irregularity, as an exceptional device, will serve to throw regularity into relief, and, on the other, a succession of irregularities constitutes, in effect, a new form of regularity. The alternation of styles is a powerful means of musical expression, since in music, more than in any other art, contrast plays an active part in the structure.

*   *   *   *   *

It goes without saying—we lay stress on the repetition—that the utilisation of these divers new rhythmic processes for purposes of musical composition will be possible only after a careful process of assimilation. The

initiation of musicians, susceptible only to *external* phenomena, into the harmonic devices of men like Debussy,
Schönberg, or Stravinsky, can inspire only artificial,
insincere, and consequently inexpressive productions.
Similarly, the application of the many means of modifying rhythms by doubling and tripling the speed or
slowness of isolated beats, by dissociations or irregular
groupings of sounds, etc., will produce only illusory
effects of virtuosity, so long as this new technique is not
sufficiently engrained in the composer as to be directly
and unconsciously subservient to his mental processes.
It is to be feared that much water will flow under the
bridge before our rhythmic education will have sufficiently penetrated and modified mentalities and organisms
for its potential effects to be employed with ease and
grace. Our primary concern—as we have said before—
is that musicians trained in the methods of yesterday
should devote themselves to the study of those of to-
morrow. Not until then will pianoforte masters realise
the beneficial influence of education by and in rhythm
on the study of instrumental technique, and teachers
of composition appreciate the necessity of ever more
closely co-ordinating sound and movement—ear, feeling,
and temperament.

MUSIC, JOY, AND THE SCHOOL (1915)

*The school in relation to society and the family—The nervous system and sensi-
bility in general—What is music ?—Various musical pedagogues realise
their deficiencies and the need for reform—The present curriculum—
Essence of music—Rhythm and tonality—Personal rhythmic experiences
and mental development—What should be taught in music lessons at
primary schools ?—The ear and temperament—The joy of self-knowledge
—Joy and will-power—Joy and the social sense—Good habits—Art and
school fêtes.*

SCHOOL is a preparation for life : in other words, the
child, on leaving school, should be in a position not
only to fulfil the divers obligations of social life, but
also to exercise his will in his practical affairs, according
to his particular temperament and without impinging on
the rights of others.   And the training at school of his
brain, body, will, and sensibility, should be undertaken
simultaneously ; no one of these four indispensable
factors being neglected in favour of another.   Imagine
the horrible, possible consequences, for example, of
developing body at the expense of brain !   And of what
use is brain without will ?   And again, must not brain
and will combined remain ineffectual, so long as they are
not regulated, controlled, and harmonised by moral
sensibility ?

I contend that schools ignore the training of sensibility, with deplorable results on the development of
character.   It is—to say the least of it—strange that
with the existing prevalence of neurasthenia, no attempt
is made to direct the boundless desires arising from ill-
controlled feelings ; that, in newly-developed countries,

where, for the most part, will-power is concentrated, with a marked absence of scruple, on the attainment of commercial success, educationalists show no anxiety to awaken the moral sense of the coming generation, while in countries where too long established traditions have a cramping influence on the development of individuality, no resort is made to expedients for arousing temperament. And yet the means are at hand whereby the coming generation might be trained to a greater flexibility of spirit, a firmer will-power, an intellect less dry and exclusive, more refined instincts, a richer life, and a more complete and profound comprehension of the beautiful.

A mere professional musician should perhaps hesitate to approach a problem of such enormous scope. So many pedagogues regard music as a mere secondary branch of knowledge, entitled only to the last and least place in the school curriculum : a poor, beggarly subject, scarcely worthy of notice. And yet the greatest minds of ancient and modern times have assigned to it an educational rôle of the highest significance. To the charge of trespassing on the domain of education proper, the musician has only to invoke the authority of Plato and most of the Greek philosophers. He might likewise refer to Montaigne, Helvetius, Locke, Leibnitz, Rousseau, Goethe, and Schiller, for evidence that every healthy educational system—that is, every system based on the intimately reciprocal reaction óf body and mind, feeling and thought—assigns a pre-eminent place to music and the arts subservient to it.

The fact that in our schools not more than one or two hours a week are devoted to music, goes far to show that the word " music " has acquired an entirely new significance in our own educational system : it has come to stand for the mechanical production, or, rather, reproduction of sounds—a practice that depends exclusively on imitation, and the end and aim of which is to cram the child's mind with a certain number of

Crescendo of Movement

sentimental tunes of the stock pattern. This certainly is a conception of music very different from that associated with the great names mentioned above. For these masters music represented a sort of compromise between inspiration and form, the art of self-expression by personal rhythm.

Far be it from us to bring charges against any one. We have no desire, in freely expressing our profound convictions, to offend a host of educationalists, many of whom, incidentally, are entirely at one with us in the matter. These, we believe, hold, as we do, that in many cases relegation of music to the background of the school curriculum is due to lack of musical knowledge on the part of the teaching staff. It is gratifying to us to know that a considerable number of members of the teaching profession recognise the inadequacy of their education in music, and declare that, themselves never having received a good musical education, they are unable to bestow such on others. It is beyond dispute that, at the present time, there is, almost from all sides, an urgent call for the reform of our musical education. Yet the greatest confusion prevails as to the means of effecting this reform ; otherwise it would be simply unaccountable that, despite the protests of all musicians, not music, but a mere imitation of music, continues to be taught in most schools. No heed is paid to the appeals of competent authorities ; and, whenever this important question is raised, the dullest dilettantism appears to preside over, and too often to have the last word in, the discussion.

We shall be told that music occupies too modest a place in the school curriculum to admit of the reforms urged by specialists, no matter how beneficial these may appear to be. We entirely dissent from this view. One cannot have it both ways. If one's daughter complained that the height of her heels—as ordained by the current fashion—prevented her from walking properly, one would reply : " Then you must scrap them—unless you prefer to make yourself ridiculous." And to the proposal that music lessons, throughout the whole course of training, must be limited to one hour a week, we likewise reply : " Rather abolish music altogether from your time-tables." One must have time for everything—for music as for every other branch of study. If you regard music as superfluous, leave it alone ; but if you attach importance to it, and the conventional time-tables prove an obstacle, remove the obstacle.

Before everything else, one must make sure that the teaching of music is worth while. And there must be no confusion as to what is to be understood by " music." There are not two classes of music : one for adults, drawing-rooms, and concert-halls, the other for children and schools. There is only one music, and the teaching of it is not so difficult a matter as scholastic authorities are apt to suggest at their congresses. Under an ideal social system, every one will make it his duty to dispense his art and learning freely about him ; every true musician, both composer and artist, will devote an hour daily to the giving of music lessons for the benefit of the public ;—then, and not till then, will the problem be solved. We have a long way to travel before that point is reached. Yet, may we not legitimately ask of those upon whom the whole musical training of our youth depends, that they shall at least regard music not as a pastime, but as an art ;—that they shall treat it, and teach others to treat it, with respect, if not with love, as becoming to an art that, in a well-organised social scheme, should impress every manifestation of beauty with the *cachet* we call style ?

So long as society is badly organised, so long will man be unable to give thought to beauty. Once given the opportunity, he will become a devotee of art, so far as his innate capacities will allow him.

It is not the function of education to develop isolated

individuals.   Its aim is far removed and higher : nothing
short of the progressive development of the race, the
perfecting of its thought and taste.   One cannot cure the
disease of ignorance by increasing one's own knowledge.
It is a question of taking precautionary measures for
future guidance, of influencing the outlook and disposition of the coming generation, and so moulding it as to
ensure the transmission to future generations of a strongly
social instinct and more intense love of truth.

To confine musical education to the teaching of a few
patriotic songs is to give the child "an idea of the
ocean by showing him a drop of water in a glass."   A
tune is nothing other than a feeling expressed in a particular language—music.   What is the use of giving
children sentences to learn by heart in a language of
which they are ignorant ?   This absurdity is enacted
daily in our schools in the name of music lessons !   We
shall be told that this is an exaggeration, that the lessons
are not confined to the teaching of patriotic airs, that
children are also taught to read music at sight.   Admitted
that in some schools children actually *are* taught to read
music.   But how are they taught ?   It is not so much
the result as the method that matters (for our present
purposes).   It is possible, by means of certain mathe-
matised and muscular processes, to contrive to read
music without possessing the slightest feeling for tonality.
But it is precisely feeling for tonality that should be
created before everything, forming, as it does—apart
from rhythm—the whole essence of music.   Tonality is
the vertebral column of harmony.   A melody, deprived
of all time and rhythm, may yet express feeling by
means of gradations and contrasts of tone and of modulations.   A method that professes to teach children to
read music, and is not based on the study of tonality or
scales—the relations between tones and semitones—must
be dismissed as inadequate.   It may produce certain
ephemeral results, but it can never contribute to the

musical progress and general development of the race. And yet, as educationalists, our aim must be ever in that direction. This alone justifies, in the first instance, our forcing children to attend school. In their homes, they are surrounded by the influence of tradition; school widens their horizon, teaching them that man's duty does not consist in working for the passing moment, but involves preparing for the future.

The most important element in music lessons should be their general effect of awakening in the pupil a love for the art; for that purpose it is necessary—passing from the general to the particular—to initiate him into the two primordial elements of music: rhythm and tone.

Rhythm is the basis of all vital, scientific, and artistic phenomena. It produces alike the element of order and measure in movement and the idiosyncrasies of execution. The study of rhythm conduces to the formation of an individuality for all purposes of life—that is, a manner of expressing oneself according to the rhythm most natural and native to one's being, which again is largely dependent on one's constitution, blood circulation, and nervous system.

Rhythm is ignored in our present educational system. A vague attempt is made to inculcate some idea of time, but children leave school without knowing the meaning of rhythm. No one, surely, now doubts that rhythm originates in the body itself! And it is worth noting that the most gifted of all artistic peoples, from the rhythmic point of view—the Greeks—in marking the rhythm of their verses, designated the rhythmic unit by the term "foot," which usage has passed into most modern languages. And yet we have long ceased to scan verses by means of bodily movement, and rhythm has become a purely intellectual conception. That is why children find it so difficult to acquire a feeling for music-rhythm in reading at sight. And we are reduced to the necessity of deliberately severing, for purposes of school training, the two fundamental and equally important elements of music—movement and tone. To teach them simultaneously would confuse the child and compromise the whole effect of the training. The child must there- fore forego the study and analysis of keys, until he is well practised in rhythmic movements. The image of these experiences in corporal rhythm, impressed and re-impressed on his mind, will awaken and develop his rhythmic consciousness; just as, later on, the image of the tonal experiences of the ear, likewise repeatedly engraved on the memory, awakens and develops a feeling for tone. This comprises all that is required in the way of musical education at school.

We now propose to put a few simple questions; by the replies to which, we may judge whether the present system is worth preserving, or whether a reform of musical education is really necessary.

1. Are you of opinion that the child should learn the meaning of words before he is taught to read or write them ?

The answer will probably be in the affirmative.

2. Do you believe that a child will instinctively shun any disagreeable sensation—for instance, that he will keep away from fire before he has been burnt ?

Answer: No.

3. Do you believe that an oyster, encrusted in shell, can understand the delight of a hare in scampering over meadows and woods ?

Answer: No.

4. Do you believe that a myope could follow with the naked eye the flight of an aeroplane crossing the frontier ?

Answer: No.

5. Are you of opinion that one can hear music better with a good than with a bad ear ?

Answer: Yes.

6. Are you of opinion that, by training, even mediocre faculties may be developed ?

Answer : Yes.

The unanimity of the replies all intelligent folk will return to these questions justifies us in declaring that the present system of musical education should be completely reformed. We must begin by setting children exercises in hearing music ; for, strange though it may seem, in very few countries is this the present procedure !

We must again apologise to those of our colleagues who have improvised hearing-exercises in their particular classes. We realise that many of them share our views, and we are extremely gratified. But we are now speaking of our school syllabus, according to which music lessons comprise making children hear what they do not understand, read what they cannot understand, and write down what they have never learnt or felt.

I may be told that in every class there will be found some pupils who hear and understand perfectly. Granted; but they do so not as a result, but *in spite*, of the training. It does not follow, in our opinion, that any one who can read music competently must necessarily be musical. A person without any feeling for music may read with great facility, while another may read extremely badly and yet possess exceptional musical gifts.

The essential is that one should have a good ear, and so be able to appreciate the infinite nuances of pitch and of dynamism of sounds, developments and oppositions of rhythm, and contrasts of tonality ; * and that musical training should develop inner hearing—that is, the capacity for hearing music as distinctly mentally as physically. Every method of teaching should aim, before everything else, at awakening this capacity. We hold also that it should conduce to the development of the individuality, and the perfecting of the whole mechanism of thought and feeling ; achieving, in short, the co-

* See Chapter V., p. 71.

ordination of experience and memory, experience and imagination, the automatic and the conscious, the conscious and the requisites of temperament and fantasy.

The training of sensibility and temperament should precede that of the ear, for rhythm (a product of the balance of active nervous forces) is a fundamental element of music, as of every other art, and, indeed, of every vital manifestation.   And even if his hearing faculties should later prove insufficient to qualify the child to pass for a musician, in the ordinary sense of the word, the training we advocate will have served to enable him, so to speak, to enter into his individuality.   Initiated into the marvellous mechanism of his body, given to him for consecration as a worthy dwelling-place for the soul—confident of achieving without effort or preoccupation any and every movement suggested by others or of his own volition—the child will experience a growing yearning to make full use of the abundant forces in his control. His imagination will likewise develop as his mind, released from all constraint and nervous disquietude, gives full rein to his fantasy.

Functioning develops the organ, and the consciousness of organic functioning develops thought.   And as the child feels himself delivered from all physical embarrassment and mental obsession of a lower order, added to the sense—acquired by the practice of combining his individual efforts with those of the rest of the class—of participation in a collective movement, he will conceive a profound joy of an elevated character, a new factor in ethical progress, a new stimulus to will power.

I call this joy "elevated," because it will not be based on external circumstances.   It will be distinct from pleasure, in that it becomes a permanent condition of the being, independent alike of time and of the events that have given rise to it; an integral element of our organism.   It will not necessarily be accompanied by laughter, as is gaiety; it may quite well make no

external display ; it will flower in the hidden recesses
of the ego, in the mysterious garden of the soul, where
the sap of our individuality is secreted, a sap that cannot
be.squandered—which may be applied in every direction and never exhausted. Joy arises in the child the
moment his faculties are liberated from any restraint,
and he becomes conscious of his control over them, and
decides on the direction in which that control shall be
exercised. This joy is the product of a joint sense of
emancipation and responsibility, comprising a vision of
our creative potentialities, a balance of natural forces,
and a rhythmic harmony of desires and powers.* Germi-
nating in the creative faculties, innate or acquired, this
joy increases in proportion as our powers develop and
our will frees us from the shackles that have burdened
us from birth. The gift of self-knowledge, conferred on
the child by an education calculated to cultivate every
vital spiritual and physical faculty, will produce a sense
of liberation and independence. This self-knowledge
will mean that his education has effected a thorough
co-ordination not only of imagination and its practical
activities, of perceptions and feelings, but also of the
different kinds of impulses and emotions. Who could
resist a feeling of joy at acquiring the power of rapid
association of ideas, the capacity of more speedy and
clearer-sighted analysis of the motives of future actions,
and more distinct presentiment of the effects of present
ones ? " Joy," in Bergson's words, " is at once heat and
light." In certain exceptional persons this light glows
from birth. But this is not the case with many children,
and it is the function of teachers, by care and perseverance, to create in their obscure souls the ray of joy
which at first may glimmer faintly and intermittently,
but which eventually will illuminate and keep ablaze
a whole hearth of light and heat, ever increasing in

* " Joy is a soul-force." . . . " Joy illuminates thought." . . .
" Joie et Action," by Henri Bois, Société a'édition de Toulouse, 1910.

warmth, lustre, and beneficence. This light will illuminate not only the present, but the future. It will guide humanity along its present path and to its ultimate destination. Not from without do we receive and assimilate it: it must arise from within ourselves, and irradiate from the centre of our being. We cannot contain it. Irresistibly, it must spread its lustre upon those about us: not only those in our immediate neighbourhood, but upon apparent strangers. Who, indeed, possessing this quality of radiance, could resist a yearning to exercise it for the benefit of others? How should even the most hardened egoist be content to keep to himself an influence exuding with such force and such splendid spontaneity from the springs of his being? The more joy we inherit, the more we are tempted to impart it among those to whom it has been denied. And so, like the soldier of Marathon, who bounded away, his heart leaping with ecstasy, to spread the glad tidings, till, disregarding and gradually exhausting his powers, he collapsed at the moment of announcing the victory, but who expired in the joy of having accomplished his mission,—so we, too, must expend our forces not only in exulting over our hardly regained faculties and the joy that has come to birth in us, but also in freely disseminating this joy among our comrades.

And how is this joy created and nurtured and made durable? Simply by the realisation of our ambition to utilise to the full all that is capable of utilisation in us, and to master, by unceasing endeavour, new proclivities producing, in their turn, subconscious impressions of such force as to burst forth from us, pervading our whole environment. Our whole lives depend on habits. Our misfortunes arise from bad, as our joys from good ones. The mere rectification by an effort of will of some habitual tendency, however insignificant, will serve to give us the self-confidence necessary for undertakings of far greater scope. Who can achieve the little, can achieve the great. Once the child has planted his foot firmly on the path of progress, he will find it comparatively easy to keep a straight course, without wasting his energies. The difficulty is not so much to exercise powers as to *will* such exercise. Once arrived at our destination, what matters the time we have taken! The essential is that we should have been able to make the journey, and have known where we were going. Only good habits have maintained us while on the march. The more we cultivate these, the more our power increases. Joy is attained with the first step towards progress. Thenceforward, it will intensify unceasingly; rendering us capable of the highest and most unexpected achievements. Finally, combining with our subconscious forces, it will take firm root, and, following the inevitable law of life, bring forth buds and fruits and flowers.

It stands to reason that the attainment of this permanent state of joy, at once sensorial, emotional, and intellectual, must intensify the child's imaginative and artistic faculties. Æsthetic emotion is a product of the refinement of the senses, susceptibility of the nervous system, and mental flexibility. Whatever the child's natural artistic proclivities, a conscientious study of the phenomena of movement, both in himself and in nature, cannot fail to produce a more vivid comprehension of art as a whole. Art is compound at once of imagination, reflection, and emotion. Reflection tempers and refines the imagination; imagination gives life to style, and emotion ennobles and sensitises the products of sensation, reflection, and imagination.

The question may be asked whether it is really worth while to train hundreds of young people in artistic pursuits for the purpose of public performances. Certainly, in these troubled times, little thought is given either to art or to the stage. But this has been a characteristic of all periods of abnormal stress. Besides, artistic studies are not designed solely for the training of professional artists : they aim also at forming a public capable of appreciating artistic representations, of entering into the spirit of them, and of feeling the emotion they may have served to express. Scholastic instruction is not enough. Training of the senses and mind alone can raise the public taste to such a pitch that, in the ideal of Adolphe Appia (one of the purest artists of our time), the public shall actively collaborate in symbolic and poetic spectacles presented by men of genius. For my part, I am convinced that education by and in rhythm is capable of awakening a feeling for art in all those who undertake it. That is why I will continue my agitation for its introduction in our schools, and for the enlightenment of our educationalists as to the important and decisive rôle art should play in popular education.

So far as pictorial, architectural, and sculptural art is concerned, it is not enough that there be schools in which the representation of lines, colour, light and shade, relief and grouping, is taught : the students of these schools must be trained to respond with their whole being to the rhythmic movement that raises, sets, balances, harmonises, and animates works of statuary, architecture, and pictorial art. Nor is it enough to teach students of our conservatoires to interpret masterpieces of music with their fingers. Before everything, they must be initiated into the sensations that have inspired the composition of these works, the movement that gave life to their emotions, and the rhythm which has regulated and refined them. A Bach fugue is a dead letter to those who are unable to feel in themselves the conflicts produced by the counterpoint, and the sense of peace and harmony evoked by the synergies.

A true pedagogue should be at once psychologist, physiologist, and artist. The complete citizen should leave school capable not only of living normally, but of *feeling* life. He should be in a position both to create and to respond to the creations of others.

IX

RHYTHM AND CREATIVE IMAGINATION
(1916)

The man of genius and the crowd—Futility of teaching rules of construction and classification before awakening artistic imagination—Technique and invention—Temperament and style—Order and balance—Methods and life—The individual ethic—The integral muscular sense—Irregularity of time-values—Organisation of work.

INDIVIDUALITY of style, originality of technique, and imaginative power do not of themselves constitute the quality of genius in a work of art. The distinction between a man of genius and a man of talent is that the latter remains isolated from artists specialising in branches of art other than his own—isolated, moreover, from the common thought of the people to whom he belongs, even though he be associated with a school, or, for that matter, the founder of one. A genius is the direct product of a general spiritual and social development—the representative of a "*milieu*"—and his work constitutes the spontaneous expression of the soul of a race. His power consists in uniting in one comprehensive movement the individual movements of isolated minds ; in grouping in a single mighty rhythm the particular rhythms of his contemporaries. Often enough the æsthetic effects of the man of talent present a more vivid appearance than those of the creative genius : the latter being less ostentatious because more serene, less picturesque because more composite. Too many artists, in expressing complex emotions, will be found to sacrifice their innate sense of form. Too many, again, only possess a sense of form from lack of

138

imagination. Reasoning is so much simpler than imagining. The admirable offices of logic in concatenating ideas are, however, a poor substitute for the rapid processes of spontaneous emotions, creative of vivid images, thrown out haphazard in their violent course, forming in their fortuitous groupings ever new effects of combination. No adequate attempt is made in our schools to develop children's imaginative qualities; on the contrary, they are suppressed by a continual insistence on analysis, co-ordination, classification, and labelling. In our conservatoires, students are expected to bow before the hallowed traditions and proprieties of technique, style, and imagination. Admittedly, licence does not necessarily conduce to beauty. Admittedly, one of the functions of education is to produce clear and ordered mentalities, trained in logic and analysis. But let us not set the cart before the horse ! What is the use of learning to construct before you are given material with which to construct—of knowing all about classifications before you have any ideas to classify ? A musical work without form, but revealing qualities of passion and vitality, is surely superior to a correct but stereotyped harmonic exercise ! True originality is the product of individual ideas, not of picturesque processes of expression. Before inculcating the means of æsthetic expression, would it not be advisable to put your future artist into contact with life and nature, encouraging him to study their rhythms, to absorb and identify himself with them—and *then*, if you like, to interpret them ?

If it be at all possible, on a careful analysis of the works of master musicians from the point of view of phrasing and shading, to deduce, from observation and comparison of characteristic passages, any general rules of interpretation, there should yet be no question of attributing to these rules the character of definite laws, or of imposing them on students as such. In a great

number of cases, the strict application of general principles
of style will produce an interpretation of the particular
passage to be phrased, accurate in its expression. But,
where art and feeling are concerned, accuracy is not
enough ; the artist must interpret music in his own
way, guided by natural instinct, to which he should
subordinate his whole individuality. The only law of
shading beyond dispute is that of *contrast*. This is the
foundation of all rules of musical expression. But no
rules can compensate for lack of temperament, and the
master's first care should be to awaken the temperament of his pupils, to cultivate their æsthetic sense,
and to develop their individual characteristics by every
means in his power. He should therefore be careful,
in expounding a new rule, to point out that this rule
may be, in practice, subject to innumerable exceptions,
and that an adequate musical interpretation is not so
much an intellectual as a spiritual matter ; he should
invite his pupils to suggest other interpretations, to each
of which he will accord a fair hearing—even if it appears
to him wrong—so as not to discourage them, and to
preserve their predilection for individual expression.
Undoubtedly æsthetic feeling develops somewhat late in
children, and it is therefore indispensable to formulate
certain general rules for guidance ; but the master should
point out that these rules may be replaced by others, and
that the interpretation of any particular melodic passage
may vary according to the character of its predecessor
and successor, in the same way as, in instrumental exercises,
the fingering of a scale will vary with the notes on which
it commences and finishes. In short, the master should
teach his pupils the art of shading and phrasing in the
same way as a professor of counterpoint—a real artist,
and not a pedant—would initiate his pupils into the
composition of fugues, while indicating that the classic
rules and formulas are nothing until they are vitalised
by artistic feeling, love, and pursuit of beauty.

Far from me be the desire to limit the time given to studies in technique, analysis of styles, and processes of notation in the time-tables of schools of music. Every musician must be acquainted with the trade secrets of his calling, and, before inventing for himself, must have learnt to imitate and reproduce. But not all invention is of a creative nature. A sound education should furnish the student with the means of extracting only such parts of his reading and analysis as will be useful to him, enabling him to strike out his own path instead of following the beaten track. Undoubtedly classical musical studies are indispensable ; but too often the method of conducting them in conservatoires is suitable only for those already acquainted with them, and in whom the master has already awakened the instinct for individual development and the distinguishing of processes congenial to their particular temperaments. Too many imaginative faculties are aroused quite late in life, owing to masters having demanded only the execution of formulas, and encouraged a mere imitation —first voluntary, later involuntary—of the methods of composition bequeathed to us by predecessors of different temperament, instead of inducing instinctive elementary researches, founded on the consciousness of actual physical and emotional capacities. Much has been written on the art that will follow the cessation of hostilities, as though the War itself must exercise an immediate influence on art. The determining factor in any new developments of style will be our *attitude* after the War ; and the extent to which we seek, in the period of reconstruction and reparation, to react from past impressions, and to throw off every previous constraint, purifying ourselves of effete doctrines and automatic thoughts and productions—and so becoming capable of expressing forcibly, and in an individual manner (though, where necessary, also collectively), our new emotions—freed from, obsolete forms and methods of education, and alive in every limb to the acute consciousness of the present, and fore-knowledge of the future.

One of the first concerns of the education of the future will have to be the extrication of the rhythms congenial to particular individualities from the influences tending to restrict their free expression, and the restoration to the child of the exclusive control of his temperament. A constant appeal will be made to his imagination ; his nervous system will have to acquire the necessary flexibility to prevent the wealth of images issuing through its agency from inducing a state of hypersensitiveness. The body, instinct with motor force at high pressure, will have to be prepared to execute every behest of mind, and, after every such execution, to keep a sufficient reserve of energy. Many parents at present shrink from having the creative imagination of their children developed. They are afraid of their becoming "artists," under the impression that it is impossible to be an artist without possessing a "kink." And if it were ? Is not this "kink" the root of all wisdom ? Artists, in their wanderings over unknown countries of their own creation and transfiguration, may surely be pardoned an occasional deviation. Their Philistine brothers have no merit in never losing their way, since they keep vigorously and stolidly to the beaten track, victims—if they only knew it—of their lack of imagination. And yet creative artists possess qualities of memory and accuracy which would secure them the high regard of the Philistines, were these to suspect their existence. A painter, for example, recalls every detail of the images that have arrested his eye ; his mind classifies, assorts, and combines them, and transforms each active element into idealised forms charged with emotion. But the essential is that his work should be grounded in feeling. Too many of us are on our guard against artistic emotions, afraid of falling, in following our natural instincts. Our people will only become really artistic through an education in temperament and sensibility. Grace and naturalness are commonly supposed to be incapable of conscious acquisition. As a matter of fact, the natural in art is nearly always the result of careful selection, and a host of eliminations, sacrifices, transpositions, and changes of place—all of which relate very definitely to the conscious. The order, symmetry, and art of preparation and balance, that constitute the harmony of a work of art, depend largely on the manner in which the artist has learnt to subordinate each of the rhythmic elements of his theme to a general synthesis and rhythmic unity. Rhythm is the live essence of feeling, the fundamental impulse of a movement in the form impressed on it by the first emotional reaction. Elementary rhythm requires the consonance of each of its subdivisions to enable it to retain its power of animating a continuously harmonised movement. Rhythm and metre are the bases of all art. "Poems," said Emerson, "are a corrupt version of some text in nature, with which they ought to be made to tally. A rhyme in one of our sonnets should not be less pleasing than the iterated nodes of a sea-shell, or the resembling difference of a group of flowers."

It is always interesting to distinguish the personality of an artist beneath the divers forms of his creation, to watch its modifications according to the whims of his æsthetic instinct, to follow the successive experiences dictated by his temperament. But the human value of a work of art does not lie in its display of originality in manner and style : it depends on the sincerity of the pursuit, and the disinterestedness of the love, for beauty which it manifests. There is no dearth of artists, whose sole motive is an ambition to develop their "ego," and who love nature only in so far as she enables them to express and vary their personal fancies. The great creative minds, confronted with beauty, become oblivious of everything that does not partake of beauty. They concentrate on expressing the emotions it calls forth. They

humble themselves before it, becoming its passionate
and faithful devotees. They are prepared to sacrifice
themselves for it ; they seek ever to raise themselves
to its level ; they lay bare their hearts for beauty to
take possession of them. What are all our methods
and systems, what matter if instincts be primitive or
cultured, what is all technique and science, without *love*
—love for life in beauty, and beauty in life ? Certainly
there exist laws which enable the artist to furnish a perfect
form for the images recorded by his intuition ; there are
fundamental principles of ordination of lines, of juxtaposition and coalescence of colours and sounds, but in
the completed work, nothing of all this science should
be manifest. Alone, the feeling of rhythm—that is, the
true, ideal, creative essence, the fundamental harmony of
nature—should reveal itself : a direct, spontaneous, and
faithful reflection of beauty.

It is the painter's function to diffuse himself in the
objects he sees, his works constituting an apparent
expansion of the intense curiosity for the rhythms of
life and nature that animates his artistic consciousness.
This continual preoccupation with movement in pictorial
art should commend itself to musicians. Painters must
also, like them, acquire the art of associating and dissociating movements, of accentuating consonances, creating
counterpoint, treating human emotions symphonically,
and selecting appropriate gestures and attitudes for
their expression in " orchestration."

"Rhythm is everywhere," as all artists are agreed ;
but this sacred principle must not be allowed to remain a
mere statement. Only rhythm can assure the unity of
human faculties and constitute that *ethical individuality*—
if I may be permitted the term—the possession of which
reveals our divers potentialities, and transforms the
human organism into a confluence of ideas, sensations,
and faculties—a living harmony of independent entities
voluntarily united.

Creative imagination in every branch of art was obsessed, in the period before the War, with the research for novel effects, completely out of touch with normal life.—(Or was it that life itself had so lost touch with its natural rhythms that the artist was no longer capable of rhythmicising his work realistically?) On the rising generation falls the duty of seeking to create mentalities, clearer, more in conformity with instinct, and, at the same time, more disciplined; likewise temperaments at once richer in power and more conscious of their composition. Musical education of the future, for instance, will no longer confine itself to the laws of syntax and vocabularies, but will comprise the development of means of spontaneous expression, and the art of combining and harmonising them by the process of elimination and selection known as style. Music must become once more a living language, a vital manifestation of thoughts and emotions. And, for this purpose, greater scope must be allowed in its study for the qualities of effusion, propulsion, and repercussion, that characterise tonal expression by sound.

Musicians of to-morrow must try to develop the art of regulating planes, pursuing lines, and determining and controlling pace. And this development will depend on a new orientation, that has yet to be created, to replace the conventional methods of thematic development (killed for all time by Debussy) by an architecture satisfying at once the needs of emotional imagination and the exigencies of form. All young painters to-day are unanimous in their desire and resolve to discard the artifices of camouflage decoration in favour of all that is unchanging and permanent in form; that endures throughout the ages; to harmonise elements rightly proportioned, to select only subjects directly inspired by emotion, and to retain only essential sensations completely and distinctly realised·*

* *Vide* the interesting work by Ozenfant and Jeanneret, "*Après le Cubisme*" (*édition des Commentaires*).

Young musicians will aim at the same ideal, concentrating primarily on the control of emotions, on the limitation of mere easy imitation of exceptional, accidental, and decorative elements, renouncing the effects of mere virtuosity that obscure the really human property of conceptions, and spiritualising music by every possible means. They will be unanimous in discarding, in order to return to nature, *i.e.* to elementary emotions and simple expression, every development of an intellectual and didactic order, and every æsthetic process issuing from a momentary fancy rather than from a deep-seated sensibility, varying in the most natural, flexible, and elastic manner. . . . But these new conceptions depend on a unification of spiritual and corporal faculties, that can be achieved only by an assiduous training in movements in time and space, and a diligent cultivation of the muscular sense.

This training alone can convey to the mind a feeling for time duration—one of the elements of music most intimately allied to sensibility (for only a feeling for movement can reveal to us the laws by which modifications in the acuteness of sounds unite with modifications in their time and dynamic force). Only the possession of a powerful muscular sense can enable the hearer to substitute for the emotional state of the moment a condition that will respond to the motor sensibility of the composer, and only such a sense can endow the latter with the capacity of expressing himself spontaneously, without permitting theories of a literary or mathematical order to trespass on the domain of purified physical sensations. The hearer of a work of music should be able to say : " That is *yourself !* " But he can only sense this constitution of the work, if it really appeals to him, by means of emotions, mutually and genuinely experienced, and sacrifices freely accepted.

The muscular sense is at present so imperfectly developed, both in the composer and in the interpreter, that the latter—especially a pianist—usually disregards the expressive potentialities of time-duration ; while the former, in many cases, is unconscious of the short-comings of most of his agogic effects. In particular, *rubato* effects are nowadays so exaggerated by pianoforte *virtuosi* that the intimate relations subsisting between the energy expended (accentuations) and the changing forms of the sounds (time-values) are utterly distorted. The pianist, playing without orchestral accompaniment, is apt to follow his whim in modifying the sequence and alternation of time-values and accentuations that constitute musical rhythm, and by so doing deprives himself of an infinite variety of means of expression. Incessant vagaries of *rubato*, compared with the processes of imagination, are as the buzzing of a fly against the window-pane to the soaring flight of an eagle.

In fact not only the æsthetic expression inherent in nuances of time, as conceived by the composer, but also the dynamic force itself, is thus vitiated—nuances of time and energy being inseparable. Vagaries in the distribution of sound-durations can only attain æsthetic value by contrast, at the right moment, with an ordered interpretation scrupulously observant of the relations in time between the various sounds—just as the æsthetic value of a *crescendo* and a *diminuendo* is only established by reference to a *piano* or a *forte*, and the emotional value of a modulation depends on its contrast with a fixed and persistent tonal state.

Would not the most indulgent of critics reprimand a pianist who exercised his humour for fantasy to the point of sprinkling a melody in C major with profuse sharps and flats, " padding " simple chords, or transposing minor into major themes? And yet we could name a host of critics, including the most exacting, who neither condemn, nor even mention, the complete disregard by most pianists of time nuances ! This is an inconsistency only explicable in the light of the ignorance of most musicians of the physical laws which govern agogic shading. This ignorance is, fortunately, likely to be dispelled in the near future, now that so many thinking musicians are coming to realise the importance of the active and receptive functions of the motor organism, and the existence of natural laws governing the relations between movement and sound — the two mutually fundamental elements in the musical expression of human emotions.

We are in the habit of jotting down fleeting impressions, of sketching instead of finishing compositions, of merely noting instead of arranging rhythms. The cult of picturesque details has supplanted that of form proper. Educationists should bear in mind that, while rhythm plays a preponderant rôle in art, serving to unite all manifestations of beauty and animating them with the same throbbing life, it should constitute a no less important factor in general education, co-ordinating all the spiritual and corporal movements of the individual, and evolving in the latter a mental state in which the combined vibrations of desires and powers are associated in perfect harmony and balance. "Only the soul can guide the body, along the path the mind has traced for it."

X

RHYTHM AND GESTURE IN MUSIC DRAMA —AND CRITICISM (1910–1916)

The Individual Artist.—*The trinity of word, gesture, and music— Musicalising of muscles—Stairs and inclines—Adolphe Appia's method— Nuances of movements—The training of audiences—Relation between musical and corporal dynamics—Nudity and the purification of bodily interpretations.*

Criticism —*Universal ignorance of the laws of plastic interpretation— Orchestration of the human body—Conventions and inconsistencies—Vanity of impressionistic judgments—The rôle of the critic.*

The Crowd.—*Passion-plays in Switzerland throughout the ages—Open-air festivals—The rôle of the crowd in music drama—The laws of collective gesture—Relations between the crowd and the individual artist—Mass dynamism—The polyrhythm of crowds—The training of a chorus— Gesture and lighting.*

THE INDIVIDUAL ARTIST

SINCE Richard Wagner (following Gluck) prescribed for lyric drama the classic trinity of word, gesture, and music, and set himself to define the ideal method of interpreting his works and, like Grétry, to lay the foundations of a school of lyric-dramatic art, the public, under the influence of its critics and amateurs, has concluded that, to the everlasting glory of the contemporary stage, sound, movement, and speech have been definitely united in the creation of an art-form analogous to the Greek Orchesis, and that all goes well in the best of all possible worlds.

It may nevertheless be worth while to inquire whether the mere presence of the three classic elements in a lyric work suffices to establish their unity. Actually a cursory analysis of modern lyric works—including those of Wagner—must bring home to the most optimistic that the classic unity has not been achieved, and is incapable of achievement under existing conditions of musical education.

To unite word, gesture, and music, it is not enough that the music should be intimately allied to the word, nor that the word and the gesture should correspond. It is necessary in addition that physical movements and sound movements, the musical and the plastic elements, should be co-ordinated. If we now examine either the works or the productions of the modern theatre, we shall find ourselves forced to admit that this last union has not yet been effected.

Just as verbal expression, the poetic interpretation of the text, demands precise and definite gestures, so *musical* expression, constituting the atmosphere of the piece, exacts of the actor a similar and absolute physical submission to the rhythm that produces it. Every movement of musical rhythm should evoke in the body of the interpreter a corresponding muscular movement ; every mood expressed in sound should determine on the stage an appropriate attitude ; every orchestral nuance, every *crescendo, diminuendo, stringendo* or *rallentando* should be impressed on the interpreter and *expressed* by him, as occasion demands. I say, as occasion demands, because naturally, as the purpose of the text does not require an appropriate gesture to each word, so not *every* musical rhythm calls for its physical interpretation. It is, however, essential that it should produce a mental attitude, that it should develop in the mind of the interpreter a particular image that shall animate his whole organism, if we really wish to see the ideal unity effected—if we wish to bring music into the heart of life. We have only to visit any of our principal opera houses and study the play of the performers, while listening to the orchestra, to perceive at once that there exists a barrier between the orchestra and the stage, and that the orchestral music acts as a mere accompaniment to the song or to the attitude of the actors, and does not really enter into them and inspire their movements. The music rises, swells, breaks out in grandiose resonance; the gesture either does not follow the *crescendo* or does not convey it to the spectator. The music subsides, dies away, whispers and murmurs as in a dream—the attitude on the stage reveals a muscular tension which is *fortissimo!* Even musical rhythms that characterise not soul-movements, but simple motions of the body, such as walking or running or sudden arrests or starts, are not realised on the stage—or are realised incorrectly, which is worse! Certainly there exist opera singers who feel the necessity of this union of gesture and music, and who endeavour to express rhythms of sound by muscular rhythms. But they do not succeed for want of a special training, as necessary to this end as is a special finger training to enable a musician to express himself through the medium of an instrument. Not every musician requires to express music in movement; but it is obvious that an opera singer, to be a complete artist, must possess this faculty of realising rhythms plastically. Unfortunately, if his education is incomplete, that of his public is much more so; that is why so many non-rhythmic singers attain success in spite of this deficiency. It will not always be so; a new point of view is already in course of evolution; the study of the relations between time and space is engaging the attention of numerous æstheticians, and the time is not far distant when lack of rhythm will be counted as serious a flaw in a singer's equipment as tonal inaccuracy.

Before dedicating one's body to the service of art, it should be deemed necessary to perfect its mechanism, to develop its capacities, and to correct its shortcomings. It is not enough that these capacities function intuitively, as is the case with many gifted individuals; it is necessary in addition that they should be exercisable consciously, and not depend on momentary nervous impulses. Again, it is essential that the nervous system itself should be trained and regulated so as to give the brain complete liberty of control over muscular movements. All movements of the body, its gait, gestures, and attitudes, should be studied not only on a flat surface, such as the boards of a stage, but on different planes, on inclines of different degrees (where practicable), and on staircases,* in such a way that the body may familiarise itself with space, its plastic manifestations adapting themselves to the material conditions dictated by the action, and eventually imposing on the painter a new conception and treatment of scenery. Finally the organism should become an instrument of musical resonance so vibrant and of such susceptibility as to be capable of spontaneously transposing into attitude and gestures all the æsthetic emotions provoked by sound rhythms.

In his "*Mise en scène du drame Wagnérien*" (pp. 44–45) Adolphe Appia, prophesying in 1895 the collaboration of rhythm and drama, quotes two significant details from the representation of the third act of the Walkyrie.

"Wotan arrives in a terrific cyclone that subsides as he reaches the summit. The Walkyries have concealed Brünnhilde among them and seek to appease their father. The musical passage is quite short, but the incomparable

---

* Adolphe Appia first gave me the idea of evolutions on a staircase, and the Russian painter Salzmann designed for my exercises a highly ingenious set of units, whereby a whole series of practicable staircases could easily and speedily be constructed. Distinguished producers such as Reinhardt, Granville Barker, and Gémier came later to adopt our methods, but only Gémier appears to me to have utilised them to really vital effect. Nowadays one sees staircases on all stages, but the producers do not know what to do with them, nor can the actors either perform or repose on them with ease. Appia wrote : " Stairs by their straight lines and breaks maintain the necessary contrast between the curves of the body and the sinuous lines of its evolutions ; their practical uses offering at the same time distinct facilities of expression."

polyphony is meant to be accompanied by an action that impresses it on the eye, without however obliging the maidens to separate from each other. It is effected by a light counterpoint, in which the successive entries mark the timid supplication in a highly individual manner ; *each Walkyrie should time her entry a beat in advance of the score.* The last bars expand irresistibly ; the vocalists should interlace their movements corresponding to the score, and by way of further accentuation, the whole group extended before Wotan *might straighten itself and recoil on the hard chord* that recalls the abrupt voice of the God. One cannot, in this scene, carry too far the minute search for new musical developments."

It would appear to be easy to train artists according to these indications ; but this is not the case. The clearest comprehension by the actors of these directions by no means assures their execution. To make with apparent ease a step in advance of a particular note, he must have gone through a whole series of exercises in advancing and halting, aiming at the acquirement of the various kinds of balance of the body, pose of the feet, and muscular innervation of the legs necessary to interpret the different sound tempi in all their shades. The gait of the actor must accord with the musical movement, and the rhythm of his steps must fall quite naturally into the rhythm of the sounds. The most perfect musician may be absolutely incapable of effecting a *rallentando, accelerando,* or *rubato* in walking, corresponding to the acceleration, abatements, and fluctuations of his musical imagination. Nor would he be able to change his attitude in a given time—say, over a crotchet or a quaver—without having studied plastic anacrusis, that is, the laws of preparation of movements. He must next practise movements of the arm *in all degrees of rapidity and energy,* first simultaneous and corresponding movements of both arms, then the same movements executed by the arms in different directions—finally different movements simultaneously, one arm, for example, making an angular, the other a circular, movement. In this form of exercise, movements of apparent simplicity prove exceedingly difficult to execute. To raise one arm in sixteen beats of an *adagio* while half lowering the other in the same space of time requires a perfect acquaintance with every shade of muscular innervation and, in addition, considerable practice, before this double action will convey an impression of naturalness and ease. To one practised in the correlating of movements in time and space, the sight of a gesture completed before or after the beat of a musical rhythm produces a positive æsthetic pain. It is not until the arms are capable of being moved with complete freedom that their movements can be combined with leg movements. An infinite number of combined exercises have been contrived, the study of which must inevitably produce harmony of all habitual movements, thereby conducing to grace, which is only another word for ease and naturalness, and which is attainable only through knowledge of our physical possibilities. The factor co-ordinating arm and leg movement is respiration. Singers confine their use of the diaphragm to the production of the necessary breath for the larynx, and yet breathing is not only an invaluable medium of physical balance, but, in addition, a highly powerful agent of dramatic expression, and apart from the rapid movements of costal respiration by which our lyric artists so frequently express their emotion in love scenes, there exist a whole host of other movements of the torso, produced by the breath, complementary to the movements of arms, legs, and head. The latter should also be submitted to special exercises, all the more so since vocal exercises by no means encourage suppleness in the neck. . . . But the mastery of body movements constitutes a mere virtuosity, unless those movements are employed to help out facial expression. The same gesture may express ten different sentiments according as the eye gives the clue. The

Scene from *Les Souvenirs*.   Geneva, 1918 (1)

correlating of body movements with facial play must, then, also be made the subject of a special training ; but this should not be undertaken until repeated exercises have brought music into direct communication with the organism — vibrations of sound evoking analogous vibrations in the tissues and the nervous system, which the body, susceptible of musical emotions, has learned to transform into plastic emotions and to realise æsthetically.   The mechanism of the body is nothing until it has become subservient to the sensibilities, the development of which a diligent study of the translation of musical rhythms into physical movements is almost certain to promote.

*   *   *   *   *

As soon as interpreters have learnt to express with their bodies every nuance of the orchestra, it must inevitably follow, that, after some hesitation and misunderstanding, the public will come to appreciate the lyrico-plastic unity thereby achieved, and will feel the necessity of initiating itself into this new medium of interpretation by an identical training.   The time is near/ when the, as it were, antinomy that subsists to-day between plastic rhythms and sound rhythms will shock an audience in the same way as a false note in a chorus or a wrong beat in an orchestra.   A new mentality will evolve, the old tastes will change, the traditional conception of scenic exigencies will be modified, and eventually people will wonder how it was ever possible that such a divorce should have been allowed to subsist between the stage and the orchestra, between musical conceptions and physical realisations.   Composers will then abandon current dramatic forms to adopt others more conformable to truth and nature.   They will no longer permit their imaginations to give to gestural and ocular expressions and attitudes a musical form of which the rhythm and the movement are incapable of plastic realisation.   Custom has trained them to regard all music without words as the expression of inner feelings. Their imagination would often suggest more effective interpretations if they could command a visual representation of them in gesture and facial play, in place of this accepted suppression. Muscular dynamics must render musical rhythms visible, and musical dynamics plastic rhythms musical. Gesture must define musical emotion and call up its image. And to that end we must educate our bodies in rhythm and by rhythm. It is not necessary that we should be perfectly formed : the essential is that our movements should be harmonised, and that our habitual motions should be refined ; in short, that we should be artists. We have all of us muscles, reason, and volition ; consequently we are all equal before Rhythm. We must vocalise our movements and establish a communion between them and music. To that end it is ·necessary that we should learn to know our bodies, and that is why, without sharing the views of æstheticians who, in respect of costume, advocate complete return to the customs of Greek antiquity, I myself favour for my plastic studies a return to quasi-nudity when exercising in private. Nudity provides not only a medium of control indispensable for purposes of physical expression, but is in addition an æsthetic element inducing the respect for the body that animated the great Greek philosophers. In proportion as the idea of sex subsides in the fervour of the artist, and in the passion for complete absorption in beauty and truth of expression, so our bodies take on new life, and we feel lack of respect for nudity to be a sin against the spirit. Once our operatic singers have learnt to understand the intricate mechanism of their movements and the intimate relations between their bodies, their minds, their desires, and their æsthetic instincts, they will emancipate themselves from the prejudices at present encumbering them, thanks to their education and heredity, and will regard their bodies as mediums of elevation—as instruments of pure art and beauty. No longer will the

Philistines snigger at the sight of Isadora Duncan dancing with bare legs. Thenceforth critics will have to insist on the young Siegfried discarding his miserable pink tights, and on the Rhine Daughters assuming the authentic garb of water-sprites. Purified by art, we shall see in the body the collaborator of conscience, an agent of noble will and pure imagination, an instrument of wisdom, beauty, art, and truth. The interpreter will no longer seek art and beauty outside himself, he will have to induce beauty and truth to descend into him, to dwell with him, to become an integral element in his organism. Such are the benefits I anticipate from the cult of rhythm, as a result of which authors and actors, repudiating the old worn scenic conventions, will recover the purity of plastic sensation, will ally in their art the sensibility of the musician with that of the sculptor and painter, and will free themselves—thanks to a real education, on principles pure as nature and truth— from the tyranny of meaningless virtuosity, lying gestures, and intellectual perversities.

* * * * *

CRITICISM

The progress of the art of gesture is unfortunately retarded by the ignorance of critics touching the powers of expression possessed by the human body. Certainly it is possible to appreciate the merits of a symphony without being capable of playing all the instruments of the orchestra—and to recognise the merit of a singer or pianist without having studied singing or the piano. It is moreover true that sound visual, intellectual, and artistic faculties may make up for want of technical knowledge, in criticising human gesture, whether individual or collective. But the opinions of people uninformed as to the multiple resources of the human frame can never have other than a subjective value, and should not have the power of influencing the education of

either artist or spectator. A musical critic can admittedly
interest the public in recording the impression produced
on him by such and such orchestral work, although he
understands only approximately the mechanism of each
instrument—but he will be unable to explain why certain
things displease him without an appreciation of the tone
and character of the different agents of sound, an
acquaintance with the laws that regulate the art of grouping instruments, and a knowledge of the essential
principles of musical construction.

Human gesture and its orchestration conform to
elementary principles of nature, dynamic, rhythmic, and
agogic, which it is absolutely necessary to understand
before one is justified in formulating a decision as to
their artistic worth. Criticism of a work or its interpretation, in so far as these are the direct product of
emotion and temperament, can only be of relative value.
On the other hand, that which is the result of intellectual
qualities, sense of form, intuition of dynamic or rhythmic
effects, can be analysed. But to be in a position to
analyse it, one must know something of the matter in
question. By so much as the subjective opinion of a
great creative artist interests us from the psychological
point of view, by so much the impressions of a negative
spirit, a critic who has never made any personal contribu-
tion to art, leave us cold. On the other hand, we can
take an interest in an analysis based on first-hand knowledge. Every human body comprises more numerous
potential orchestral effects (concatenation, juxtaposition,
opposition of gestures and attitudes, and changes while
stationary or in step) than the most complex symphonic
body. To what extent, and in what manner, could and
should this human orchestra ally its rhythms to those of
the orchestra of sound ? That is the question we have
to consider.

No musical critic would hold it right for the clarinets
to play in a different key from the rest of the orchestra,

or for a pianist to execute his part in a concerto in a different style from that adopted by the instruments accompanying him. . . . Yet we do not find two critics in a hundred commenting on the confusions of style, time, phrasing and shading that may persist between the movements of a *corps de ballet*, or of a solo dancer professing to interpret a musical piece.

Not only is their eye so accustomed to the regular arm movements, extended, contracted, undulatory, and sinuous, that constitute the means of expression possessed by ballet dancers, that any really vital gesture, any effect of dynamic muscularity, offends them æsthetically; but their minds have so deliberately accepted the disharmony between the physical movements and the sound rhythms, that their ears positively cease to listen to the music once their eyes compel them to follow the spectacle, and *vice versa*. It seems to them quite natural that on the stage the human body should be perpetually trying to repudiate the laws of gravity, that the ambition of the dancer should be to imitate the bird, instead of to transfigure the man, to produce the picturesque and artificial, instead of to ennoble and refine the gestures of natural life. We still look back with bewilderment and regret to interpretations (quite pretty from the pictorial point of view) of classical and modern compositions, applauded by capable musicians who simply did not perceive the abyss created by the dancers between the orchestral and physical symphonies. The truth is, musicians have no conception of the capacities of the human body, and neither their sight nor their muscular sense is sufficiently acute to warn them of the errors of style committed, and of the nuances disregarded. The trouble is that so many critics, imagining themselves to possess intuitive knowledge, consider physical movement of such secondary importance as a medium of artistic expression, that they do not hesitate to hold forth *ex cathedra* on texts of which they do not even suspect the meaning! "How few people," said Varvenargues,

"are capable of comprehending every side of a question !
There, it seems to me, is the most common source of
human error."

Each time we attend a display of dancing, we are
staggered by the incoherence of the spectators' opinions,
and the contradictions of their sentiments. Those who
object in the concert hall to the technical acrobatics of
instruments, applaud it in the dancer. Those who oppose
transcriptions and arrangements of classical pieces,
approve the most horrible travesties of them as performed by the artistes of the ballet. Those again who
complain of the inadequate delicacy of touch of certain
pianists, pass, without turning a hair, the crude, exaggerated, and frantic gestures of opera singers ! Others
who are dependable authorities on the pictorial or sculptural representation of the human form go into raptures
over the affectations and abnormal dislocations of living
and breathing bodies. Finally, there are critics, and
these are the worst, so perverted in taste and steeped in
the artifices of conventional choreography, that, far from
recognising the absurdity of these displays, they remain
impervious to the efforts of progressive artists to reform
the dance as a simple and natural expression of emotion.
Once these professional critics have written of a dancer
that he has grace, a good carriage, balance, and temperament, they have said everything ! It never occurs to
them to consider the degree of sympathy he has shown
for the musical thought it was his business to interpret.
And yet as much importance should be attached to the
processes of plastic interpretation as to those of musical
execution.

But there, again, what divergencies of opinion these
musical critics exhibit ! According as nature has made
them "rational," "emotional," or "imaginative," and
psychologists such as Dr. Charles Odier can classify them
as technicians and theorists on the one hand, senti-
mentalists and emotionalists on the other (or sub-classify

the "imaginatives" as "rationalists," "impressionists," and "intuitionists")—the works and interpretations are perceived and analysed by them in a hundred and one different ways. Fortunately, the value of a musical criticism does not depend on the nature of its conclusions, but on the simplicity and sincerity of the musician who makes it.

There is no inferior art of criticism, but there are inferior methods of practising that art. Every man who wishes to devote his life to the public appraisement of artistic works and interpretations should make it his business to be well informed and to move with the times. Unfortunately, too few critics appreciate the importance of their vocation. Many of them imagine that their critical faculties are definitely formed, and that they have nothing more to learn. Some apparently consider their task to consist in picking out, and exposing indiscriminately to public ridicule, defects in the works of all kinds presented to them. It should rather consist in trying to get to the bottom of these works and considering to what extent they may, in spite of their defects, be made to serve the purposes of art. As La Rochefoucauld put it: "a sensible person sees things as they require to be seen. He gives them their own value, and causes them to exhibit to him the side from which they may be viewed to best advantage. . . ." There are few such "sensible people" in the realm of criticism. To say "such and such a piece pleases or displeases me," without further elucidation, is the prerogative of the least educated music-lover ; it is the critic's function to fathom the author's motives, and to explain them to his readers, without stressing his own personal preferences. From this point of view, Robert Schumann, who could "discover" a genius of so antipathetic a tendency as Berlioz, proved himself a model critic ; while the articles of that disinterested enthusiast, our contemporary, Camille Mauclair, at once critic and creator, guided alike by principle and impulse, command the respect of artists of the most divergent tendencies, and exercise a thoroughly wholesome influence on the progress of art, as a whole.

The practice of censuring any artistic conception that does not happen to conform to their particular temperament does not commend itself to those who feel it their vocation to cultivate the tastes of dilettantes unacquainted with the diversity of musical form, and unconscious of its affinity with the multiple forms of emotional life. But those critics who aspire to produce work of lasting educative and persuasive value, find it necessary, before hazarding an opinion on a work of unfamiliar character, to make specially careful inquiry as to its "intentions," and as to the qualifications of its creator.

It is easy enough to pronounce a hasty judgment, based on one's education or one's particular preferences, but this rudimentary mode of informing the public is more suitable for "reporters" of art than for conscientious and sensitive analysts, concerned to appreciate the point of view of the creator. Unfortunately, with three-quarters of the writers on musical matters, book learning and an ambition to shine in the public eye by a display of erudition or cheap paradoxes, take the place of the real requisites of a serious and conscientious critic—a passion for all forms of artistic endeavour, curiosity as to individual modes of expression, a capacity to assimilate new forms of art and to extract the essence of the ideas underlying them, and the will to withdraw from one's own personality in order to commune with other and different personalities.

It does not follow, however, because we refuse to be impressed by slaves of a school or style who condemn every work that does not conform to it, that we have any more respect for those who carry eclecticism to an extreme and set themselves to discover beauty where it does not exist. Only it is more common to find a critic failing to find beauty in a work because he does not want

to find it, or through lack of beauty in himself.   Instinct
is not everything—the faculty and the desire to analyse
would modify many of the "instinctive" prejudices of
those who undertake the task of enlightening public
opinion on the productions of classical or contemporary
music.   In the words of that shrewd artist, Jean Huré:
"The art of criticism consists in recognising beauty
wheresoever and in whatever diverse forms it may conceal
itself."   And, before him, Leonardo da Vinci wrote:
"Love is born of Knowledge."

It is all important that the majority of critics should
agree as to the essential qualities required for the art of
dancing, and the principle that should underlie the various
techniques involved.   It is a matter of the reciprocal
influence of rhythms and feelings in sound and plastic;
a constant exchange of psychic currents and sensorial
repercussions.   There may be a diversity in the external
means of expression, dependent on the individualities of
the executants, but all dancers who are real artists—no
matter how divergent their manners of bodily expression
—must be guided by the same motive, the interpretation
of *music*.   The soul of music radiates, in an equal degree
of intensity, from all dancers worthy of the name of
artist; but just as the focus of light makes a different
impression according to the degrees of atmospheric
resistance, and the processes of sifting and reverberation
necessitated by the various obstacles interposed between
it and our eyes—so the radiating influence of vital music
may appeal to spectators in different aspects, arising
from the diversity of the physical agents of response in
the dancer, whether in the structure of his limbs, or in his
nervous system or temperament.   To the spectator
accustomed to the varieties of physical mechanism, these
differences in the types of gestures and attitudes will not
matter.   Whatever the imaginative variations in the
embodiment of musical ideas and feelings, he will be
able to recognise whether the latter really inspired the

corporal movements, and to distinguish fusion from mere juxtaposition, creation from imitation, sincere synrhythm from vulgar synchronism, spontaneous response from considered adaptation. Every musical work comprises an element of inspiration, and another of thematic development and architecture. This latter element depends on the intellect and physique, and may be expressed differently by dancer interpreters, according as their aptitudes or understandings have formed their various techniques. But the inspiration present at the creation of the music should be revived in the transposition of musical rhythms into movements in space; the same breath should animate both sound and corporal expression. A dancer of the old ballet school should be able to express the soul of music as faithfully through the medium of the traditional processes to which his limbs are accustomed, as an Isadora Duncan by her immobility, or a Sakharoff by his polymobile effects, *provided that soul has been absorbed by each of them.*

In the same way the really artistic spectator will not allow himself to be influenced by his personal predilection for a particular technique, any more than an ideal audience of absolute music will be biassed by tastes in harmony, construction, or orchestration. We cannot, of course, control our likes or dislikes, but these should not intrude upon a general appreciation, relating to the intrinsic value and sincerity of the artistic manifestation in question. Moreover, the mastery of technique being a *sine qua non* for purposes of representation of a work, we must be careful not to confuse idiosyncrasies of artistic style with that mere poverty of expressive resources which, alas! is the idiosyncrasy of so many so-called artists. One cannot construct a work of art on inspiration alone; the most profound thought may be distorted by deficiencies in the vehicle of its externalisation. That is why an artist should never obsess himself with any particular method, but should be constantly experimenting with those which have not come instinctively to him. And the same applies to a critic, whose analytical faculties should be adaptable to all forms of style.

The understanding of art does not depend on study however profound. It is possessed completely only by those whom taste and temperament have made capable of responding to elementary emotions, whatever the nature or construction of the work, its harmonic or tonal system, or its rhythmic processes. Without this, it is impossible either to judge or to understand a piece of music.

We may find evidence of this in the fact that the interpretation of an unknown piano work will often seem to reveal to us great interpretive powers in a pianist whose execution of works with which we are familiar disappoints or displeases us. Similarly many conductors who have a prejudice against a particular piece eventually discover its beauties as a result of having it repeatedly played to them. May we not conclude from this that certain critics who after a first hearing pronounce such and such a piece to be deficient in form would change their opinions if they took the trouble to study the score or even to acquaint themselves with the motives of the composer? However, they prefer to pride themselves on their subjectivity, forgetting too often that subjectivity is only justifiable on the part of powerful and creative personalities. How many critics are mere " grousers," confined to a negative attitude out of sheer creative impotence! One thing or the other: either a critic is himself creative and accordingly entitled to express preferences and judgments founded on his temperament, or his function is that of an observer and recorder, in which case he must confine himself to studying, comparing, analysing, and directing attention without drawing conclusions. To attain the right to deliver arbitrary judgments, he must be very sure of himself, follow an inflexible line of conduct, resist the temptation to modify his judgment out of friendship or personal bias, and keep his own personality and temperament severely in control.

"Dionysius," relates Rabelais, "would ridicule pedants who are pleased to expose the faults of others and to ignore their own ; musicians whose flutes preserve harmony but whose manners do not ; rhetoricians given to expounding justice without practising it."

If dramatic and musical critics, instead of constantly lamenting the deterioration of the art of gesticulation in drama, would take the trouble to analyse the correlations of gesture with musical rhythm, they would learn that there exist apart from individual gestures, collective gestures, and that without a careful study of these last no representation involving movements of a chorus can attain a really musical or artistic character.

THE CROWD

The individuals composing a chorus, however gifted, will never produce a really dramatic effect so long as they act independently of one another. Forty persons each making a different gesture, fail to convey the impression of a common emotion. Their gestures are lost in space. It is with the choric element as with music drama as a whole, each of its elements should be able to fuse with the others or temporarily withdraw from them, as necessity dictates. The gesture of a crowd should be the result of a number of modifications, almost imperceptible, of a fixed attitude imposed on all its participants. In modern spoken drama, each individual member of a crowd can act independently and gesticulate according to his fancy to give the impression of, for example, a festival, a strike, or a battle ; . . . and we regard as masterpieces of this kind the extraordinary productions by M. F. Gémier of *The Merchant of Venice* and *Antony and Cleopatra*. But in lyric drama the crowd has an entirely different function. It must express the emotions of a whole

community, to which end a very special process of training is necessary.

This æsthetic education of a chorus, the study of
the laws which govern collective gesture and movement,
and which form an integral part of any system of
rhythmic exercises, deserves the special consideration of
all my compatriots who are gymnasts, singers, or sports-
men.   More than in any other country, in Switzerland
popular spectacles involve the participation of numerous
supers, and the happy influence of these "Festpiele," to
employ the German term, has long been recognised by
our psychologists, pedagogues, and even theologians.

*   *   *   *   *

From the twelfth century onwards, the Swiss organised
performances of Passion plays to which actors and
audience repaired in procession, singing and dancing.
These performances originally took place in churches,
later they were carried into the open air.   In certain
cases the spectators took an active part in them, and we
have an account of one in which the Pilate, reviled
by two hundred actors, with difficulty escaped with his
life.

In the fifteenth century, the colleges organised
dramatic fêtes under the influence of the humanist plays
of Terence, and the performances of Passion plays
increased.   At Lucerne in particular they involved the
participation of hundreds of people ; at Einsiedeln, the
audience sang in common with the chorus ; at Berne
the poet and painter, Nicholas Manuel, produced panto-
mimes and carnival plays ; at Zurich, Josias Murer, in
his *Siege of Babylon*, and Halzwarth, in his *Saul*, brought
"a whole army " into play.   Indeed, pitched battles were
fought in the course of the action, and the text indicates
that in the last act " the populace, appeased, with one
accord ceases fighting, lies down, and falls asleep."   There
existed even at that period, then, a system of rhythm
applied to crowds.   The   stage   directions   are   highly

significant in this respect. The trumpets sound, the populace fights, attacks, retires, argues, murmurs, takes oaths, dances, and forms processions, thus playing in the piece a rôle as important as that of the leading actors.

These traditions have not been lost. If the colleges of music have decayed, and the mystery plays have practically disappeared, we may set against them those great patriotic festivals of extraordinary vitality and beauty, organised by the cantons on the centenaries of their entry into the confederation. Phenomena of nature have also inspired some wonderful demonstrations such as the unforgetable festival of winegrowers. We may therefore pride ourselves that our country possesses a natural instinct for grouping crowds and making them live in dramatic action. In the open air, under the glare of the sun, in the prodigious framework provided by a glorious landscape and sky, in scenes where nature herself furnishes every gradation of height, depth, and density, processions pass, dance-circles are formed, men and women fall on their knees in devotion, without requiring any particular technique of representation. But in a restricted area everything is different, and the framework of a space artificially confined creates special conditions of movement and grouping. Would our Swiss artists but undertake the interesting task of studying the relations of defined and lighted space with musical rhythm and physical movement, they might divert the dramatic art of Switzerland into an entirely new channel. The works are there—only the stage-technique is wanting. The impressive last scene in Chavannes' *Guillaume le Fou* signally failed to produce the requisite effect at the Comedy Theatre owing to the producer regarding the chorus of Swiss peasants as an assemblage of isolated men, each retaining his individuality, instead of treating them as one individual, a synthetic entity. Let us, then, consider the most practicable method of bringing the crowd into direct relations with the underlying motives of lyric drama by means of a refining process applied to its rhythmic potentialities.

*   *   *   *   *

We have all of us admired, at gymnastic displays, the wonderful living picture formed by hundreds of young men moving in step to music ; the synchronism of their gestures produces a sensation at once emotive and æsthetic, and yet these gymnasts are quite unconscious of creating an artistic effect. Their-sole aims are discipline and hygiene. They cultivate movement for its own sake, and give no thought to it as a medium for the expression of emotion. On the stage, in lyric drama, the crowd of supers also cultivates collective gesture, but in the interests of ideas. It sustains a double rôle, not only supporting the dramatic action, but, in addition (as in the plays of Æschylus), communicating the thoughts of the poet or expressing the emotions of the spectators, thereby forming an intermediary between the stage and the auditorium. When it plays an active part in the drama its movements constitute gestures of action. When it bears the rôle of confidant of the hero or of mouthpiece of the religious or philosophic truths contained in the play, its gesture partakes of the nature of music.

The collective gesture of action may consist simply of a repetition by each member of the chorus of an individual movement prepared in advance, or even in the merging of a number of individual gestures independent of each other. But where a musical gesture has to be made with the object of indicating a situation or creating an atmosphere, these individual gestures must be unified, each member of the chorus discarding his personality to subordinate himself to the whole. In other words, the producer must orchestrate the diverse movements of the actors in such a way as to obtain unity of collective gesture. Before studying the laws by which this orchestration may be effected simply, clearly, and naturally, yet in such a way that these skilfully contrived collective movements retain an essentially human character, we must first understand the laws which establish the harmony of individual gestures.

*   *   *   *   *

No physical movement has any expressive virtue in itself. Expression by gesture depends on a succession of movements and on a constant care for their harmonic, dynamic, and static rhythm. The static is the study of the laws of balance and proportion—the dynamic that of the means of expression. According to François del Sarte, dynamic harmony depends on the relation that subsists between all agents of gesture. Just as in music there are consonant and dissonant chords, so in mimic art we find consonant and dissonant gestures. "Consonant" movements are produced by the perfect co-ordination between limbs, head, and torso, the fundamental agents of gesture. Exactly the same is the case when it is a question of harmonising different motive elements of a crowd.

A crowd may act either independently or conjointly with a soloist. In the former case, it may express an affirmative or a negative attitude, showing hesitation or the reverse ; when acting with a soloist, it introduces an element of opposition or encouragement or even of argument (that is to say, a mixture of acquiescence and resistance).

In the collective movement of a crowd we have to observe both changes and successions of attitudes. Just as, in the individual, changes in the position of an arm or leg may become unæsthetic when accompanied by superfluous movements of the shoulders or incongruous facial play, so also changes of gesture and attitude, while walking or running, of a collection of individuals, will produce a harmonious effect on the spectator only by a subordination of each individual gesture in favour of

Scene from *Les Souvenirs*.   Geneva, 1918   (2).

the whole. The crowd must be considered by the producer as an entity, a single individual, with many limbs. The simultaneous execution of individual gestures will not of itself express the collective emotions of a crowd. Fifty persons slowly raising their arms will only produce the effect of a single strong line. In order to convey the impression of a whole people raising its arms, the gesture of each isolated actor should carry on the gesture commenced by his neighbour and transmit it to a third in pursuance of a continuous movement. Similarly where it is desired to manifest an impetuous tendency, a single step forward taken by each member of the chorus will by no means suggest the advance of a whole crowd. To accomplish this, the rear members must remain stationary, other members taking a slight step, others again a longer, and yet others more than one step forward in such a way that the whole space is occupied and, in consequence, the group is extended.

It is the same with dynamic gesture. The impression of a common release of energy does not depend on the amount of muscular effort contributed by each individual member. An effect of *crescendo* could be obtained without any increase of energy on the part of individuals by a simple shrinkage of the group analogous to that of the contraction of a muscle, or, on the other hand, an extension which will cause it to occupy a larger area. Generally speaking, dynamic effects are obtained by modifications of space, and emotive effects by interruptions of continuous symmetrical formations. A single person rising gently out of a kneeling group will produce a stronger impression than if the whole rose at the same moment. The effect will be increased tenfold if, while he rises, those who remain kneeling bow themselves to the ground. Just as every gesture of the arm attains its maximum significance by the opposition of another limb, so a collective gesture should be set off by carefully contrived contrasted gestures. An advancing body will

convey a far stronger impression of its forward direction
if simultaneously other bodies are seen retiring.

Thus polyrhythm ought to play a highly important
part in the training of stage crowds; not alone polyrhythm
as applied to the chorus, but that formed by counterpoint
between the gestures of the individual actor and those
of the crowd, opposing continuous slow movement to
lively and irregular movement, linking in canon gestures
and steps, producing all manner of variations of attitude.
The study of the relations between stage gesture and
space demonstrates the need of dispensing with painted
representations of artificial dimensions in favour of real
inclines and staircases * which permit the body to vary
its attitudes in pursuit of balance.   But it is not enough
to have provided actors with material conditions more
suitable for bodily movement.   The essential is to give
them the special education required for the utilisation of
such conditions.   This education must adjust the relations
between space and time; hence it will be essentially
musical, for music is the only art that teaches time-nuance.
The chorus must reproduce the elementary rhythms of
music; it must give form and a framework to the
individual actions of the protagonists.   In an orchestral
ensemble, full freedom is allowed the individual musicians
in interpreting the dominant motives of the work, but
their lyric expansion is continually restrained and toned
down by the necessity of respecting the general form and
of preserving the balance of the interpretation as a whole.
As we have said, it is the chorus that creates the atmosphere
in which the individual artists perform; the latter must
obviously be permitted freedom of individual action, but
only so long as they keep within the limits imposed by
the æsthetic and emotional atmosphere of the piece.
For the rest, each individual whether in the chorus or
outside it must sacrifice his particular idiosyncrasies of
expression in the interests of the general impression;

* See page 152 of this chapter.

Scene from *Les Souvenirs*.   Geneva, 1918 (3)

the crowd retaining its special function of pointing the
similarity and contrasts between the imaginary lives of
the *dramatis personæ* and the ordinary lives and rhythm
of the spectators.

The special training for choruses proposed by Appia
twenty years ago and since practised by us, aims at giving
performers the necessary flexibility for adapting themselves
spontaneously to all the rhythms, however complex,
called into play by the inspiration and what we may be
permitted to call the "music" of the creative imagination.
This education should be imposed likewise on conductors,
producers, and specialists in stage painting and lighting,
whose efforts should combine to produce an impression
of unity, for they can remain independent and isolated
only at a serious risk to the work as a whole.

*   *   *   *   *

Stage lighting does not generally attempt more than
a picturesque imitation of the effects of nature, hardly
venturing outside the scope of scenic decoration. Its
action, allied with music, however, would create new and
varied possibilities of expression. Discarding its habitual
function of representing the various shades of day and
night, it might participate directly in the dramatic action,
accentuating sudden changes of feeling, whether impulses
or reactions, permeating the decorative space with its
emotive qualities. We might thus be shown a crowd at
first enveloped in relative darkness entering little by little
into a zone of light; different elements of the crowd
disporting themselves in variously lighted parts until the
collective gesture begun in twilight emerges into the
triumphal light of day.

Light is the sister of music. . . . To reinforce the
crescendo of the one by strengthening the other, to
harmonise all their qualities of shading, phrasing, and
rhythm, would be to convey to an audience, by a combination of sound and light, a maximum of æsthetic
sensation and to provide actors with undreamt facilities

of expression. Provided, naturally, that actors should not come to use these new methods mechanically, that they should remain real artists. For art is not a particular method of expressing or transcribing life. It is "life itself and the means of experiencing it." The development of sentiment and temperament does not unfortunately enter into any actual curriculum of artistic education. That is a grave mistake, and it seems incredible that so few artists and critics should recognise it. So far as we are concerned, if we earnestly desire these reforms it is because, to vary the maxim of La Rochefoucald, "we know perfectly what we want."

XI

HOW TO REVIVE DANCING (1912)

Definition of dancing—The so-called " classical " dance, and the negation of gravity—Acrobatics of gesture—Metre and rhythm—Excessive isolation of music from dancing—Dancers and composers of ballets—Creation of choreographic style—Phrasing and pace of dancing—Divers exercises in fusion of music and moving plastic—Gesture and expression—Sincerity and travesty—Plastic polyrhythm—Fiction and fact in the theatre—The dance of the future.

DANCING has always, from the time of Lucian to that of Goethe and Théophile Gautier, been described in dithyrambic and aerial terms, calling up vague dreams of a supernatural order, in which bodily form, emancipated from the laws of gravity, floated high above the realities of human existence. These are not the terms in which I propose to frame my discourse on the dance to-day ; my object is to determine within what limits the art of dancing may approach, in its conception and by purely human means, governed by physiological laws, the art, at present in full course of development, from which it very directly derives, namely, music.

There exist, and there will always exist, exceptional beings who, naturally gifted in music and moving plastic, imbued with the joy of living, and permeated with the profound impression of beauty derived from human emotions, contrive to render sound rhythms visible, and to re-create music plastically, without any special training, guided solely by their intuition, and by the unconscious subordination of their physical faculties to their imaginative and emotional capacities. These are spoilt children of fortune, and education is only wasted on them.

Numerous normal individuals are attracted to the art of choreography by a natural taste for plastic expression —frequently for mere bodily movement—and devote themselves to dancing, without acquiring the numerous faculties necessary for the practice of this independent and profoundly human art. For these, the training in vogue among dancers is hopelessly inadequate. The possibility of raising the standard of this training is my present concern; only by the raising of this standard, and, in consequence, of the mentality of dancers, can the dance be restored to its ancient glories.

I desire to confine myself, in this study of the conditions and possibilities of a renaissance of choreographic art, to the technical side of my subject, and may be pardoned, I trust, for omitting the usual metaphorical and lyrical flourishes.

*   *   *   *   *

Dancing is the art of expressing emotion by means of rhythmic bodily movements.—It is not the function of rhythm to render these movements expressive, but merely to control and refine them, in fact to make them artistic, by means of a "conscious change of their relations"—in Taine's expression. From remotest antiquity we find the dance accompanied by forms of music, aiming at the rhythmic regulation of gesture, evolutions, and attitude. This musical accompaniment may not be strictly necessary, as I will explain in a moment; but once we admit that the art of dancing involves a fusion of rhythmic sound and movement—just as, in lyric art, we find the spoken word allied to music—we are forced to the conclusion that the state of decadence in which dancing has sunk in our time is due partly to the exaggerated development of bodily virtuosity at the expense of expression, and partly to the absolute negation of the principle of unity of corporal plastic and musical rhythm."*

In stage dancing, as may still be witnessed in the more important operatic performances, bodily movements tend neither to express feelings nor to transpose sound movements. They rarely harmonise at all with the music which is supposed to have evoked them, and the limbs that execute them are not even themselves in harmony. The arms ignore the movements of the legs, or rather they have the air of refusing to follow the latter in their evolutions. They confine themselves to maintaining balance, and might as well belong to a different body. As to the legs, their rôle would appear to consist in repudiating the weight of the body. One can understand how, by eliminating from their drawings the representation of certain muscular contractions, painters contrive to dispel the impression of weight, with the definite object of conveying an illusion of immateriality (in the ascension of saints, flights of angels, etc.). But dancers, without knowing it, merely emphasise the material aspect of the body in seeking to negative its weight by a series of leaps and bounds. These are only effected by strenuous efforts of contraction. The immaterialisation of a body can only be expressed in dancing by the graduation of dynamic *diminuendos* in limbs other than the legs, since the latter, in the course of the dance, are bound to be contracted. This immaterialisation, incidentally, cannot possibly be conveyed to the audience unless the dancer is sincerely and

---

* Training in (so-called) "classical" ballet dancing aims at the acquirement of a certain number of automatisms, of an acrobatic nature, which can be linked together in various ways. The function of the *maître-de-ballet* consists in adapting them to the divers forms of music they are intended to interpret. Once dancers have passed their final examination, their technique is regarded as finished, and any artistic development considered superfluous. Throughout their career they continue to exhibit to the public the virtuoso effects acquired in their training, and which constitute what is popularly known as the art of *choreography*.

N

completely absorbed in immaterial thoughts. But spiritual faculties can never be developed normally and completely in a dancer who specialises in restricted movement and particularly in the realistic movement of leaping.

A complete thought, an association of ideas and feelings, a "state of soul," can only be interpreted by a body wholly absorbed in that thought. Just as, in opera, mere aimless singing, wholly concerned with virtuosity, conveys to artists an impression of insincerity and futility, so bodily movements, where not inspired by the need for externalising feelings or interpreting a really vital piece of music, constitute a form of ridiculous stage acrobatics. Dancing and mimicry, in relation to the modern stage, have become inferior arts (in pantomime, gestures serve merely to express conventional feelings and realistic actions) through specialisation in purely technical effects. Of what avail the variety of these effects, or even the care of certain dancers to produce them synchronically with the measured cadences of the orchestra? Not measure, but rhythm, assures the originality of musical expression. It is futile for dancers who are not artists to make their steps exactly correspond with the musical phrasing—their movements express not music, but merely its external forms deprived of all vital impulse. Rapidity or slowness of sound or bodily movement can only become expressive when made to represent a state of concentration or excitement produced by stimulating and emotive mental images. A slow walk or a light run can only produce an æsthetic impression where the general pace of the interpreter indicates to the spectator the relations between the visible movements and the concentrated state of mind and soul that has evoked them. If the speed of the walk or run be influenced by immaterial causes, the general attitude of the whole body will be similarly influenced—which only proves the insincerity of most of the regular dancing steps, for which only the leg-muscles are required, and which furnish an analogy to the audacious scale passages so justly tabooed from modern instrumental music.

*   *   *   *   *

There is no longer any necessity to plead the case for the old operatic ballet ; the case has already been judged and lost ! The public has ceased to take any interest in choreography, and artists no longer regard it as an art ; but the deplorable part is that neither artists nor public appreciate the real grounds of their contempt. We find them still extolling the merits of individual dancers of repute, from which we might conclude that the decadence of choreographic art lay, in their opinion, in the inferiority of the standard of dancers. Very few performers are conscious of the discord existing between musical metre and rhythm, and the manner of expressing them plastically. The gulf separating the orchestra from the stage appears to them a normal state. The notable efforts of Isadora Duncan to revive Greek dancing seems to them all that is required to reform the art of ballet ; they do not notice that these dances are quite uninfluenced by music, and could dispense with music altogether ! Others —including quite well-known artists and critics—preserve, or affect to preserve, an unshaken confidence in the choreographic traditions, despite the complete divorce of these from their musical principles, which are based on a sincere research for natural musical expression. In short, the dancing public of to-day appears to me in an analogous situation to an audience at the opera that did not notice when (1) the rhythms of the vocal text did not correspond with the musical rhythms, supposed to give them their value, and (2) the artistes sang in a different key and time from the orchestra.

Wagner strenuously combated the lack of unity between poesy and music, and accomplished something of a revolution. In the same way, artists, conscious of the gulf that separates corporal language from sound rhythms on the stage, should concentrate on bringing home to the public the real cause of the artistic inferiority of which they cannot fail to be conscious, and impressing on them that if dancing is no longer an art, it is only because the fundamental laws of sound and plastic æsthetics are no longer regarded.

The music of movement, like the music of sound, aims at expressing the common emotions of humanity.

The music that is within us, and which is composed of our natural rhythms, and of the emotions that determine the sensations peculiar to our temperament, may assume different forms, according to the capacities of individuals. In dancing, it must transpose itself at once into sound and movement. Sound-music regulates, controls, and refines plastic, which otherwise would be abandoned to the anarchy of movements. In addition, it strengthens expression by means of its stimulating properties. Plastic, on the other hand, renders sounds visible and gives them a human touch.

In the modern ballet, music and dancing are separated owing to the isolation of musical and choreographic training. This has been the case for so long that there exists very little ballet music suitable for dancing, and very few bodily rhythms involved in dancing that can inspire composers with original musical ideas. There is no common ground between dancers and composers for the ballet, nor any *rapport* between rhythms in time and those in space.*

* If you point out this state of affairs to a painter, he will tell you, with apparent logic, that, from his point of view, the sight of harmonious movements is more important than the sound of adequately harmonised music, and that this juxtaposition of different elements seems to him to destroy the unity of the plastic impression. Undoubtedly—assuming he lacks a normal feeling for music!—nothing can be more legitimate than moving plastic dispensing with music, and drawing all its resources from the human body. The trouble is that non-musical dancers, incapable of interpreting the music which is supposed to be inspiring them, are not content to dispense with, and contrive rather to parody, it. One thing or the other, either they regard music as a mere agent of control over movements, in which case

Once it is admitted that bodily movements should be controlled by musical rhythms, it becomes important that the latter should be susceptible of corporal realisation. If we examine the present-day ballet music, we find that the time-units are commonly too short to enable legs and arms to express them synchronically, whence we may conclude that composers of ballet are unacquainted with the instrument for which they are writing, and are producing music, the greater part of which is impracticable for its proclaimed purposes. They accumulate technical musical devices to dissimulate their lack of understanding of the human body, and its potentialities of expression.

On the other hand, we find that when, in the course of ballet music, passages suitable for expression by the body *do* occur, the dancers do not even attempt to reconcile their movements with the rhythm of the music, and content themselves with adapting the conventional interpretation. This leads us to our second conclusion, that ballet dancers are ignorant of the laws of sound rhythm, in relation to those of plastic rhythm, and find themselves—confronted with music—in the situation of a village fiddler able to repeat by heart a certain number of airs which have been crammed into him, but who, placed in an orchestra, knowing nothing of the laws of musical prosody, would seek to adapt these airs—as best he could—to the music he was set to read, and which was a dead letter to him. These two conclusions bring us to a third, viz. that if we wish to instigate a revival of dancing as an art, we must provide an education that will enable dancers to understand the music they are set to express plastically, and familiarise composers with the laws of balance and bodily movement in all their nuances. Only in this way can there be any question of an adequate rhythmic and plastic expression of emotion,

any instrument of percussion will serve their purpose, or, accepting music as a genuinely inspiring force, they must submit themselves to its impulses, and spare us the revolting spectacle of its prostitution.

for only when we are thoroughly versed in the multiple signs of a language can we effectively employ these signs to express our feelings.

*   *   *   *   *

The art of musical rhythm consists in differentiating time-durations, combining them in succession, arranging rests between them, and accentuating them consciously or unconsciously, according to physiological law. The art of plastic rhythm is to designate movement in space, to interpret long time-values by slow movements, and short ones by quick movements, regulate pauses in their divers successions, and express sound accentuations in their multiple nuances by additions or diminutions of bodily weight, by means of muscular innervations.

The dancer-student (and by the term dancer I imply every interpreter of music by means of bodily movement, including operatic singers and conductors) should therefore undergo a double and parallel training, as a result of which he will acquire a knowledge of, and sensitiveness to, music, and an understanding of the rhythms that inspire it, together with the faculty of interpreting these plastically, without sacrificing their style—that is, the alterations the composer has effected in the relations of the rhythms as between themselves. It is these alterations that express his emotions, and all the dynamic and pathetic nuances comprising the emotional element in the music should be executed by the dancer by means of *modifications in the regularity of muscular movements effected by his own sensibility.* These modifications can only be produced as a result of special exercises, and the following seem to me indispensable for giving the artist a consciousness of his movements, and making it possible for him to vary and combine them artificially without strain.

In the first place, the dancer must be rendered capable of walking in time, whatever the movement be—which is by no means as easy as might be thought. Dancers, as a rule, do not know how to walk slowly, they cannot keep balance, and the virtuosity of their legs is confined to quick movements. If one carefully watches Isadora Duncan, in other respects the sworn enemy of mere technical virtuosity, and a seeker after naturalistic effects, one will notice that she rarely walks in time to an *adagio*, almost invariably adding involuntarily one or more steps to the number prescribed by the musical phrase. This arises from her inability to control the transfer of the weight of the body from one leg to another in all variations of pace. She disregards the laws of gravity which, from the corporal plastic point of view, create the laws of balance. The only art in space hitherto known to us, architecture, is based on the laws of gravity and balance. The human body is intended likewise to submit itself to these laws, and various muscular innervations are there for the purpose. Ordinary stage dancers are incapable of walking slowly; we have all seen them waddle back to the wings, like ducks, after their turns. Choreographic training deforms the natural play of their joints. In my exercises in measured walking—to me the A B C of a choreographic training—the student learns to control the harmony of the active muscles, and their complements, from the slowest *largo* to a lively *allegro*, and to practise *accelerandos*, *ritenutos*, and *rubatos*, in walking, without losing his balance. In addition, different kinds of walking are evoked by the different pace of musical phrases and adapted to *staccatos*, *legatos*, *portandos*, and the like effects of the music. There exist here as many variations as in the bow strokes of a violinist, and the same comparison will enable us to follow the special exercises and training necessitated by the different styles of walking and halting, whether abruptly or slowly. To attack a phrase on the violin by an anacrusis of three semi-quavers necessitates a different position for the bow, and a different kind of muscular activity from that required for an attack on the semibreve played *pianissimo*, or on a crotchet played *forte*, and followed by a rest. The study of repressions of steps is of even more import- ance, inasmuch as the cessation of movement constitutes, for dancing purposes, a potent means of creating con- trasts and of introducing polyphony in the expression of feelings. In many respects, the dance may be compared with a *concerto* for violin and orchestra, in which the soloist engages in a dialogue with the other instruments, and where now one, now another of the two protagonists remains silent for a moment to enable his interlocutor to speak. In dancing, however, the dialogue is conducted in two different languages : plastic phrases respond to musical phrases. The essential is that artistic and æsthetic emotion should be expressed ; for the rest, plastic language has no less and varied resources than that of music.

* * * * *

To return to our exercises in walking : it goes with- out saying that these are not confined to a flat surface, but are practised on inclines strewn with objects, and on staircases of every kind and dimension. Once we are concerned with utilising the whole body for the expres- sion of human emotion, it becomes obviously absurd to deprive it of opportunities of freely disporting itself in its divers modes of activity. The walk of a man will vary according to the surface on which he is moving ; it is therefore necessary that, in the theatre, he should be given practice in moving on different kinds of surfaces.* Have you ever seen children dancing on a grassy slope ? And do you know the deep impression made by the sight of a crowd of men laboriously climbing a mountain ?

Preliminary exercises in walking should be executed without the aid of the arms. These are reserved for other than the purely balancing functions to which ballet dancers devote them. The arms form the principal medium for the expression of feelings called up by

* See Chapter X., p. 152.

dancing, and lend themselves to an infinite number of combinations of movements. I should say that the symbols forming the language of gesture are almost as numerous as those of the language of articulate speech. The study of gestures, their oppositions and combinations, is, however, unknown in operatic ballet circles where the arms serve only to maintain balance. Dancers of the Duncan school employ more varied, beautiful, and numerous gestures, but they are usually confined to antique models, reproducing the attitudes of Greek statues, and by no means asserting the personality of the dancer, or expressing spontaneous and sincere emotion. Apart from that, they operate in space, without order of sequence ; they are never led up to, they occur at haphazard ; they are not the inevitable product of nuances of feeling dictated by the music ; finally, they fail to interpret the mentalities of contemporary human beings.

In studying diction, the pupil is taught carefully to modulate his voice according to his temperament, and not in imitation of the vocal nuances conceived by others. The same applies to the study of gesture, which should depend on the shape of limbs, the force and flexibility of muscles, and the particular dispositions of the joints. To give an idea of the infinite number of combinations of gestures, let us take the movement of raising the left arm and holding it vertically above the head. This gesture may vary in form and expression, according to the divers inclinations of the torso and head, the degree of tension or flexion of the elbow or wrist, the position of the fingers in the hand, open or closed, and the displacements of the torso or other parts of the body. Again, while raising the left arm, the right may remain stationary or sink in contrast, or bend to the right or left or rear, in every nuance of tension or flexion. These various combinations of the arm may assume a totally different significance, according as the actor's eye is directed to the left arm, right arm, elbow, wrist, or fingers. They produce varied impressions according to the degree of resistance of the inhibitory muscles, and the slowness or rapidity of the movements (one arm may be raised slowly while the other makes a rapid gesture). Yet again, while the left arm is being raised, the right may execute quite a number of movements, and each of these gestures may be seen in a different aspect, according to the successive directions of the eye. Finally, the divers positions of the legs will further modify the pace and æsthetic significance of the arm gestures. According as the weight of the body is on the leg placed in front, or to the rear, and to the degree of inclination, and the condition of flexion or tension of the legs, the whole attitude will vary in meaning and value. Each of these detailed modifications in the position as a whole may, in its turn, be combined with other alterations of the original attitude, from which may be seen that the vocabulary of gesture does not lack variety. The important point, for artistic purposes, is that, according to the feeling that evokes the gesture and the physiognomic expression produced by the mental attitude, each of the varieties of gesture we have mentioned will assume a distinctive character, and reflect diversely the multiple nuances of human emotions.

*   *   *   *   *

Gesture itself is nothing—its whole value depends on the emotion that inspires it, and no form of dance, however rich in technical combinations of corporal attitudes, can ever be more than a mere unmeaning amusement, so long as it does not aim at depicting human emotions in their fulness and veracity. One has only to consider in this light our present operatic ballets, and the psychological effect of their activities, to realise that they outrage human dignity, arousing only the paltriest emotions, of an effeminate tendency, and eliminating the elements of vigour, initiative, courage, aggression, and revolution in favour of a sentimental and artificial pretty-prettiness. The man plays a negligible rôle and is really superfluous. The stimulating conflicts between resolution and weakness, doggedness and resignation, masterful love and tenderness, struggles, perilous enterprises, the slow but sure advance of Progress, the overcoming of obstacles, resistances, and compunctions, the victories over self—all these must give way to the conventional travesty (or what is one to call an art in which Siegfried, Renaud, and Tristan are represented by women ?) in which the man, conscious of the decadence of choreographic art, dare not assert his virility, nor affirm his dignity of authority, nor manifest plastically his innate æsthetic qualities, the instinct for domination and for tenacious resistance. What more repulsive spectacle can there be than that of the male dancer assuming feminine graces ? The eternal conflict of the sexes must be the keynote of the revival of the dance, and the latter can only recover its social influence and character of human truth, when the eternal adversaries, whose oppositions and reconciliations form the basis of all vital dramatic art, are adequately represented and staged.

Who can doubt but that, once balance has been restored, the divers nuances of expression will only appear in individuals capable of feeling emotion, when brought into contact with art, under the influence of sincerely felt sensations and sentiments ? Part of the dancer's education will have to be devoted to his nervous system ; special exercises habituating the nerves to transmit the orders of the brain to the limbs entrusted with their execution, and establishing by means of rhythm a vital and regular circulation—covering all nuances of movement—between the divers agents of the organism. Numerous automatic movements must be created, and made subservient to the conscious will, under whose direction they may be applied or withheld, combined, opposed, or superposed. The sub-conscious manifestations of individuality will also have to be developed, while not over-burdening the nervous system, nor destroying the plastic harmony of the organism. Before all else, the plastic interpreter of musical emotions must, however, be made capable, by virtue of an artistic and moral training, of deeply sensing these emotions—for any attempt at expression on the part of one not genuinely inspired by music is a sham. . . . Consider the admirable Russian dancers, with their fiery temperament, their grace, flexibility, and undeniable rhythmic qualities—watch them on occasion discard their dizzy gyratory effects to bring out the lyric essence of a dramatic situation! Their movement at once loses all ease and sincerity. Sentiment is replaced by sentimentality, natural expression by grandiloquence, each gesture of passion, shame, desire, suffering, is exaggerated to an extreme. A constant *vibrato* animates their movements ; a continuous crude expansion asserts itself ; the immodesty of simulated emotion is exposed in all its nakedness ! Does this mean that the dancers lack science, tact, and intelligence ? Not in the least. The cause of this exaggeration of attitudes and gestures is the lack of a close co-ordination between their sensibilities and those of the musician. The music does not directly re-act on their sensitive faculties, does not irresistibly inspire the natural means of bodily expression ; they are unable to express music, through incapacity to *take it in.*

The interpreter is no true artist unless he is capable not only of *giving,* but—once having received, humbly and joyfully, the "message" of the work—of creating anew what he has received, and of conveying to others, transfused, the essence of that message and of himself.

To the majority of ballet dancers, music is only a pretext for decorative effects in moving plastic. Beauty of gesture is sought in no other interest than that of the æsthetic application of their physical resources. They do not realise that no attitude can produce an impression of sincerity and beauty, unless it is the product of a state of mind—or indeed, of soul. The research for external grace excludes every effect of simple and natural beauty. This latter is the product of inner physical and intellectual effort, tending to the pursuit after higher, universal elements. Before expressing music, the dancer should be capable of living, and of responding to its impulses, in a completely disinterested spirit. The body is never so beautiful as when reflecting beauty of thought and the spontaneous stimulus of life. As Wagner said : "Only life can create a real need for art, and can furnish art with both matter and form."

The dancer-artist should make use of his whole body in expressing his emotions through music, and, inversely, in expressing music through his emotions ; it is therefore indispensable not only that all his limbs should be trained, but that his sensibility and musical intelligence should be adequately developed. A special education, aiming at awakening a feeling for the relations between movements in music and those of the muscular and nervous system, should be imposed not only on dancers, but on all artists pre-eminently concerned with rhythm, e.g. instrumentalists, singers, producers, and conductors. This education will result in the formation of live and sensitive beings, in control of their temperament, and capable of externalising and refining swift and acute sensations, and of understanding and loving the music whose many emotions they are set to interpret. The executive artist will constitute no longer a mere instrument, but a human being, capable of conveying his feelings—or the feelings of others—in a beautiful form, to a public he is able both to interest and stimulate. The present training of dancers is long and arduous. And what does it produce ? The execution by the legs of a number of small, quick—and ugly—movements without expression or delicacy ; the power of effecting prodigious leaps, like frogs, and revolutions like spinning-tops ! In arm gestures, as we have already explained, the dancer is entirely deficient ; adequate facial and ocular play can never be achieved so long as the subject is uncultured in feeling and thought. And even the acrobatic dancing, that constitutes the triumph of our *premières ballerines*, is confined to flat surfaces. As we have pointed out, specialisation in exercises of virtuosity has not even initiated dancers into evolutions on divers forms of surfaces and on staircases, to say nothing of walking slowly and with grace.

If only we had the enterprise—artists and public alike —to repudiate the anti-æsthetic spectacles so consistently presented to us on the operatic stage ! If only our composers and conductors had the courage and keenness to insist on ballet masters learning music and teaching it to their dancers ! The facts speak for themselves : the majority of dancers concerned with interpreting music do not know their notes, or, if they do, have no real understanding of music, of the intimate relations of which with plastic art they are completely ignorant.

Plastic polyrhythm is unknown in our ballet dancing. The art of contrasting movements and attitudes is still in an embryonic stage. The simultaneous execution of slow movements with the same movements at double, triple, or quadruple speed has never been attempted. The nuances produced by the co-operation of a large number of individualities in the expression of a single composite emotion cannot be achieved so long as those individualities remain incompletely developed, or even, as is often the case, without power of expression.

The very bodies of the most gifted and fully trained dancers are hampered in their strivings towards complete power of expression, by the artificial light, devoid alike of subtlety and truth, in which they are obliged to execute their movements. It is virtually impossible for them to express themselves plastically without the support of lighting effects, which at once reveal, and inspire them, creating an atmosphere in space analogous to that created by the play of music in time.   The present system allows for no play of natural shadows, no contrast of delicate movements with firmly silhouetted attitudes, no attempt at representing a *crescendo* by a gradation from darkness to light, directly inspired by the music—no connection between the space wherein the dancers disport themselves and the rhythms they execute, between the respective emotions created by the environment and the action.

    *   *   *   *   *

In an exhibition of dancing to which several arts collaborate in harmony (moving plastic, music, decorative staging) it is highly desirable to avoid any conflict between the artificial and the real.   Reality will always hold the spectator's attention more forcibly than artifice, making the latter unsatisfactory and ridiculous.   For this reason the three dimensions of space should never, in a setting for dancing, admit of an imaginary perspective of the painter's creation—nor will the real and vivid light which reveals the reality and vividness of those three dimensions in moving plastic suffer imaginative lighting effects in the staging.   Similarly, the rhythm of moving plastic should be spared the competition of imaginary but fixed movements of statuary and painting.   Existing stage decoration is the mortal enemy of real rhythm executed by the human body in the three real dimensions of space. Decoration in two real dimensions and a fictitious depth is out of place in a space involving real depth ; while a lighting which suppresses shadows compromises the real value of plastic and movement.   The setting for a display of dancing should be of a genuinely plastic nature, and the lighting, the aim of which should be to reveal the bodily rhythms in the most natural way, should fall from heaven, or break from the horizon.

Since all sources of expressive movements in moving plastic are of an imaginative nature, a direct contact with reality should not be permitted to compromise the illusion, and destroy the imaginative effects conveyed through that medium of expression. The illusion should be produced by the expressive action confined to time and space, musical atmosphere and light. The flowers a dancer stoops to pick must be fictitious and exist only in his imagination, or in the music which dictates the gesture of picking flowers ; neither real nor artificial flowers should be laid on the ground. The smell of these fictitious flowers has no real existence. You may convey it by the same gestures as those expressive of the joy of breathing the fragrance of life ; you do not require to have the stage sprinkled with perfume ! * The sources of joy, sorrow, despair, and energy have no real existence in the scenic representation of these passions, or at least exist only in the actor ; but all the impressions which have moulded his thoughts and feelings are expressed by his attitude and movements, by the proportion of their duration, and their accentuation, by the combination of the degrees of lightness and weight of his various limbs, and by the collaboration of his muscles, the servants of his temperament. In that sense the means of expression are realistic, and anything forming part of the setting, outside space and light, becomes a lie. As opposed to pantomime, which cannot dispense with real objects, because the relations between man and his environment are therein specialised to an extreme, natural dancing generalises feelings and emotions, expressing them in their elementary form. That is why the causes of these feelings lose their intensity in being made manifest; their meanness renders unconvincing and disproportionate the lyric grandeur of their expression. For example, fear in face of the dangers of nature is experienced by all human beings ; but such dangers, as represented by material means in the restricted space of a stage, can only admit of the presence of individuals, not of *mankind*. The art of living plastic (the Greek *orchesis*) is the product of

* As in certain exhibitions of Dada and Negro dancing, and the like.

impression transformed into expression, and does not
confine itself either to the concrete or the abstract.   In it
the body must serve always to express the life of the soul.
Consequently, thoughts and feelings which cannot be
entirely externalised by its natural motor forces are outside its province, pertaining to that of the conventional
theatre, which is concerned with the individualisation and
specialisation of the circumstances and forms of matter
surrounding the individual.

Dancing must be completely reformed ; in this, as in
so many other domains, mere ameliorative measures
seem to me to be utterly futile.   The art is in a state of
decay, and must be rooted out, and replaced by a new
one, founded on principles of beauty, purity, sincerity,
and harmony.   Both dancer and public should be trained
in feeling for bodily forms ; the courageous and noble
efforts of Isadora Duncan and her disciples to restore
plastic purity, by the idealisation of the quasi-nudity of
the human body, must not be allowed to succumb to the
clamour of protests from hypocritical or ignorant philistines.   Bodies trained in the refined realisation of rhythmic
sensations must learn to assimilate thought and absorb
music—the psychological and idealising factor in dancing.
Doubtless it will be possible one day, when music has
become ingrained in the body and is at one with it, when
the human organism is impregnated with the many
rhythms of the emotions of the soul, and only requires
to react naturally to express them plastically by a process
of transposition, in which only appearances are changed—
doubtless it will be possible at that stage to dance
without the accompaniment of sounds.   The body will
suffice to express the joys and sorrows of men, and will
not require the co-operation of instruments to dictate
their rhythms—itself comprising all rhythms and expressing them naturally in movements and attitudes.
Meanwhile, the body must submit to the intimate
collaboration of music, or rather, be willing to yield,

without restriction, to the discipline of sounds in all their metrical and pathetic accentuations, adapting their rhythms to its own, or, better still, contriving to oppose plastic to sound rhythms, in a rich counterpoint never before undertaken, and which must definitely establish the unity of gesture and symphony. And thus the dance of to-morrow will become a medium of expression and poesy, a manifestation of art, emotion, and truth. . . .

A Plastic Exercise (i)

XII

EURHYTHMICS AND MOVING PLASTIC (1919)

The art of the Eurhythmist is self-sufficient—Analysis of the art of moving plastic—Muscular consciousness and instinct for attitudes—Table of elements common to music and moving plastic—Rhythms musical and intellectual—Arhythm—Possible amelioration of music-corporal interpretations — Sequence of attitudes — L'Après-midi d'un Faune, Russian ballet, and continuous movement—Visual and muscular experiences.

Classification of elements common to moving plastic and music—Dynamics —Agogics (division of time)—Division of space—Relations between time and space—Division of time and space in relation to the situation of the individual in space—Sequence of gestures—Gestures from the æsthetic point of view—Plastic and musical value of gesture—Gestures of groups— Rhythm and human society.

RHYTHMICS aims at the bodily representation of musical values, by means of a special training tending to muster in ourselves the elements necessary for this representation—which is no more than the spontaneous externalisation of mental attitudes dictated by the same emotions that animate music. If the expression of these emotions does not directly react on our sensorial faculties, and produce a correspondence between sound rhythms and our physical rhythms, and between their expulsive force and our sensibility, our plastic externalisation will become mere *imitation*. It is this that distinguishes eurhythmics from the old systems of callisthenics, musical drill and dancing. All external effects of corporal expression, born of an understanding of rhythmic movement and music, are the inevitable product of a state of emotion quite free from æsthetic ambition. Their manifestation satisfies the exigencies of art, since art consists of magnifying ideas and emotions, and giving them a decorative form and style, while developing their vital qualities and rendering them susceptible of communication to others. The eurhythmist is he who both creates (or re-creates) artistic emotion and experiences it. In him sensation humanises the idea, and the idea spiritualises sensation. In the laboratory of his organism a transmutation is effected, turning the creator into both actor and spectator of his own composition.

If, once having achieved the corporal representation of musical rhythms (by means of the transformation of metaphysical sensations into manifestations of a muscular order and *vice versa*), the eurhythmist tries to modify these effects so as to externalise their form and impress them visually on the spectator, the eurhythmic training changes its character and assumes an æsthetic and social significance. And the pursuit of perfection in the interpretation, *via* the body, of musical emotions and feelings, enters the region of what, as distinct from the arts of painting and sculpture, we may call *moving* or *living plastic*. Eurhythmic exercises enable the individual to feel and express music corporally, for his own pleasure, thus constituting in themselves a complete art, in touch with life and movement. A training in moving plastic renders the eurhythmic mediums of expression more harmonious and decorative, and refines gestures and attitudes by a process of successive eliminations.*

The conventional ballet training concentrates on harmony and grace of bodily movements, without insisting upon the particular mental state, inevitably

* We have often remarked that Eurhythmics cannot be judged from the mere sight of movements executed by its students. Eurhythmics constitutes an eminently individual experience. Moving plastic is a complete art directly addressed to the eyes of spectators, although directly experienced by its exponents. The impressions of a Eurhythmist may be conveyed to spectators particularly sensitive to the "feeling of movement"; the plastic artist *aims* at conveying his impressions to the public.

conducive to these movements, on the part of the dancer. Education by and in rhythm aims, before all else, at producing in the student a psycho-physical sensibility, calculated at once to create the need and furnish the means of spontaneously externalising musical rhythms genuinely felt, and interpreting them by any means inspired by a perfect knowledge of the relations of space, time, and weight. The conventional dancer adapts music to his particular technique and a number—in reality very restricted—of automatisms; the eurhythmist *lives* this music, makes it his own—his movements quite naturally interpreting it. A training in moving plastic will also teach him to select, among these movements, those most expressive and suitable for producing effects of a decorative order which will convey to the spectator the feelings and sensations which have inspired them. The main thing is that the emotions, which have inspired the sound rhythms and the form in which they have taken shape (also the processes of a geometrical and architectural order which have determined the harmonies and developments), should be reproduced in their plastic representation, and that the same life force should animate sound music and the music of gesture alike.

Once the limbs are trained, once the senses and mind have been awakened by rhythm, the nervous resistances eliminated, and the divers forces of the organism connected by a continuous and powerful current, it becomes necessary to complete the muscular sense, the feeling for space and familiarity with its laws—as well as that for shades of time—by the acquisition of æsthetic qualities and of the instinct for divining the results certain movements will produce on others, and which enable the plastic artist to realise with his limbs gestures and attitudes he has previously imagined. Placed before a mirror, he should see reflected the perfect plastic expression of a preconceived *ensemble* of lines and curves; for, just as merely being musical will not enable a man to create music, so the mere possession of a feeling for plastic beauty and emotion will not suffice to transpose emotion and beauty into external forms of physical movement. While acuteness of visual powers and a cultivated decorative sense enable a draughtsman to convey graphically the beauty of the human body in movement, these qualities will by no means serve to enable him to represent those movements through the medium of his own body. For that purpose he will have to acquire, by means of a special training, the inward sense of decorative line and form, balance and dynamism, necessary for plastic representation.

Every visual or auditive activity begins with a simple registration of images and sounds, and the receptive faculties of eye and ear will only develop an æsthetic activity when the muscular sense is sufficiently developed to convert the sensations so registered into movement. As we have said elsewhere, and frequently, movement is the basis of all the arts, and no artistic culture is possible without a previous study of the forms of movement and a thorough training of our motor-tactile faculties. It was this discovery that led us to precede lessons in solfège by a training of the nervous and muscular systems, according to the laws of time and rhythm ; the same phenomenon shows us the danger of undertaking the study of moving plastic (corporal solfège) without reiterated experiences tending to the acquisition of a host of qualities producing collectively a feeling for space in time, and time in space, by means of movement.

A point is reached when moving plastic becomes completely musicalised by the study of the multiple elements of an agogic and dynamic nature which constitute the expressive language of sound. It will then seek to create forms of movement at once decorative and expressive, *without resort to sound*, by the exclusive aid of *its own music*. Doubtless these mediums of musical expression can never become really complete without the

A Plastic Exercise (2)

co-operation of whole groups of people, for it is a matter not only of endowing the human body with all the divers mediums of expression possessed by the art of music, and of making that body the direct agent of thought and creative emotion, but also of harmonising and orchestrating several bodies in movement.

The elements common to music and the modern ballet are exclusively time and, more or less as an accessory, rhythm. The elements common to music and *moving plastic* are :

Music.	Moving Plastic.
Pitch.	Position and direction of gestures in space.
Intensity of sound.	Muscular dynamics.
Timbre.	Diversity in corporal forms (the sexes).
Duration.	Duration.
Time.	Time.
Rhythm.	Rhythm.
Rests.	Pauses.
Melody.	Continuous succession of isolated movements.
Counterpoint.	Opposition of movements.
Chords.	Arresting of associated gestures (or gestures in groups)
Harmonic successions.	Succession of associated movements (or of gestures in groups).
Phrasing.	Phrasing.
Construction (form).	Distribution of movements in space and time.
Orchestration (*vide* timbre).	Opposition and combination of divers corporal forms (the sexes).

*　　　*　　　*　　　*　　　*

All the rhythmic elements in music were originally formed after the rhythms of the human body ; but in course of time the types and their combinations were varied and multiplied to the point of spiritualising music, and their muscular origin was eventually lost sight of. The body became unaccustomed to them in proportion as the preponderance of purely intellectual education

increased ; and so it has come about that the majority of
rhythmic models taken from modern music, even ballet
music, are no longer capable of interpretation by the
body. Certain types of music may be associated with
bodily movements, but not vitally interpreted by them,
nor what one may call plastically transposed. In our
ballets, sound movements are developed concurrently
with corporal movements ; the music acts as an accompaniment, and not as a collaborator ; it neither inspires,
penetrates, nor animates the gestures, movements, and
attitudes. That is why so-called "classical" dancing
does not constitute a complete art, nor contribute to the
progress of the art. In fact, the ballet dancer possesses
intuitively neither intellectual nor physical rhythms, his
virtuosity being formed from a combination of automatisms that his emotion cannot replace, at will, by spontaneous rhythmic manifestations. The composer of
ballet music, for his part, has only intellectual rhythms
at his disposal, and these are likewise automatised to
such a pitch that he cannot interrupt a development of a
purely musical character in his score in favour of spontaneous rhythms, of a corporal origin. Dancer and
musician alike are slaves of time, as unversed in nuances
of time-duration, as in the dynamic relations of sound
and corporal movements. The composer may observe
the conventional musical rhythms, but is a-rhythmic
from a muscular point of view. The dancer, for the
most part, is a-rhythmic both from the muscular *and*
musical points of view, for lack of an education that
would enable him both to break his automatisms (or
adapt them to modifications of time-duration), and to
incorporate and later externalise sound rhythms with
complete ease and flexibility. Let me explain what I
mean :

To be *a-rhythmic* is to be incapable of following a
movement in the exact time required for its normal
execution ; to hurry it here or delay it there instead of

keeping it at a uniform pace ; not to know how to accelerate it when acceleration is necessary, nor to draw it out when protraction is necessary ; to make it rough and jerky instead of smooth and continuous, and *vice versa* ; to commence or finish too late or too soon ; not to be able to link a movement of one sort on to a movement of another sort—a slow to a quick, a flexible to a rigid, a vigorous to a gentle, movement ; to be incapable of executing simultaneously two or more conflicting movements ; not to know how to shade a movement, that is, to execute it in an imperceptible gradation from *piano* to *forte*, and *vice versa*, nor to accentuate it metrically or pathetically at the points fixed by the requisites of the musical shape or emotion.   All these deficiencies, without exception, may be attributed either to inability of the brain to issue its orders sufficiently promptly to the muscles responsible for the execution of the movement, inability of the nervous system to transmit these orders accurately and smoothly to the right quarters, or inability of the muscles to execute them infallibly. A-rhythm arises, then, from a lack of harmony and co-ordination between the conception and the execution of the movement, and from the nervous irregularity that in some cases produces, and in others is the product of, this dis-harmony. With some people, the brain may conceive the rhythms normally enough, having inherited a supply of clear and distinct rhythmic images, but the limbs, while perfectly capable of executing these rhythms, are hampered by a disordered nervous system. Others suffer from the inability of their limbs to execute the perfectly distinct orders of the brain, and this ineffectual nervous functioning eventually produces a breakdown of the system. With others again, who possess perfectly sound nerves and muscles, the clear registration, in the brain, of durable images is impeded by inadequate education in rhythm. *The object of rhythmic training is to regulate the natural rhythms of the body and, by their automatisation, to create definite rhythmic images in the brain.*

* * * * *

Some considerable time must elapse before the desired renaissance of rhythm in music can be accomplished,* but I claim that a relatively short time should suffice for a rhythmic training to reform musical, dramatic, and choreographic interpretations. In the first place, theatrical performers—actors, singers, and dancers—who undergo a course of such rhythmic training should at once realise that, without it, a satisfactory and rhythmic musical expression is out of the question. Nine-tenths of the auditors of an opera are unaware of the constant conflict between the orchestra and the action. Singers and dancers alike impose their gestures and attitudes, utterly regardless of time, on music which either they do not understand, or else understand imperfectly. Their feet are set in motion when they should remain stationary, their arms are raised when they should be motionless, their bodies no more harmonise with the music than would their throats if they sang out of tune or time, or suddenly began an air from another opera, while the orchestra continued to play from the original score! And these deficiencies are the product alike of the clumsiness of limbs ill-trained in rhythm and of a mind insufficiently cultivated, and consequently ignorant of the intimate relationship between movements in space and movements in time. I challenge any singer, be he the greatest genius in the world, to interpret plastically and with rhythmic feeling the simplest music, before he has undergone a special education designed to make his muscular actions correspond with sound movements.† This training should be accorded all operatic singers of the future, and should be taken in conjunction

---

* See Chap. VII., p. 110, "Rhythm and Musical Composition."

† The dissociation of movements of the larynx from those of the limbs is even more difficult to achieve than that of arms, legs, and head.

with their vocal training. The results would be such, I am persuaded, as to make it appear incredible that at any time the study of bodily rhythms should not have formed part of their dramatic training.

This rhythmic training should likewise have a place in the education of conductors, producers, and operatic composers, who should be initiated into the many resources of that most expressive instrument, the human body, before attempting to set it music to interpret. The relations between sound rhythms and plastic rhythms must also be taught all dancers, whose art, as fore-shadowed by Grétry, Schiller, Goethe, Schopenhauer, and Wagner, will thereby be ennobled, made at the ¦same time more human and more poetic, and will cease to be what it is to-day—a mere amusement for the legs, devoid alike of intellectual value, æsthetic or musical feeling, and social or artistic interest.

*　　*　　*　　*　　*

But ignorance of musical rhythm is not the only cause of the inferiority of artistic manifestations in which the body plays a part. Another mistake which tends to discount the sovereign importance of the body in our stage performances consists in taking as models for bodily movements attitudes stereotyped by painters and sculptors.

Often when present at displays of dancing, frantically applauded by eminently artistic spectators, I have wondered why my musical taste was offended, and why, despite the undoubted talent of the performer, a feeling of discomfort was awakened in me, as well as an impression of something artificial, something prepared and unnatural. I have heard painters, endowed with admirable judgment, express their enthusiasm at the splendour of the attitudes, the refinement of the gestures, the harmony of the groupings, and the audacity of the acrobatic movements; and while admitting these qualities, while bowing before so much artistic feeling, sincerity, ability, and knowledge, I could not bring myself to feel the slightest æsthetic emotion, and could only accuse myself of coldness, lack of understanding and philistinism.

A production of Debussy's *L'Après-midi d'un Faune* a few years ago revealed to me the cause of my misgivings and distaste. A procession of nymphs moved slowly on to the stage, pausing every eight or twelve steps to enable their charming attitudes (copied from Greek vases) to be adequately admired. On continuing their march in the last attitude assumed, they would attack the following attitude—at the moment of the fresh pause in walking—without any preparatory movement, thus giving the jerky impression that would be conveyed at the cinema by a series of movements from which the essential portions of the film had been suppressed. I then understood that what shocked me was the lack of connection which should be present in every manifestation of life heightened by thought. The exquisite attitudes of the Greek nymphs followed each other without any attempt at linking them by a human and natural process. They formed a series of pictures, most artistic in effect, but voluntarily deprived of all the advantages obtained by time-duration—I mean *continuity*, the potentialities of slow development, the easy preparation and, as it were, inevitable climax of plastic movement in space—all of them essentially musical elements, and which alone assure truth and naturalness to the union of gesture and music.

Guided by this experience, I analysed in the same way the movements of various dancers of the highest distinction, and noted that those among them who were most truly musicians, while endeavouring to follow the pattern of the music in the most scrupulous manner, had no more regard for the principle of continuity of movement and of plastic phrasing than the nymphs mentioned above. I mean that in the play of their limbs the point of departure was the attitude and not the movement itself.

Musicians will follow me : in composition of a contrapuntal nature, the lines of the polyphony are not
embroidered on a canvas formed of chords, chosen, fixed,
and linked together in advance. On the contrary, the
chords depend on the outlines and patterns of the melody.
The ear does not sense and analyse them as such, until
the parts cease moving and become sustained notes. In
moving plastic the same thing should happen. Attitudes
are pauses in the movement. Every time that, in the
uninterrupted sequence of movements forming what
might be called the "plastic melody," a punctuation
mark is inserted, a pause corresponding to a comma,
semicolon, or full stop in speech, the movement becomes
static and is perceived as an attitude.

But the real perception of movement is not visual ; it
is muscular, and the living symphony of steps, gestures,
and consecutive attitudes is formed and controlled not by
the agent of mere appreciation—the eye, but by that of
creation : the whole muscular apparatus. Under the
action of spontaneous feelings and irresistible emotions,
the body vibrates, starts into movement, and eventually
assumes an attitude. The latter is the direct product of
the movements which prepare it, whereas in choreographic
art of the present day, movement is only a bridge con-
necting two different attitudes. Thus there exists, in the
art of dancing, as at present understood in our theatres,
a confusion between visual and muscular experience.
Dancers * choose models for their attitudes among
masterpieces of sculpture or of painting, and take inspiration from Greek frescoes, statues, and paintings, ignoring
the fact that these works are themselves the product of
a special cultivation of style—of a sort of compromise
between the relations of movements, a series of diminutions and sacrifices which have enabled their creators to

* In several of her plastic interpretations, Isadora Duncan instinctively surrenders her body to continuous movement, and these are always
the most vital and stimulating of her dances.

convey the illusion of movement by synthetic means. But if it be necessary for the plastic arts, deprived of the help of the time element, to produce a synthesis by means of fixed corporal attitudes, it is against truth and nature for the dancer to adapt this synthesis as the starting point of his dance, and to try and re-create the illusion of movement by juxtaposing series of attitudes, linked, each to its neighbour, by gestures, instead of resorting to the source of plastic expression—which is movement itself.

Specialists in the visual arts may be justified in appreciating the present mode of dancing which, with the magic of colours, the startling contrasts of lighting, and with the help—as it were non-material—of the flowing lines of light or heavy drapery and costumes satisfies the most refined decorative exigencies, and furnishes the eye with an exquisitely picturesque enjoyment. But is this enjoyment of a spiritual and emotive order? Is it the real and direct product of deep and sincere feelings? And completely as it satisfies our yearning for æsthetic pleasure, does it saturate us with the creative emotion of the work?

Bodily movements are a muscular experience, and are appreciated by a sixth—the muscular—sense, which controls the multiple nuances of force and speed of those movements in a manner appropriate to the emotions that inspire them, and which will enable the human mechanism to refine those emotions, thus rendering dancing a complete and essentially human art.

Eurhythmics undoubtedly is based on muscular experience, and eurhythmicians watching exercises performed by fellow-students do not follow them merely with the eye, but actually with their whole being. They enter into close communion with the spectacle they are watching, experiencing thereby a joy of a peculiar nature, and a yearning to move, to vibrate in unison with those they see expressing themselves in physical movement. In short, they feel awakening and palpitating in them a

Study in Leaping (1)

mysterious music, which is the direct product of their
feelings and sensations. This music of the individuality
would suffice to control human movements, if mankind
had not lost that sense of order and of the shading of
physical expression, without which a revival of the dance
can never be achieved. There is no tradition of corporal
movements, and, as we have seen, modern dancers borrow
from the fine arts a cult of attitude which substitutes
intellectual experiences for spontaneous feelings, and
relegates dancing to a secondary plane in the realm of
art. There is only one way of restoring to the body the
complete scale of its means of expression, and that is to
submit it to an intensive musical culture, to give it
complete control of all its powers of dynamic and agogic
expression, and the power to feel all shades of tone-music
and express them muscularly. A special education will
liberate the music imprisoned in the soul of the artist—
the *individual* music that, entering into and fusing with
the music to be interpreted, gives it an increasing life,
so much so that the individual rhythms of all the
interpreters of a choreographic work achieve a collective
emotion that is the very genesis of style. As Elisée
Reclus puts it : "The people, of which we form part,
moves in consistent rhythm ; in each of us an inner
music, the cadences of which resound in our breasts,
controls the vibrations of our flesh, the movements of
our steps, the impulses of passion, even the course of our
thoughts ; and all these activities have only to unite in one
harmony for a multiple organism to be constituted,
comprising a whole crowd, and giving it a single soul."

* * * * *

This is not the place to analyse in detail all the
elements indicated above as being common to music and
plastic, nor to set out all the exercises designed to
awaken in the mind the sense of a fusion of these two
arts, superficially so different. I would commend to the
reader, desirous of familiarising himself with these exercises,

my book on Moving Plastic,* and will here confine myself to establishing certain fundamental relations between the two essential musico-plastic elements. (1) *Dynamics* (so-called)—that is, the science of gradations of force ; (2) *Agogics* (time-division)—that is, the science of gradations of speed. This latter involves a further element, (3) *the division of space*, these two conceptions being inseparable in defining movement.

It goes withont saying that the dynamic is closely related to the agogic element, and that the gradations of force are often inseparable from those of speed or slowness. But, for the sake of accuracy, we will consider each of these two concepts separately in the following tentative essay in classification. This classification does not claim to be definite, nor to comprise the whole of the questions relating to plastic. It is intended simply as a lucid, if abstract, exposition of the fundamental elements of moving plastic and their relations to music. These two arts, plastic and music, being essentially of a dynamic nature, it is natural that a study of the gradations of movement should be based on music. We will therefore designate as " musical movement " every movement conforming to the dynamic laws that govern music.

DYNAMICS

The function of dynamics in music is to vary the gradations of force and weight of sounds, whether abruptly, by the effect of sudden contrasts, or progressively, by *crescendo* and *decrescendo*.

The instrumentalist, entrusted with the interpretation of these musical-dynamic gradations, must possess the mechanism necessary for producing sound in all its degrees of force—for increasing and diminishing it according to the composer's intentions. Where the

---

* *Exercises de plastique animée.* Lausanne : Jobin & Cie. London : Novello & Co., 160, Wardour Street, W.

Study in Leaping (2)

instrument chosen for the interpretation of music is the whole human body, this body must have acquired a perfect knowledge of its muscular potentialities, and be capable of consciously exercising them. This will necessitate a profound study of technique in relation to musical dynamics : a training in the differentiation of joints, of which each must be exercised separately ; a training in muscular contraction and decontraction of the whole body, or of one of its limbs, or indeed of two or more limbs, operating with conflicting muscular gradations ; finally, a training in balance, flexibility, and elasticity.

In the majority of gymnastic systems of a hygienic or athletic character, dynamics dispenses with the help of agogics—that is to say, the movements are practised *quâ* movements, the instructors paying insufficient regard to the modifications introduced by differences of time-duration in the preparation for muscular activities. As will be seen from the succeeding section treating of the division of space by relation to division of time, it is only by the practice of special exercises that one is enabled to precede any bodily movement by a precise preparation ensuring its perfect execution.

The precise preparation and linking together of movements depend on the harmony of the nervous system. A good gymnast is not necessarily a eurhythmician and plastic artist. The training in corporal dynamics should therefore be completed by a study of the laws of agogics (division of time) and of the division of space.

DIVISION OF TIME ("AGOGICS") AND DIVISION OF SPACE

The function of agogics in music is to introduce variations in the duration of time, and to shade sounds in all degrees of speed, whether metrically (by a mathematic division of each sound into fractions of a half, third quarter, eighth, etc., of its time-value) or pathetically (by pauses—*rubato, accelerando, rallentando,* etc.).

Of all organic agents of agogic expression, the fingers are the best qualified to interpret quick passages—far better than the wrist that guides the violinist's bow, or the feet that operate the pedals of the organ. The aptest instrument for the execution of very slow sounds is the breathing apparatus, productive of the music of the voice and of wind instruments. The whole human body constitutes the ideal musical instrument that is most capable of interpreting sounds in every degree of time : the light limbs executing the rapid, the heavy limbs the slow, passages. It may achieve slow effects, unusual in music, by flexible succession of gestures, attitudes, and displacements ; and, moreover, may, by means of dissociated movements of separate limbs, interpret no matter what polyrhythm.

Unity in the division of time is achieved in bodily movement in the same way as in music. As regards division of space, we can only formulate a general principle—the application of which must be left to the initiative and whim of the teacher.

As we have seen, moving plastic is based on movement, and not on attitude. Its alphabet will therefore be composed of signs representing not the attitudes, but the passages from one attitude to another. The body in an upright stationary position may be regarded as the axis—so far as movements of the torso and head are concerned—of an imaginary sphere, which we divide by nine radii. Each of the radii (that is, the distance between the centre, and no matter what point on the circumference) may be subdivided into x notches. The sphere itself may be divided into eight horizontal segments (*planes*).

Each of these divisions is regarded as a resting-place, marking the boundaries of movements ; but in practice, each of these marks serves to represent the

distance between the starting-point and no matter which
of the resting-places. We also have occasion to utilise
these nine guiding-points as *lines of movement :* thus the
forearm may be made to follow line 8, while the arm
follows line 3, etc., and the torso, head, and arms can
be manœuvred differently in each of the eight horizontal
planes. When we add that we have devised eight ways
of utilising the joints of the arms, it will be appreciated
that the number of combinations is incalculable.

The space to be covered by the legs may also be
divided into eight planes, and the space within range of
the thigh into nine radii.

For the body in motion, we employ five steps of
different lengths, and thus create a great number of combinations of movements and new attitudes : each step
forwards, backwards, or sideways, modifying the position
of the body in relation to an arm fixed in a point of
space. To make ourselves quite clear, imagine the arm
outstretched in a horizontal line, the forefinger pressed
against the wall. To make a step backwards involves a
forward attitude for the arm ; to kneel down makes an
oblique line, etc. The point fixed in space is not
necessarily concrete, and in all our exercises in direction
in space the body evolves about an invisible and
imagined point.

DIVISION OF SPACE IN RELATION TO DIVISION OF TIME

A gesture executed in *x* time necessitates a given
muscular force. This muscular force is the product of
the relations between the action of the synergic and the
inhibitory muscles ; thus if a gesture executed in a
certain space of time is to cover the same distance in
a shorter space of time, the activity of the inhibitory
muscles is reduced, while that of the synergic muscles
increases, and *vice versa* (whether the movement be made
vigorously or gently, the proportions remain the same).

Thus, once one has decided to assume a definite attitude without stiffness, it becomes necessary to obtain from the muscles in question a sort of compromise between these two conflicting activities, and to exercise control over their relations, in such a way as to express the gradations of time and weight by appropriate movements.

Most novices are apt to make their gestures or steps either too late or too soon. The former—which is the most frequent case—arises from a surplus of activity in the inhibitory muscles ; the latter from an inadequacy of that activity.

DIVISION OF TIME AND SPACE IN RELATION TO THE SITUATION OF THE INDIVIDUAL IN SPACE

1. If we now consider not one moving body, but several bodies in motion at the same time, we are obliged to take note of the relations of these bodies between themselves. The student must adapt his movements to those of his comrades, mindful ever of the general effect. Movements are thus both perfected and simplified. The nuances of energy of each body in isolation have no influence on the general nuances effected by the group as a whole. By this means, a group of men can produce an impression of *crescendo* by an extension (the men spreading themselves out) or by a shrinkage (the men pressing together analogously to a muscle contracting). And *vice versa*.

2. To the same category belongs the study of the estimating of space to be covered : the space in which the body operates serves as a frame, to the dimensions of which the movements have to adapt themselves. Exercises in estimating space will depend on the *tempo* and on the nature of the rhythm of the movements.

3. It is of equal importance to set students exercises in composition (developments and successions of geometrical figures) to accustom their minds to conceive

ensemble effects in a given space, and teach them to apply them for decorative purposes.

PROGRESSIVE SUCCESSION OF GESTURES

The reciprocal relations between the elements constituting moving plastic, form the *phrasing* of movement.

In music, phrasing is a collocation of elements dependent on one another, constituting a more or less complete entity. In moving plastic, we may say that "every set of gestures in logical succession constitutes a phrase." In other words : if one gesture results from another, the two form a phrase.

Take, for example, the movements effected by a wood-chopper. In order that his two gestures—the raising and dropping of the arms—should form a single phrase, the first must be the preparation for the second, the second the inevitable result of the first. Any interruption, however slight and imperceptible, will suffice to produce two phrases—except, of course, where the interruption does not imply a real break, but takes place while the body is, so to speak, in suspension. (We shall return to this case later.) The moment the movement is interrupted, a fresh effort of the will is required for its resumption, which effort of will, being primarily independent of the preceding movements, may be exercised at any moment, regardless of the latter. It is not, therefore, the *result* of that movement.

We term *anacrusic* any action that discloses its preparation in such a way as to give this visible preparation the appearance of the act itself. The inevitable result of this preparation is subservient to the laws of gravity. As examples, we may mention the movements of the wood-chopper or blacksmith, and the actions of pulling and pushing, etc.

We term *crusic* any action the preparation of which is concealed in such a way that the result of this preparation appears as the real beginning of the action. The spontaneous movement that constitutes the action itself inevitably produces an involuntary and less emphatic movement—the reaction ; for example, the actions of rowing, reaping, planing, turning a lathe, drawing a bow, throwing a stone, etc. It goes without saying that the majority of actions may be at once crusic and anacrusic : that is to say, that the reaction from one movement may be the preparation for its successor.

SUCCESSIONS OF GESTURES FROM THE ÆSTHETIC POINT OF VIEW

The Plastic Value of the Gesture.—There is another element that should be mentioned with crusic and anacrusic actions, and that is the starting-point of the corporal phrase.

Voluntary actions should be localised—that is to say, the willing of a movement to be effected should be concentrated first in one or other different parts of the body or limb to be moved, so as first to distribute the effort and eliminate every useless muscular action from the movement, and then to adjust the effort.

In the movements of manual labour, this localisation is usually unconscious. Thus, with the wood-chopper raising his axe : if it is heavy, the starting-point of the movement will be in the back, which, in making the first effort, enables the arms to lift the axe more easily than if the effort had been confined to the hands ; if the axe be light, the hand holding the implement makes the first effort, and inevitably brings the rest of the arm into play. It is this localisation that gives the movement its plastic value. This principle is at the root of all æsthetic concatenation of movements. But once a movement is realised as part of a succession, the localisation is not essential, and its adoption becomes more complex. For instance, take again the gesture of raising the arm : the

Group Exercises

gesture may be effected so as to give the impression that the act of volition determining it has its starting-point either in the breathing, the arm, the forearm, or the hand, and that the parts of the body where the spontaneity of the first movement is not evident have been brought into play by the localised preparatory action.

If the movement to be effected is of no emotional or intellectual significance, generally speaking, it links in action heavy with light limbs.

The trunk being the heaviest limb of the body, and that first influenced by emotion, owing to the action of the diaphragm, it follows that the most important and common instigator of all movements is the breathing.

Breathing is at the basis of every manifestation of life, and plays as well æsthetically as physiologically a rôle of the very highest importance in moving plastic. (*Vide* in my book on Eurhythmics,* the chapter devoted to the different modes of breathing ; see also the little volume on my method, entitled " Breathing and Muscular Inervation " † (with anatomical diagrams).) It may be said in general that, even in cases where breathing does not engender the movement, the phrase will begin with an expiration and end with an inspiration.

Movements may, however, have their starting-points in other parts of the body. The torso, arms, legs, hips, hands, shoulders, may alike give the impulse to the movement. And once the attitude is assumed with its starting-point in one or other of the limbs, breathing will assume the function of modifying the intensity of the arrested gesture.

* " Eurhythmics," Part I., " Rhythmic Movement." London : Novello & Co., 160, Wardour Street, W. 1.

† *La Respiration et l'innervation musculaire,* Lausaune : Jobin & Cie. ; London : Novello & Co.

PLASTIC AND MUSICAL VALUE OF GESTURE

Every time our conscious will selects a starting-point for a movement, a new phrase is begun. We have already pointed out that the characteristic of a phrase is its collocation of elements dependent on one another and culminating in a rest. But these elements may be linked in succession in a manner more or less constant. Precisely as a literary phrase may be composed of different sentences, separated by commas or other punctuation marks, so plastic phrases may also comprise sentences independent of each other, separated by pauses. These pauses cannot be confused with the ends of phrases, since the body remains in a state of suspended animation : it is made apparent that its movement is to be continued, but the moment of continuation is not definitely indicated.

These points of suspension—plastic punctuation marks—correspond to accentuations in music, and stress the culminating points of musical phrasing. These culminating points—" rhythmic " points, as Mathis Lussy calls them *—are the climaxes of *crescendo* and *diminuendo*, the ascending or descending lines of which are more or less sudden or slow, complex or simplified. They depend not only on dynamics, but also on the harmonic succession of sounds. Corporal phrasing at these moments becomes absolutely of the same nature as musical phrasing, and, while achieving expression by its own technical processes, models itself on, and identifies itself with, the latter. We may find, especially in classical composers, a host of examples of musical passages lending themselves to corporal phrasing.

*   *   *   *   *

All the above indications relate to the corporal movements of a single individual. There remains to analyse

---

* *Le Rhythme musical*, Heugel, éditeur, au Ménéstrel, 2 bis, rue Vivienne, Paris.

the opposition of attitudes and gestures of two or more bodies in movement, two or more groups of individuals, a soloist and a group, etc. A host of combinations suggest themselves; and these, in their reunions and sequences, form what one may call the "orchestration" of human movement. The dynamic principles are quite different from those of a single muscular apparatus, and the guiding in space of an *ensemble* of plastic artists modifies the direction of the gestures of each isolated artist. A new polyrhythm is produced, compound of movements and lines, and the expression of which, even more so than the polyrhythm of a single body in motion, brings home to us the fact that moving plastic and music are two arts of the same nature, capable of heightening each other's effect, even if not created for that purpose. In endeavouring to express with the body the emotion evoked by music, we feel this emotion penetrate our organism, and become more personal and vital as it sets in vibration the deepest fibres of our being. The student, by gradually training his body in the dynamic and rhythmic laws of music, becomes more musical generally, and eventually capable of interpreting sincerely and spontaneously the intentions of the great composers, on no matter what instrument he may choose. The marching, running, and dancing to fugues of Bach will not constitute a *lèse-majesté* against that profound genius who composed expressly for the harpsichord; this corporal interpretation does not profess to render the complete thought of the master and to substitute an arbitrary mode of interpretation for the means of expression selected by him: it is merely a matter of the substitution, for the purely intellectual analysis of the work, of the experience of sensations of the whole organism. To bring out the different parts, dissociate the polyrhythms, realise the *stretti*, and oppose the nuances of dynamic contrasts will become for the student a perfectly natural process. All the structural details of the phrasing and shading will be made clear, because felt by the body—and so become organic. In short, the student will have the music within him, and his instrumental interpretation will become more convincing, spontaneous, vivid, and individual.

Again, the rhythmic and dynamic faculties of the body will expand as they take their starting-point in music—the only possible field of development. In fact, music is the only art, directly founded on dynamics and rhythm, which is capable of giving style to bodily movements, while permeating them with the emotion which has inspired it and which it in turn inspires. Once the body has become musicalised and saturated in rhythms and their nuances, moving plastic will gradually evolve into a higher and self-sufficient art.

*   *   *   *   *

It should also furnish the public with the opportunity of expressing its æsthetic will and its instinctive love of beauty in evolutions and combinations of gestures, steps, and attitudes, forming veritable festivals—musical and rhythmic. How fine is the sight of a host of men or children executing the same gymnastic movement in time ! But how much finer the effect of a crowd, divided into distinct groups, of which each takes an independent part in the polyrhythm of the whole ! Art thrives on contrasts, and it is these contrasts that form what we call the *values* of art. In a plastic display, the æsthetic emotion is produced by the opposition of lines and the contrasts of time ; and it is a powerful and really human emotion, because directly inspired by the mechanism of our individual life, of which we may retrace the image in the rhythmic evolutions of a whole populace.

Rhythm, as we have said, is the basis of all art ; it is also the basis of human society. Corporal and spiritual economics are a matter of co-operation. And once society is properly trained, from school upwards, it will itself feel the need for expressing its joys and sorrows in

Geneva Festival, 1914

manifestations of collective art, like those of the Greeks
of the best period. We shall then be offered well-
organised festivals, which will express the popular
æsthetic will, and where divers groups will perform in
the manner of individuals in a form at once metrical and
individual—that is to say, *rhythmical*, for rhythm is
"individuality given style." There are such wonders to
be created in the domain of collective rhythmic movement. So few people realise that this domain is almost
unexplored, and that a whole people may be made to
execute movements in order and symmetry without presenting the aspect of a battalion of soldiers ; that it may
counterpoint the musical design in a hundred different
ways by gestures, steps, and attitudes, while conveying
an impression of consistent unity and order. A generation of children trained in rhythm would prepare for itself
and for us undreamt-of æsthetic joys.* There is no
greater happiness than in moving rhythmically and
giving body and soul to the music that guides and
inspires us ; and it is virtually created by the possibility
of conveying to others what our own education has given
us. What can be more gratifying than to interpret
freely, and in an individual manner, the feelings that
actuate us, and which form the whole essence of our
personality — of externalising, without constraint, our
sorrows and joys, our aspirations and desires—of allying
eurhythmically our means of expression with those of

* I may be pardoned for mentioning, as a matter of record, my
Festival vaudois of 1903, in which, at Lausanne, under the direction of
Gémier, a chorus of 1800 persons took part, according to my principles
(long before the productions of Reinhardt) ; also the *Festspiele* of
my school at Hellerau, where for the first time, in 1911, I achieved, in
Orpheus, and other works, a polyrhythm of crowds on staircases
and inclines. Later, the performances of the *Fête de Juin*, in 1914,
at Geneva, where, apart from the dramatic scenes produced by Gémier,
the lyric parts of my work (text by Albert Malche and Daniel Baud-
Bovy) were interpreted by 200 rhythmic students, entrusted with the
plastic expression of the orchestral and choral symphony on a flat
surface, tiers and monumental staircases.

others—to group, magnify, and give style to the emotions inspired by music and poetry ? And this gratification is not of a passing, artificial, or abnormal order : it is an integral factor in the conditions of existence and the progress of the individual. It cannot but contribute to the raising of the instincts of the race, and the permeation of the altruistic qualities necessary for the establishment of a healthy social order.

XIII

To my friend,
PERCY INGHAM.

MUSIC AND THE DANCER (1918)

*The Philistine and the dance—Ignorance of the public—The muscular sense—
Dancing and imitation of clear-cut plastic attitudes—Qualities of emotion
and style—Nuances of force and flexibility, and their relations with those
of time—Opposition of gesture—Rests—The construction of a dance—
Space and direction—Conventional techniques — Dancing and musical
thought—Intellectual music and " living" music—Choreographic literature—Creation of a new musico-plastic style—The composers of to-morrow.*

CHOREOGRAPHIC performances have been for some years
past on the increase in every country, and the public
appears to be taking more and more to them. We
regard this as a healthy sign of the times.

In the old days, the provincial philistine would have
believed himself lost if his presence at a local performance of dancing had been discovered. Possibly he is
beginning to wonder to-day if dancing may not be—or be
capable of being—as pure and expressive as any other
art ? Doubtless snobbishness plays its part in this new
interest ; but the cult of sport is also partly responsible.
A training in gymnastics for hygienic purposes may
have awakened his interest in æsthetic gymnastics.
Unfortunately, this latter requires more encouragement
than is accorded it in contemporary sporting and society
circles if it is to contribute to the progress of
plastic art.

It has been said that in matters of choreography light
comes from the North. We, for our part, have always
found the ballet audiences at Moscow and Petrograd

221

content with a mere ocular amusement, and it was certainly not their influence that inspired certain talented Russian dancers to seek new outlets for their art. In fact, they constitute the most frivolous, inconsistent, and reactionary of any public, and the very last to regard the dance as other than a superficial entertainment. In other countries—in Sweden, France, Switzerland, Germany, and England—the public has far better judgment, discerns in dancing a higher medium of expression, and is only perplexed at not being able to explain the satisfaction it derives from its various forms. One has only to mingle with the audience in the intervals, or at the close, of a performance to appreciate their embarrassment at not knowing whether they have enjoyed or disliked the dancing, whether or not to yield to their first impression. The reviews in the Press the following morning set them at ease, and form the basis of their ultimate judgment. They have no suspicion that the critics—whatever their erudition and artistic taste in other branches—know as little as themselves in matters of dancing. Journalists, completely out of touch with the art of movement, regard themselves as authorities in matters choreographic ! As to those who specialise in drama and the ballet, they are so perverted by their familiarity with the old routine that they prove even less competent than the others to distinguish the sincere endeavours of genuine artists to restore natural dancing, from the pretensions of the swarm of opportunists on the make.*

It is hardly possible to appreciate any art without a

---

* It is significant that musical critics, who have received no ocular training whatever, consider themselves fully qualified to judge musico-plastic performances designed to appeal simultaneously to eye and ear ; while on the other hand, non-musical plastic experts do not hesitate to lay down the law on artistic manifestations, in which music plays a preponderant rôle. It is obvious that the criticism of performances involving a fusion of the arts of music and bodily movement should be entrusted only to individuals qualified to appreciate and analyse each of the separate constituents of this artistic combination.

certain understanding of the phases of its evolution and the laws of its technique. How is one to produce any sort of constructive criticism on the decadent dancing in vogue to-day, or to appreciate new reforms, unless one feels the need for these reforms, and attempts to ascertain and analyse the source of that feeling—and, before all else, to establish the nature and purpose of the art that for the last fifteen years has been steadily deteriorating?

In analysing painting and music, our eyes and ears—however badly trained—provide us with the points of comparison necessary for any serious attempt at an objective appreciation. But fully to appreciate the style of human movement, we require a special—the *muscular* —sense, complemented by what scientists have called the kinæsthetic or stereognostic sense (or simply sense of space), and what Professor L. Bard, of Geneva, has recently and aptly described as sense "of gyration." Neither conventional gymnastics, sport, nor lessons in deportment and grace suffice for this purpose, the movements they produce having no direct relation with the multiple nuances of agogics (variations in time) and of dynamics. On the other hand, our instinctive appreciation of human attitudes, lines, and gestures is warped by a conventional education restrictive of all spontaneous corporal expression, to say nothing of a long addiction to stock theatrical fare.

Numerous dancer-artists have trained themselves to assume attitudes borrowed from Greek statuary, and have sought to revitalise them, in reconstructing plastic masterpieces challenging comparison with the original. But we must remember that the isolated figures of classical sculptors were each and all directly inspired by the highly complex art of *Orchesis;* an art which, according to Lucian and Plato, consisted in "expressing every emotion by means of gesture." The fixing and elaborating of the supreme climaxes of dancing and gesticulation is fatal to the continuity of movement, and destroys the logical

succession of attitudes.* It is therefore not enough for
the modern dancer to reproduce certain decorative
classical attitudes—which, in the Greek *orchesis*, would
merely indicate pauses—in order to resuscitate and
rhythmicise the life that animated classical dancing. Nor
will a public, that has been soundly educated in movement, be satisfied with the choreographic performances of
the present day, which consist of a series of charming
plastic themes and graceful attitudes inconsistently and
artificially linked in succession. It will demand, apart
from the quintessential emotion,† the qualities of style,
form, and development of contrasts and gradations
required for manifestations of any complete and vital
art.

Every really musical spectator should be able to
judge whether a virtuoso has adequately analysed the
work he is professing to interpret to convey its message
and general emotion—or whether he has merely studied
the different passages, one after the other, without
attempting to animate the whole with a consistent
impulse of organic life.

The spectator of a plastic interpretation should also
demand from the dancer general qualities of form and of
gradation in development, and not be content with the
successions of isolated effects, and " moments," without
cohesion, to which too often dancers of the new school
confine themselves ; and choreographic composition
should be as carefully formed as musical or pictorial
composition. Its life and emotion should be given style,
and this style will depend as much on the position, value,
and proportion as on the intensity of its expressive
elements. In a conception of moving plastic, the

---

* See page 204, lines 15 *et seq.*

† A curious phenomenon : many artists, who demand qualities of
refined emotion and feeling from music and painting, express themselves
as satisfied with interpretations of dancing from which emotion—
voluntarily or involuntarily—has been entirely excluded.

executant requires not only all the resources of corporal technique, but in addition a training in their careful and conscious application, in the subordination of particular to general effects, the combination and contrasting of the latter, and the modification or even elimination of particular elements, in accordance with absolute principles, the observance of which (whether spontaneous or deliberate) produces *style*.

The significance of an arm gesture depends on the contrasting or parallel attitudes of the head, the other arm, legs, and torso, the divers motions of breathing, variations in balance produced by the displacement of the weight of the body—and the time occupied in their deployment. To an untrained spectator, none of these nuances will be noticeable.* His only concern is that the arm should be rounded and graceful. Just as an auditor whose hearing faculties are undeveloped must fail to appreciate melodic and harmonic successions, and the divergences of sound relations, so the spectator who lacks an adequate visual training can follow only the general outline of a gesture, and is incapable of distinguishing its relations in space, and sensing the greater or lesser muscular intensity. I recall, after a display by Isadora Duncan at the Châtelet Theatre, hearing people, of artistic repute, confine their remarks to the physical proportions, and, in particular, the bare feet of the dancer—which is equivalent to an audience at a pianoforte recital confining its attention to the qualities of the instrument, and ignoring those of the interpreter.

Confronted with the delicate shading of gesture effected by dancers like Sakkaroff, the untrained spectator will exclaim : " It's the same thing over and over again," without perceiving that in fact these artists are performing before him the whole scale of variations of a single gesture. And he will applaud, in other dancers, a gesticulation over-elaborated and lacking in rests, which

* See Chapter XII., pp. 214 and 215.

Q

is the common failing of many quite sensitive and enthusi-
astic beginners. . . . And this raises the question of the
importance in plastic interpretations of the elimination of
useless movements, the installation of rests, the distribution of expressive effects over localised parts of the
organism, counterpoint, phrasing, polyrhythm of associated
and harmonisation of synergic movements. . . .

Another factor in plastic unity and order to which
too little attention is devoted is the understanding of
the relations between movements and displacements of
the body and the space in which they are executed. A
certain popular dancer, in particular, whom we remember
as giving us the impression of a bird fluttering frantically
about its narrow cage, in search of an outlet, was doubtless unaware of the fact that the dance of a soloist
requires to be composed with the same care for lines and
direction as the evolutions of a company, whether of
soldiers or dancers. According to the construction
of a dance, the eye of the spectator records an impression
of order or disorder, harmony or decorative anarchy.
The evolutions cannot be consigned to the impulse or
inspiration of the moment, any more than, in musical
counterpoint, the lines of polyrhythm may, without
danger, be submitted to a course of modulations and
rhythms traced at haphazard. It is important, in music,
that the repetition of a theme—in a Rondo, for example
—should be confined to a particular key ; the particular
quality of the refrain lies in the manner in which the
composer has prepared its re-appearance in the initial
key. Similarly, in the *plastic* interpretation of a rondo,
it is essential that the attitude and movements interpreting
the musical theme into corporal language should be
concentrated, at the moment of the repetition, in a fixed
portion of space. The space of which a dancer avails
himself should be a matter of careful consideration, and
his position deliberately and not arbitrarily related to the
construction and proportions of the work to be interpreted.

Every concatenation of movements and displacements of balance or evolutions results inevitably in a " resolution " (to use the musical term), a climax, in the centre or in one of the corners of the space, whether on a flat surface, or on an incline or graduated plane. An attitude transferred from one point of space to another must either gain or lose in expressive force. According to its direction, and the distance from its base, it may entirely change its significance. The pre-arranged disposition of lines constitutes a factor in the retrospective appreciation of a dance (by visual memory), of which few dancers appear to suspect the importance.

But so far we have confined ourselves to the essentially plastic side of the problem. Indeed, it is this aspect which makes the most direct appeal to both public and critics, and apparently the only appeal to dancers. The musical atrocities perpetrated by certain illustrious nonentities in the art should, to our mind, arouse the indignation of all lovers of music. There are times when protest becomes a matter of duty. And yet the majority of so-called connoisseurs object at most to the *external* side of the interpretations. We submit that a dancer has no right to be ignorant of and to despise the music which he chooses as a pretext for his evolutions. There is an intimate connection between sound and gesture, and the dance that is based on music should draw its inspiration at least as much, and even more, from its subjective emotions as from its external rhythmic forms.

A gulf separates the movements of the Greek *orchesis* from those of our modern ballet. And yet it is indisputable that the majority of the latter were originally founded on the purest classical traditions : only the spirit that animated the dances of the ancients is extinct ; life has left them. There remain only a few fundamental attitudes and positions, but how restrained and systematised ! The divers motions of the arms, for example—the innumerable symmetrical and asymmetrical positions that provided all the resources of gesticulation—have been replaced by a solitary circular movement, devoid of all expressive or mimetic value, partaking exclusively of the nature of gymnastics. The same applies to the positions of the legs, head, and torso. On the other hand, a special technique has been devised to develop the action of leaping (to the detriment of expressive walking), and has replaced the pursuit of natural balance by means of slow or quick corporal displacements by abrupt tensions on tiptoe. Dancing has become a form of acrobatics, and the arms are employed merely to maintain balance. This has produced a species of physical deformity that prevents the dancer, habituated from his youth to the processes of the traditional ballet, from cultivating an easy and natural slow gait, the divers brachial dynamisms, and, generally, the most simple expressive expedients of the dance " à la Duncan." One cannot serve both God and Mammon.

One must, however, admit that some of the ballet effects in question possess a certain grace and picturesqueness that may give rise, on occasion, to considerable pleasure. But it is a pleasure confined to the eyes, and cannot attain any really emotional or musical value.

And yet music is the basis of the most conventional dance, and we have a right to demand from dancers that elements of musical phrasing, shading, time, and dynamics should be observed by them as scrupulously as practicable. To dance in time is not everything. The essential is to penetrate the musical thought to its depths, while following the melodic lines and the rhythmic pattern, not necessarily " to the letter"—which would be pedantic—but in such a way that the visual sensations of the spectator may not be out of harmony with those of his auditive apparatus. Music should be to dancers not a mere invitation to the play of corporal movements, but a constant and profuse source of thought and inspiration *musical*, and not literary, inspiration—for the stagey effects of external imitation and the transmutation of natural musical impulses into sentimental little stories should be confined to Pantomime. Music should reveal to the dancer inner and higher forces that any intellectual analysis or pursuit of the picturesque can only weaken. It will serve his purpose only so long as he does not exploit it in the interests of an exclusively ratiocinative expression.

But it must not be inferred that, to revive musico-plastic art, it will suffice to give our dancers a sound musical training. They must in addition be made to understand the intimate connection between musical and bodily movement, between the developments of a theme, and the successive sequences and transformations of attitudes, between sound intensity and muscular dynamics, between rests and pauses, counterpoint and countergesture, melodic phrasing and breathing—in short, between space and time.

This understanding cannot be improvised, but necessitates a general training. We do not commend it to dancers who aim no higher than at the amusement of the eye or the exercise of their muscles—nor to those whose vocation consists in executing popular and national dances, the Court dances of past ages, or the capricious evolutions of the modern ballroom and café. But it is essential to every dancer who ventures to transpose works of absolute music into corporal movement. There may exist, in the theatre, an art of "decorative plastic" confined to embellishing the outlines of musical architecture, but there also exists an *expressive* plastic, the rôle of which consists in extracting from music its ideal aspirations and whole emotional life. This should not be undertaken unless accompanied by a profound respect for music as an inspiring force, and for the human organism as its potential interpreter.

We must bear in mind that plastic is never necessary to "absolute" music, which works in the deeps of the

spirit, and the emotions of which frequently suffer by
being brought to the surface. Music is certainly the
most potent agent that exists for revealing to man all the
passions that surge in the obscure profundities of his
subconscious self. Its vibrations suffice to awaken and
distribute his feelings; its tonal and rhythmic combinations constitute a special language complete without the
addition of any other agent of expression. Every phrase
directly issued from an essentially musical soul is self-
sufficient, and any attempt at strengthening the expression
by means of mediums of another order can only prejudice
its clarity and power. Why should we desire to improve
on it, when it is complete in itself? Similarly, any
direct revelation of inner feeling by means of moving
plastic can only assist the sound expression, where it is
a spontaneous emanation, and manifests itself in a
naturally emotive, eloquent, and distinct form. In so
doing it qualifies as music itself, since the art of music is
only, in R. Pasmanik's definition, the "revelation of the
quintessence of the universe."

But just as music may be allied to the word in the
form of music drama or ballad, so it may be combined
with plastic to express elementary emotion in a mixed
language. In the one case as in the other, music must
be kept within bounds, and obliged to diminish its
expressive power to enable the element with which it is
associated to assert itself, not with redundancy but in
collaboration. Combination implies assimilation; only
such poems as are designed by their authors for a musical
complement should be set to music, and only music that
has been intended by the composer to be completed by
human movement, or which is modelled on the primitive
forms of the dance, should be expressed plastically. Thus
in a great number of the instrumental pieces of the sixteenth and seventeenth century the rhythm is of a
manifestly corporal origin. The same rhythms permeate
the choral music of the seventeenth century. The

majority of the chorales of Albert, Schein, Hassler, Krieger, etc., are really dance music. Many of the French, English, and Italian works of the same epoch are of a similar character. The later Corantes, Passepieds, Allemandes, and Sarabandes of J. S. Bach were written in the form of dances, just as a number of his fugues (Nos. 2 in C minor, 11 in F, 15 in G, etc., of the "48" Book I., for example) were constructed on popular dance motifs.

All the inventions and fugues designed for amusement without regard for any intimate emotion, and the sole aim of which is to depict a sort of chase, may be interpreted by human groups in lines, fleeing from each other. The rhythmic impression produced by the rich polyphony must in my own, as well as in the opinion of such fervid Bach enthusiasts as Ad. Prosniz, Fritz Steinbach, R. Buchmayer, Ch. Bordes, etc., be thereby considerably enhanced. Nevertheless their counterpoint is often of such a strictly digital character, that a corporal interpretation can only be achieved at the cost of a fatal decrease in pace. That is why it should be essayed—as with the abstract thematic developments of the succeeding period (Haydn, Mozart)—only in an analytic and pedagogic spirit. The same risk attaches to orchestral transcriptions, for dancing purposes, of modern and romanticist pianoforte pieces. We recall with a feeling of discomfort the cumbersome effect of Schumann's Carnaval interpreted by the Russian Ballet in the style of pantomime. Dancers would do well to insist on contemporary composers writing special music for them. But the latter must bear in mind that the collaboration of gesture, while it offers them novel and interesting possibilities, imposes certain special restrictions on their freedom of expression.

We shall require the composition of a music intentionally non-rhythmic to allow for completion by rhythm of a corporal character. On the other hand, the harmonious attitudes of dancers exclusively occupied in interpreting the superficial aspect of certain soul-states might be accompanied by musical rhythms to strengthen the vital impression of their ideal representation. The dance could also be made to serve to express the Dionysian side of artistic expression, while music conveys the Apollonian side or, conversely, sounds could reproduce the frenzy of elemental passions in sensorial language, while the dance embodied their decorative forms in space. In the one, as in the other case, we should achieve a spiritualisation of matter, a pure expression of soul, an idealisation of form, and an emotionalisation of sensation.

It is always dangerous to attempt to adapt subjective music, of an essentially human character, to the physical resources of temperament. The intimate essence of a work is never wholly revealed to us when an instrumentalist—or conductor—endeavours to adapt it to his individual manner of expression. In making the work his own, he robs it of its universal emotional character. He is not interpreting, but rather transforming, re-creating, it. The inevitable coarsening of a thought cannot fail to jar on those who were familiar with it in its original form. In a musico-plastic combination, no one of the agents of expression should seek to fuse completely with another : each should endeavour to bring out the other. To obtain this result, it is necessary not only that the dancer should be completely initiated into musical science, but that the composer should utilise every one of the expressive potentialities of the human organism.

A musician would not venture to compose a violin *concerto* without a knowledge of the resources of that instrument. How then can he dare project a score for that complex instrument, the human body, without familiarising himself with its capacities for interpretation ? If he understood these, he would not limit himself to recording musical rhythms, and leaving the *maître*

de ballet to procure their imitation by his troupe, he
would produce a score wherein the miming, gestures,
movements, and attitudes of the dancers would be as
scrupulously entered as are those of the string, wind,
and percussion instruments in a symphony.

Instead of always developing the sound and plastic
movements along parallel lines, effects of contrast might
be achieved in the metre and rhythm as well as in the
melody and harmony. For instance, music arranged in
simple time (binary pulse) might be set off, as in oriental
music, by plastic motifs in compound time (ternary pulse).
To the rhythmic accentuations of each tonal phrase would
be opposed corporal accentuations emphasising other
fragments of the same phrase. Musical melody might
be applied to a harmony of plastic movements executed
by several individuals acting in concert, or in groups,
or—by way of variation—a succession of corporal movements of a monorhythmic character might be accompanied by harmonies of sound. One might devise a
whole harmonic system of gestures arranged in chords
and having their inevitable resolutions like combinations
of sound.

Effects of concord and discord, of contrast and fusion,
created by the combination of orchestral symphony and
corporal polyrhythm, might be enriched by various combinations involved in moving plastic—which demands,
before all else, the co-operation of groups of individuals.
A dancer would require to be a genius of a very high
order to dance solo to divers musical works throughout
a whole recital without producing an effect of monotony.

Too many solo dancers are content to narrate corporally a series of little stories, without attempting to
vary the medium of expression. Varieties of facial play
do not suffice to produce varieties of movements of the
whole body. There is not a single musical iustrument—
with the exception of the polyphonic piano—that could
be played, to the exclusion of every other, for two

consecutive hours, without wearying an audience. And the same applies to the solo dancer. While, on the other hand, the union of a number of dancers permits of as much variety of effects as the play of several instruments. The associations of timbres present combinations analogous to those produced by human masses differently grouped.

It remains for us to indicate under what conditions there might be created—as a contrast to absolute music—a special music adapted to gesture, and which, while distinct from the music of pantomime, would, like it, be deprived of all technical development, constructed on simple and regular lines, and would leave—at considerable sacrifice—a large scope for the collaboration of human movements. Its function would consist in inspiring and animating the body—the source of its own inspiration and animation—in acting both as its master and its servant, identifying itself with it, while preserving its own individuality.

A difficult and complex task, no doubt, but one that will certainly be accomplished, once the dancer has become a musician, and can persuade the composer to spare him the effects of merely decorative music, and devote his gifts along the lines of a more human and vital art. A new style will have to be created, product of the collaboration of two equally expressive arts, with the potential participation of a whole public trained to co-operate with the artist, and to assume a responsible part in his performances. The time is ripe—as Adolphe Appia has told us—to assert the dignity of our dramatic instincts, the triumphal gateway giving access to all the other arts . . . This "living fiction" alone can confer on us a status in the art realm, and can initiate us into the mysteries of style. This transfiguring art—the art that by its rhythm unites our whole organism to the quintessential expression of the soul—would seem to be on the wane ; but it is only a cloud that obscures it. . . . Music is always with us. Let us open ourselves to it ; we have relinquished to it the ardent expression of our inner life, let us yield to its new demands, deliver up to it, without reserve, the whole rhythm of our bodies, to be transfigured and emerge in the æsthetic world of light and shade, forms and colours, controlled and animated by its creative breath.

XIV

RHYTHM, TIME, AND TEMPERAMENT (1919)

*Balance of physical and emotional faculties—Rhythm and its characteristics;
continuity and repetition—Time an intellectual principle—Necessity for
counterbalancing regularity of movements by contrasting spontaneous impulses. Danger of stereotyping instinctive motor faculties—Rhythm and
intuition—Motor habits and character—Manifestation of divers temperaments —Table of qualities and defects of a rhythmic nature, in untrained
children—Association and dissociation of motor and auditive faculties—
Natural aptitude for rhythm and music in children of different European
countries.*

Music is the direct reflection of emotional, as of material,
life, and musical rhythm is only the transposition into
sound of movements and dynamisms spontaneously and
involuntarily expressing emotion. Consequently evolution in the art of Music must depend on the progress of
the individual, by means of a careful training in the
balancing of his physical and moral, instinctive and ratiocinative forces. As a matter of fact, very few people
would suspect that, if every form of artistic progress
depends on a general mental advance, a reform of musical
education can only be achieved through a reform of
general education. The latter in our present-day schools
lays stress on mere instruction, concerning itself exclusively with intellectual development, and ignoring the
cultivation of temperament.

A balance of the fundamental faculties of the individual
can never be attained unless, from an early age, the
organism is habituated to the free play of its forces, an
unhampered circulation of the divers currents of its

thought and motor powers, and a regular alternation—
controlled alike by sub-conscious instincts and conscious
will-power—of physical and spiritual rhythms, of which
the ensemble constitutes temperament. The man of
science should be capable at a moment's notice of
translating himself into a man of action. Indeed, the
ideal education, and that especially to be desired, now
that the war is over, is one which will enable our children
to subordinate their practical to their mental habits, and
to convert their intellectual rhythms, as occasion demands,
into physical actions of the same order. The "intellectual" should no longer be differentiated from the man
of physical capacities. There should be a medium of
free exchange and intimate union between the respective
organs of corporal movement and of thought. No longer
should our divers functions be isolated by voluntary
specialisation. A harmonisation of our nervous system,
the stimulation of slack motor centres, control of instinctive behaviour and spiritualisation of corporal manifestations, should establish a unity in our organism both for
preparatory and executory purposes. And the training
involved is neither forced nor laborious—on the contrary l
Our freedom as men of thought and action depends on
this unity of the rhythms of thought and life. A time
will come when our bodies attain—through a complete
reconquest of the muscular sense—an independence
bringing our acts into direct union with our desires.
Therein lies the cure for neurasthenia, and the recipe for
the constitution of the "whole man," whose vital expression, at once spontaneous and complete, shall have the
double character of a materialisation of the ideal, and an
idealisation of physical potentialities. The two poles of
our being will be intimately connected by a single rhythm :
the expression of our individuality. And, thereupon, art
will lose its metaphysical character, and constitute a spontaneous manifestation of our inner being, directly representing the rhythms of its life.

The characteristics of rhythm are continuity and repetition. Every motor manifestation, isolated in time, presents an exceptional and momentary emotional aspect, which is lost the moment it is repeated to form part of a continuous whole evolving at once in time and space. The two fundamental elements of rhythm, space and time, are inseparable. In certain of the arts one or other of these elements may be predominant ; in music, and in the supreme art—life, they are indissoluble and of equal importance. Life, in effect, is itself a rhythm, that is, a continuous succession of multiple units, forming an indivisible whole. Individuality may also be regarded as a rhythm, for the combination of its faculties, many of them conflicting, constitute an entity. But every life and every work of art that conforms only to the idiosyncracies of the individual is a-rhythmic, for the rhythm of art and of life demands the fusion of all traits of character and temperament.

Metre, an intellectual expedient, regulates mechanically the succession and order of vital elements and their combinations, while rhythm assures the integrity of the essential principles of life. Metre involves ratiocination, rhythm depends on intuition. The metrical regulation of the continuous movements constituting a rhythm should not be permitted to compromise the nature and quality of those movements.

The musical education, following the lines of the general education provided in our schools, is inspired by the desire to regulate sounds and harmonies, establishing the theories of the science, and reducing it to a system, all of them activities of a material order. Certainly regularity and precision of movements are sure evidence of healthy volition, but educationists are mistaken in regarding the will as the sole medium of control, begetter of a complete, individual, and well-proportioned work of art. The creation of a movement of synthetic life is a matter of temperament ; pedagogues are oblivious of the fact that a special training will develop the spontaneity of vital rhythmic manifestations, and by placing the student in a position to feel clearly every instinctive movement, and providing him with the means of subduing all the forces inhibitory of the expansion of his motor habits, will enable him also to breathe in a new emotional atmosphere, and free his emotions to attain a maximum intensity. Instead of directing musical studies towards rhythm, we limit their scope to the metrical plane. The encouragement, by assiduous cultivation, of the efflorescence of motor impulses is neglected in favour of a concentration on the creation of measured volitions. The same applies to dancing, which, in our best known academies, is confined to the acquirement of a corporal technique; the training aims at the conquest of measure, and is confined to the regulation of arbitrary successions of gestures and movements, instead of inspiring, by the development of temperament, the expansion of natural corporal rythms. Music and dancing alike are at the present day taught along mechanical lines.

A machine, however perfectly regulated, is devoid of rhythm—being controlled by time. To regulate the movements effected by a manual labourer in the exercise of his calling, is by no means to assure the rhythm of his activity. The handwriting of a copyist conveys the impression of mechanical and impersonal regularity. That of a writer, giving rein to his inspiration, records, on the other hand, the rhythm of his temperament. Versification is only the metrical side of poesy. The rhythmics of poesy depends on the underlying thought, impulse, and non-reasoning qualities. Natural dancing may be duly measured, without revealing the impulsive spirit, the physical and moral phantasy—that is, the rhythm—of the dancer. The submission of our breathing to discipline and regularity of time would lead to the suppression of every instinctive emotion and the disorganisation of vital rhythm.

The voluntary exercise of the recurrence of the beat assures regularity—and there are times when this regularity is indispensable. But to confine oneself to this form of activity would be to risk depriving one's character of all spontaneous vital expression. Time furnishes man with an instrument, which, in many cases, ends by making him its servant, influencing the dynamic and agogic elements in his movements, and repressing his individuality in favour of a conventional mechanism. The metrical regulation of bodily movements—one of the main features of most systems of gymnastics—has been made possible by the discovery that many organisms have lost their elementary character and natural impulses, and require to be remoulded through the will. But in every healthy body, the need for movement is associated with other needs of a super-metrical order (as Lieut. Hebert well understood), and the resultant expression arises from the nervous constitution of the organism. If we consider the art of movement on the stage, we must recognize that as soon as the artist—be he dancer or comedian—attempts the arbitrary and artificial regulation of his gestures, and is content to conform to the laws of measure and decorative effect, his play loses all rhythmic spontaneity. Metrical regulation must be subservient to rhythmic impulses.

The same applies to music, where the metric tradition kills every spontaneous agogic impulse, every artistic expression of emotion by means of time *nuances*. The composer who is obliged to bend his inspiration to the inflexible laws of symmetry in time-lengths comes gradually to modify his instinctive rhythms, with a view to unity of measure, and finishes by conceiving only rhythms of a conventional time-pattern. In the folk song the rhythm responds spontaneously and naturally to the emotion that has inspired it, and is not fettered by any metrical rules. Not only do unequal bars succeed each other in flexible and harmonious alternation, but the principle of irregularity of beats is audaciously asserted, in defiance of hallowed laws. All music inspired by folk tunes rings rhythmic and spontaneous, and the irresistible impulse of Russian music, and of the modern French school, is due to their instinctive return to the natural rhythms of folklore. But once this return is pre-meditated, the rhythms lose their sincerity and vital quali-ties, for, we must never forget, rhythm is a non-reasoning principle, originating in elementary vital emotions. Only the cultivation of primitive instincts, a " clean sweep " of our present selves, by a re-training of the nervous system, can give our motor organs the faculties of elasticity, re-silience, and relaxation, the free play of which will give rhythm to the expression of our emotional being.

This training is also the only one that can restore the art of dancing. The present training obliges the dancer to illustrate by concurrent steps and gestures a music deprived of rhythm by the exclusive cultivation of metre. There again we find the mechanism of instinctive motor qualities, and the intellectualisation of fundamental emo-tions. The imperative impulse evoked by a feeling can express itself adequately only by the aid of a spontaneous gesture. Once the will has intervened, the current between nerves and muscles is interrupted. Under these conditions, all exercises aiming at the automatisation of conventional successions of gestures and attitudes are prejudicial to the development of the rhythmic faculties. A renaissance of the dance can only be achieved by the subordination of *external metre* to the free and continuous expression of *inner rhythms*. Æsthetics should be born of Ethics. In the same way, musical rhythm can only flourish with the support of expressive elements issued directly from the depths of the ego and supplanting all the formulas of metre.

Apart from that, artistic feeling can only be developed with the co-operation of music, the only art inherently free from ratiocination. To suppress, by certain educative

R

means, the nervous and intellectual inhibitions that prevent the organism from submitting to the control of musical rhythms, and to teach that organism to vibrate in unison with sound vibrations, will be to liberate impulses long repressed by a mechanical training, restricting the instinctive. inspiration of mankind ; more, it will idealise our physical, and resuscitate our spiritual, forces, and thus herald the birth of a musical art at once more emotional and more vital.

        *   *   *   *   *

The rhythm of every work and of every action reacts immediately on the nature or the degree of individuality of its author, representing always the direct expression of the sensations and feelings of the individual. Doubtless it can be imitated and stereotyped, but in that process it loses its fundamental principle, being born of emotion, which can only be expressed by means directly inspired by intuition. The imitation of elemental rhythms relates to the realm of purely intellectual processes, based on deduction. As James Shelley has aptly expressed it, in an article on Rhythm and Art : " Rhythm is to intuition, emotion, and æsthetics what scientific order and logic are to the intellect. One of the essential qualities—if not *the* essential quality—of rhythm is its power of conveying the presence of life. Mechanical order, on the other hand, is objective and impersonal. . . . Time passes and is scientifically recorded by the mechanical oscillations of the pendulum. And yet for some of us time 'ambles withal,' for others he 'trots and gallops withal,' for others, again, 'he stands still withal.' "

There is an immediate connection between the instinctive movements of our body, the continuity of which forms and assures rhythm, and the processes of our psychic life.

It would seem that rhythm imprints a definite character on the speculations of thought, moulding their form of expression and dictating the language suitable for revealing the fundamental principles of sensorial life and transplanting them into the realm of emotion. It would seem, moreover, that by virtue of some secret mechanism not yet defined by psycho-physiologists, the mind possesses the power of choosing from among all the motor sensations of the individual those most congenial for transfiguration into durable impressions and definitely rhythmic images.

The more we succeed—thanks to our education—in detaching our instinctive corporal movements from the shackles forged by circumstances and environment, and preserved by heredity, the more we shall eliminate intellectual and nervous inhibitions, adverse to the spontaneous motor manifestations of our organism ; the more also will our muscular play evoke precise rhythmic images, expressive of our individuality, for the service of the mind, and the latter will contrive to record certain sequences in such a way as to confirm its momentary impressions. These sequences will vary according to the state of the mind at the moment it is engaged in fixing these images. Intuition will indicate those that must be eliminated to avoid compromising the direct expression of the temperament, as "attuned" at any given moment of our life. This attunement is capable of considerable variation, and that is why the rhythms of certain works of art may appeal to us differently, according to the moment when they are presented to us, although our mechanical processes of judgment cause us to appraise them, from the intellectual point of view, in a consistently similar manner.

The function of temperament should be to adopt spontaneously every motor manifestation capable of expressing the particular state of our organism at any given moment. To contrive, by means of a special training, to enable the child to sense distinctly the nature of its instinctive corporal rhythms, and of their divers successions, is to render him capable of sensing life itself in a more freely emotive spirit. Emotions can only attain their maximum intensity when all the faculties of the being expand in a single harmony, while nerves and muscles expend their emotive force with full, synergic, and precise power. How can we expect the child's sensibility to flourish if we do not cultivate his elementary vital manifestations from the first, and throughout his school training ? Surely it is the most bizarre of anomalies to teach him the rhythms of the speech and thought of others before enabling him to sense those of his own organism ?

* * * * *

The question of education assumes a capital importance in relation to post-war generations. This is universally recognised, and England—among other countries—has for two years already been seeking the means of according more ample space in its curriculum for experiments aiming at the imbuement of self-knowledge and the harmonisation of intellectual and ethical conceptions with the most simple means of expression, founded on a perfect understanding of their physical potentialities. The Minister of Education himself contributes to the investigation of current methods of scholastic instruction, and takes a personal interest in all research for means of developing the child's temperament, and faculties of free will. This example will certainly be followed sooner or later by all other countries. It is the duty of educational authorities to see that education does not stagnate, and to seek progress in the direction of a new system designed, at elementary schools as at the universities, to limit the number of purely intellectual subjects in favour of conveying to the minds of our future citizens what we may call their temperamental sense.

The possession of highly developed impulses and racial instincts should be supplemented by the power of controlling these faculties by an intelligence instructed in the diversity of their powers. Education must no longer confine itself to the enlightenment of pupils in intellectual and physical phenomena. It must conduce to the formation of character, assuring to children the consciousness both of their weaknesses and of their capacities, and rectifying the former as it strengthens the latter, while enabling them to adapt themselves to the exigencies of the new social order. It is no longer a question of a simple development of the scientific and analytical mentality, but rather of an evolution of the entire organism.

It is often in the most trivial actions that the most intimate traits of character reveal themselves. Motor habits betray them as distinctly as facial expression. Motor habits can be modified by education and transmit this improvement to the character. "Education without a definite aim produces an indefinite character," as Legouvé expressed it, and, conversely, one that aims consistently at the regularisation of organic functions under the control of a lucid, well-ordered, and resolute mind must inevitably influence the character in the same direction. Character is not only the direct expression of temperament, but also the product of the mind's discoveries, in relation to the general faculties of the motor and nervous systems, the control and harmonising of which form part of its functions. And, if Taine was right in affirming that "the character of a people may be regarded as the compound of all its past sensations," it follows that the acquisition of more numerous and stronger sensations, under the influence of a new education, must serve to create in our mentalities reactions inevitably modifying the essence of our character.

*   *   *   *   *

It is difficult to determine whether one race is endowed with stronger rhythmic sense than another; but it is obvious that the influences of climate, customs, and historic and economic circumstances must have produced certain differences in the rhythmic sense of each people, which are reproduced and perpetuated in such a way as to imprint a peculiar character on the dynamic and nervous manifestations at the root of every original corporal rhythm. Certain peoples, for instance, present marked differences in their muscular capacity (which, according to Peron, is greater in Europeans than in savage races) and in the nuances of their nervous manifestations. The structure of the human body also varies according to race, and must play an important rôle in all forms of motor expression.

Temperament is obviously responsible for the motor form of corporal rhythmic phenomena. Certain peoples are more nervous than full-blooded, more lymphatic than choleric, and it does not require a profound analysis or a multitude of experiments to determine the enormous influence of the fusion and association of temperaments on the phenomena of reaction and corporal expression, on variations of dynamics, agogics (that is, shading of time), and manipulations of space, produced by different aptitudes for natural rhythmic actions. The divers degrees of susceptibility of the motor organs introduce nuances into the spatial character of gestures and their dynamic expression. Rhythmic faculties are undoubtedly less highly developed in some countries than in others, but as these depend not only on the muscular and gyratory senses, but on the general or particular state of the nervous system, we may assume that they may easily be modified by training. The same applies to gifts of hearing and distinguishing of sounds which, conjointly with rhythmic qualities, constitute the substance of musical talent.

— *   *   *   *   *

Rhythmic training can make a person musical, since impressions of musical rhythms inevitably evoke some sort of motor image in the mind, and instinctive motor reactions in the body, of the hearer. Muscular sensations

eventually coalesce with auditive sensations which, thus
reinforced, add to the faculties of appreciation and
analysis. The ear and the larynx are organically related,
and their functions are connected by synergic forces
dependent on the associated nerve centres. The vibrations
perceived by the ear may be increased by the augmentation of the vibratory power of other corporal sources of
resonance; for sounds are perceived by other parts of
the human organism besides the ear.* By the association
of his motor and auditive organs a child is enabled to
imitate vocally the rhythm and melody of a song. With
those who can imitate only the rhythm, and sing the
tune incorrectly—and who are conscious of this defect—
it is practicable, indeed, generally easy, to rectify the
accuracy of the voice, once regular exercises have developed
the inner muscular sense.

* * * * *

Character and temperament are easily recognised, not
only by the speed of gestures, and the form of attitudes,
but also by the nuances of tone of voice, and the rhythms
of articulation. Children of a lymphatic tendency speak
and sing quite differently from their robust or nervous
comrades; and so with their motor manifestations.
Travellers visiting a foreign country for the first time
obtain an impression of the general character of the
people from the accent and modulation of their speech.
Consider the difference between the muscular lassitude,
the nonchalant facility, the heavy and coarse good nature
in the oral rhythms of the Vaudois, and the monotonous
recitative and hesitations of the Genevan, and his guttural
tone produced by constant nervous resistance and muscular
contractions. Again, what crispness, abruptness, harsh
and deliberate aggressiveness in the Prussian speech!
What imagination and conflict of rhythms in the impulsive

* I knew a person, deaf from birth, who never missed a musical
performance, and was sensitive not only to the dynamic but also to the
harmonic qualities of the music.

volubility of the Latin, what terseness and purity in the Englishman's modulation of vowels, what melancholy and lack of balance in the excessive contrasts of pitch in the case of the Slavs !

A child devoid of rhythmic feeling will punctuate a song in the same manner as that in which he moves, while walking and gesticulating. But there are considerable differences in rhythmic aptitudes, and innumerable gradations also in the divers manifestations of a musical temperament, in respect of faculties of intonation and audition.

We find, at one extreme, children completely devoid of rhythmic and musical feeling, to whom all sound is mere noise, and who, though intelligent generally, are sheer idiots musically—their ears impervious even to the nuances of spoken sounds (gentleness, severity, irony, etc.).

Others are endowed with well-developed rhythmic sense, marching and gesticulating in time and with ease, but are unable either to distinguish or to sing a tune.

Others—good rhythmicians—can at first distinguish tunes only by their rhythms, and cannot recognise simple successions of unrhythmic sounds. In these, once they are submitted to a training by and in rhythm, one may produce a longing to distinguish the sound of tunes, which leads in time to the attainment of this faculty.

Others, again, are born with good ear and rhythmic sense. . . . But this class may be subdivided into infinite categories and sub-categories.

Good hearers, for example, may be bad readers and singers, and *vice versa*.

Good hearers of isolated sounds or tunes become bad or mediocre, when it is a question of distinguishing chords and successions of harmonies.

Good hearers may be incapable of mentally co-ordinating and analysing their auditive sensations.

Good hearers may be able to appreciate pianoforte

music, but not that of other instruments or the human voice, and *vice versa*.

Good hearers may be subject to periods of bad hearing (nervous depressions or over-stimulations), or, again, may hear well only during a portion of the music lesson (that probably where their natural instinct does not clash with mental effort, or where, on the other hand, fatigue disturbs the mental concentration necessary to certain people to assure good hearing).

As to the divers aptitudes of a-rhythmic subjects, they are likewise of very different natures. Some of them exhibit :

(1) Ease in conceiving or seizing musical rhythms, but difficulty in expressing them.

(2) Ease in expressing rhythms with certain limbs (*e.g.* the arms) and difficulty with others (for example, in walking in time or in dancing).

(3) Ease in expressing rhythms with the voice, difficulty in executing them with the body, and *vice versa*.

(4) Ease in executing rhythms with any limb or organ separately, but not with combinations of arms and legs, arms and voice, voice and legs, etc.

(5) Ease in executing known rhythms, but difficulty in distinguishing and memorising unknown ones.

(6) Difficulty in understanding, distinguishing, and executing rhythms, but ease in continuing this execution once they are known and assimilated, and the limbs made flexible by exercises adapted to the special nature of the rhythms.

(7) Difficulty in continuing correctly for long a rhythm which has been commenced correctly.

(8) Difficulty in dispensing with constant mental control of the body (whence arises a lack of ease and smoothness in the movements or the unconscious alteration of rhythms).

(9) Difficulty in retaining the mental impression of

a rhythm without continual recourse to physical sensations.

(10) Difficulty in accustoming limbs to certain automatisms.

(11) Difficulty in interrupting automatisms, whether acquired with ease or difficulty.

(12) Ease in acquiring automatisms in certain limbs, difficulty in combining them with automatisms in another limb.

(13) Ease in imagining and then executing rhythms, difficulty in executing rhythms given by another, and *vice versa*.

(14) Ease in distinguishing and executing the most complex rhythms, difficulty in distinguishing the most simple polyrhythm.

(15) Ease in executing rhythms in a certain movement, difficulty in varying their speed.

(16) Ease in executing a rhythm without dynamic shading, difficulty in introducing any kind of emotional accentuation or nuance without modifying the form.

(17) Ease in shading a rhythm, but at the sacrifice of metrical accuracy, etc., etc.

All these difficulties arise from :

Muscular weakness—Lack of nerve tone—Muscular stiffness—Muscular hypersensitiveness—Nervous disharmony—Lack of balance due to inadequate sense of space—Excessive intrusion of critical faculties, producing continual intellectual resistance—Lack of concentration—Lack of flexibility in analysing—Deficiency of muscular memory—Deficiency of cerebral memory—Lack of will-power—Excessive energy—Deficiency of resolution—Excess of self-confidence—Lack of self-confidence, etc.

     *   *   *   *   *

I have had occasion to note all these defects and the multiple combinations of their principal elements, in children of nearly every race and type, in the course of twenty-five years' experience not only in teaching eurhythmics and developing auditive faculties, but also in producing my action songs for children, designed for accompaniment by gesture. These roundelays have been sung in every country, and I have often been amazed to note the extreme difficulty the little singers have experienced in moving gracefully to the rhythms of music, and in counterpointing the simplest melodies with gestures in time—and how resistances of every kind impede the free play of their instinctive rhythmic movements. It was the observation of this too common a-rhythm that encouraged me to pursue my physiological studies to the point of instituting a new form of education. This education aims at restoring to the child his complete corporal mechanism and freeing his "natural rhythm" (that is, the spontaneous motor expansion of his temperament), from the inhibitions which too frequently impede its expansion. I think I may claim, despite the rash criticisms of those who judge my method only from its external side, to have thus created an indispensable complement to the education of children in every country. If the children of one country reveal blemishes in the motor system not to be found in children of another country, there are also appropriate exercises to combat all forms of bad motor habits, and to transform them into new and good ones, and the teaching of eurhythmics should certainly vary according to the temperament and character of the children of every country in which it is introduced. It only remains to persuade psychologists and educationalists alike to direct their experimental researches towards the study of rhythmic aptitudes and motor and auditive predispositions. Meanwhile it may be of interest to record certain observations of a general character on the rhythmic and musical aptitudes of children of the countries I have had most frequent occasion to visit. I hasten to disclaim any scientific exactitude for these impressions.

*　　*　　*　　*　　*

Genevan children possess in general a less flexible vocal apparatus than the children of German Switzerland. Their capacity for distinguishing sounds, on the other hand, is more developed than in the German-speaking cantons, especially among the middle classes. Rhythmic feeling, hopelessly deficient in the old Genevan families, is quite normally developed among the proletariat, where it is not perverted by pronounced nervous and intellectual resistances. In German Switzerland, as in South Germany, metrical feeling is more conspicuous than rhythmic feeling, and a superficially rhythmic individuality is often marred by extreme muscular stiffness, prohibiting the dynamic and agogic shading necessary for the externalisation of natural rhythms. This stiffness is far less common in the Rhine provinces, and is only rarely found in Austria and Hungary. In these two countries movements possess an extraordinary elasticity and variety, as among the working population of certain Russian provinces. But this refinement of rhythmic feeling and capacity for shading movements is counterbalanced, in Austria by a mental versatility often disconcerting, and in Russia, among the *intelligenzia*, by a hyper-sensitiveness, producing the same inhibition as the introspective excesses that de-rhythmicise Genevan society. Auditive faculties, highly developed in Austria, are very slight in Russia, where, moreover, the vocal powers of children are frequently of a deplorably low standard. I am speaking, of course, of the children and adults whom I have had occasion to teach, and whose studies and interpretations have been conducted under my control.

In Germany, where the love and cultivation of music is more general than anywhere else, the auditive sense is certainly not more refined than in any other country. Extreme mental slowness—combined in males with an excess of self-confidence—impedes the functioning of the agents of analysis, or, at any rate, involves a considerable waste of time between sensations and deductions. This defect is compensated, especially among women, by qualities of perseverance and assimilation, rarely to be met with among the Slavs, whose sudden enthusiasms, ardent aspirations, and commendable ambitions for intellectual, artistic, and social progress are counteracted by their irresolution and constant crises of moral depression and distrust of self.

Swedish children are remarkably well endowed with rhythmic faculties, and possess quite naturally a feeling for bodily harmony. I have not had sufficient opportunity of following the development of their auditive faculties to enable me to speak authoritatively on the subject, but their musical feeling and vocal capacities are certainly above the average. The primary schools lay great stress on gymnastics, and, in recent years on music, the stimulating influence of which was perceived by their great educationalist Ling. A movement is in vogue in that country for the revival of folk-songs and dances, spontaneous representations of which by school children in the open air may be witnessed in all parts of the country. In Norway, musical instruction in schools also shows an upward tendency, while musical aptitudes are approximately the same as in Sweden. The charming old town of Bergen holds in summer a largely attended public orchestral concert twice daily, and the children emerge from their schools singing and dancing. The plastic talents of these children are no less pronounced in country districts than in the towns. One may see little peasant children, after a few months' physical training, moving with really marvellous grace and natural balance.

One finds the same ease of movement in Danes, but this quality is—with rare exceptions—not applied to such refined æsthetic conceptions as with Swedes. The obsolete cult of "grace for grace's sake" is still in force there, and the public, infatuated with ballet dancing, appreciates hardly any but external virtuoso effects. In purely musical gifts they appear to me to be entirely deficient, and Denmark requires, more than any other country, a thorough overhauling of its system of musical training in schools.

Dutch children are naturally good singers, less good at hearing, and fairly rhythmic. All these faculties are admirably developed, thanks to the constant individual efforts of several distinguished educationalists. But their æsthetic sense and taste for moving plastic are unfortunately perverted by their poverty of muscular elasticity, looseness of tissue, and defective corporal build. It is to be hoped that an intensive physical culture will lead, as in Sweden, to a development of motor aptitudes.

— The movements of English children are not restrained by any of the inhibitions encountered so commonly among Slav and Latin peoples. They have none of the muscular stiffness or mental dullness of the German, and are free from nervous and intellectual weakness, possessing a highly flexible corporal méchanism and a very special capacity for plastic and rhythmic expression. But if the development of Russian children is impeded by their hypersensitiveness and frequent nervous disturbances, that of the English suffers from a contrary tendency. Their lack of nervous sensitiveness deprives them of emotional emphasis, and their easy and graceful movements are devoid of elasticity and dynamic shading. Their muscular tension rarely attains a degree equal to the minimum among the Latins. As to their actual musical feeling, it is by no means of so low a standard as is generally asserted on the Continent. The people undoubtedly love music, and their hearing and vocal capacities are normal. As in Sweden, the old folk-songs have regained a position of honour ; it is quite common to see children dancing and singing in the streets, and their choral singing in the frequent popular performances of old English mystery plays is remarkable for its accuracy and balance. On the other hand, music is too commonly regarded, in social circles, as a mere accomplishment, and its cultivation in schools and private musical academies is largely superficial and conventional. Once the efforts of the reconstruction enthusiasts have succeeded in obtaining a due regard for music and Eurhythmics in the school curriculum, the English people will not be slow in attaining a standard worthy of the descendants of the great composers who represented it so honourably in the seventeenth and eighteenth centuries.

I have, unfortunately, not had the opportunity of studying French, Italian, and Spanish children adequately to express a definite opinion on their capacities. Musical education is very lightly regarded in their schools, and, on the other hand, their musical students rarely emerge from their respective countries. I have, however, had occasion to observe the French students of my Eurhythmic Institute at Geneva ; I have also attended performances of my children's songs in various important provincial schools, and been present at Eurhythmic classes in Paris. . . . The feeling for vigorous accentuation seemed to me far more developed than in England, but there was less ease of movement, and the stiffness of gait and gesture seemed curiously inconsistent with the mental and imaginative flexibility of the people. I do not attribute this stiffness to either nervous or intellectual causes : it is more probably due to the absurd fear of ridicule which produces, both in the family and at school, an excessive repression of physical manifestation of feeling, too often accompanied by reserve due to sex feeling. It is gratifying to find that sport has at last—thanks to the efforts of a few influential persons—entered the curriculum of masculine education, but physical culture does not yet form part of the training of children, being reserved for adults, while intellectual rather than physical or musical games are cultivated at schools. Even among the people—I speak of the Parisian people, the only ones whom I know well —dancing aptitudes are little developed, and public balls are patronised chiefly by professional dancers, whose grace is often not overmarked at that. Once let them cultivate their natural individual gifts—as they do on the stage—and they will show evidence of sufficient artistic feeling and imagination to furnish high hopes for the development of rhythmic bodily movements among the people, so soon as steps are taken in that direction. Incidentally, French children love movement, and I have noticed in several classes of suburban elementary schools with what delight the children took to Eurhythmics, and, on the other hand, with what amazement school inspectors regarded their great joy.

From the auditive and vocal points of view, the same obstacles impede the normal development of natural aptitudes. The Frenchman, as a musician, reveals artistic qualities of the first order, a highly flexible sensitiveness, an innate sense of proportion and balance, and a delicate feeling for nuances. But efforts should be made in this country to liberate music from its monopoly by an aristocracy, and to introduce it, by a greater care for the inner life of the child, to the homes of the people—where, at present, it appears to be in uncongenial surroundings. One never hears French children spontaneously singing national folk-songs on school excursions, nor is part-singing cultivated by students in their social gatherings. And yet there is no dearth of choral works available for execution.

* * * * *

It will be seen from these summary observations that rhythmic and musical instincts vary according to the natural dispositions of races.

They are not the same in Russia as in England, in France as in Sweden, in French as in German Switzerland, even in Lausanne as in Geneva.

In certain countries, dynamic feeling and the sense of intensity of nervous reactions require to be developed, and more frequent and spontaneous motor manifestations provoked ; in others, on the contrary, quite other results should be sought, nervous manifestations requiring to be tempered, and the dynamic play of muscles softened. In one country vocal training, in another the development of hearing faculties, will require special attention. In every country, Jewish children should be especially urged to undergo a training in Eurhythmics, for, while their musical faculties and artistic intelligence are in general of a remarkably high order, their a-rhythm and lack of harmony in motor and nervous functions are liable to hamper their æsthetic development and their attainment of intellectual and physical balance.

These remarks, however disjointed, are based on a whole series of positive experiments, rarely before attempted by psycho-physiologists. Every people is capable of evolving to its advantage or disadvantage according to the care with which its children are reared from infancy. Whatever the curriculum or scholastic methods in vogue, it is essential for the progress of every race that education should aim primarily at the formation of character, and the cultivation of temperament, and should comprise—with regard to music—the development of auditive and vocal faculties, and the harmonisation of motor habits.

MUSICAL SUPPLEMENT.

EXAMPLE Nº 1.

a) *Lengthening a note by half its value.*

Dot after a note

Two dots after a note.

Three dots after a note

b) *Lengthening a note by one quarter of its value.*

The second dot under the first.

A dot after the two dots, one above the other.

Two dots one above the other after the first dot.

c) *Lengthening a note by one eighth of its value.*

Three dots one above the other, etc.... etc....

d) Notation of the note-value of ¼ of a Semibreve

		2/4	
		3/4	
		4/4	
		5/4	
		6/4	
		7/4	
		8/4	
		9/4	
		10/4	
		11/4	
		12/4	
		13/4	

d) Notation of the note-value of ⅛ of a Semibreve

		2/8	
		3/8	
		4/8	
		5/8	
		6/8	
		7/8	
		8/8	
		9/8	
		10/8	
		11/8	
		12/8	
		13/8	

EXAMPLE Nº 2.

$$\frac{3}{4} - \frac{3}{\rho} \;\Big|\; \frac{6}{8} = \frac{2}{\rho \cdot} \;\Big|\; \frac{12}{8} = \frac{4}{\rho \cdot} \;\Big|\; \frac{9}{8} \;\; \frac{3}{\rho \cdot} \;\Big|\; \frac{6}{4} = \frac{6}{\rho}$$

or $\frac{3}{\rho}$ or $\frac{2}{\rho \cdot}$ | $C = \frac{4}{\rho}$ ₵ *(alla breve)* $- \frac{2}{\rho}$ etc, etc.

EXAMPLE № 3.

Theme.

1) LENGTHENING OF A BEAT. (Pause written out: Agogic accent)

2) ADDITION OF A REST. (Ritenuto, Hesitation, Agogic resistance.)

3) REPETITION OF A BEAT OR A RHYTHMIC ELEMENT.

4) ADDITION OF AN APPOGGIATURA. Extension or Expressive amplification of a melodic and rhythmic element.

5) ADDING OR LENGTHENING BY AN ANACRUSIS OR A METACROUSE ENLARGEMENT OF A MELODIC LINE.

6) EXTENDING OR SHORTENING A RHYTHMIC ELEMENT BY TWICE AS SLOW AND TWICE AS FAST. (accel. rit.)
a) DOUBLING THE LENGTH OF A BEAT.

b) DOUBLING THE LENGTH OF A BAR.

c) HALVING THE LENGTH OF A BEAT

EXAMPLE Nº 4.

Theme

a)

b)

c)

EXAMPLE № 5.

ANALYSIS AND COMBINATION OF TIME ELEMENTS CONSTITUTING A RHYTHM.

Theme. is composed of three elements.

DIFFERENT COMBINATIONS OF THESE ELEMENTS.

(musical notation examples a through t, with anacruses)

EXAMPLE Nº 6.

ACTIVITY AND REST. — CONTRAST AND BALANCE.

A) *A rhythm several times repeated, followed by a rest the value of the whole rhythm.*

1) *(musical notation)*

CONTRASTS OBTAINED BY SHORTER RESTS. (*Rest the value of one beat.*)

2) *(musical notation)*

CONTRAST OBTAINED BY A DIFFERENT RHYTHM LESS IMPORTANT (*a link to join two rhythms*)

3) *(musical notation)*

B) *An unfinished rhythm followed by an incomplete bar.*

4) *(musical notation)*

CONTRAST BY REPEATING A RHYTHMIC ELEMENT.

5) *(musical notation)*

C) *Rhythm with anacrusis. Contrast by the omission of the anacrusis.*

6) *(musical notation)*

D) *Contrast obtained by different tone quantity.* (dynamic shading.)

7) *(musical notation)*

or *(musical notation)*

or *(musical notation)* or *(musical notation)*

or *(musical notation)* ff   pp

E) *Contrast obtained by a change of harmony or melody.*

8)

F) *Contrast obtained by variation of tempo* (agogic shading).

9)

rallentando

G) *Contrast obtained by different articulation.*

10)

Legato   *sostenuto*

H) *Contrast by change of bar-time.*

11)

I) *Contrast by diminution of a rhythm* (twice as fast.)

12)

b) *by augmentation of a rhythmic element* (twice as slow)

13)

c) *by diminution* (three times as fast).

Lento

(14)

J) Rhythmic squareness of classical composers not necessary for phrase balance.
Rhythmic contrast is sufficient.

———————— 2 bars ————————   ———— 3 bars ————

15)

———— 4 bars ————   —1 bar—   —1 bar—

(Valse.)

16)

K) *Contrast obtained by the alternation of another rhythm.*

17)

L) *Two rhythms alternating and followed by an arrest.*

Rhythm A.

Rhythm B.

DIFFERENT COMBINATIONS.

1) AAB (arrest) BBA—ABAB—BBABA—

2) ABB — BABA—A —B —BAAAB

EXAMPLE Nº 7

SUBDIVISION OF LONG NOTE-VALUES INTO DIFFERENT GROUPINGS.

1) $\left(\frac{2}{\text{r}}\cdot\right)\left(\frac{6}{8}\right)$ and $\left(\frac{3}{8}\right)\left(\frac{3}{4}\right)$

a)   b)

Examples.

c)   d)

2) *The combination of a beat of* 3 ♪ *and a beat of* 2 ♪ *in a bar of* $\frac{5}{8}$

Example.

a)   b)   c)

Unequal beats may be formed on the same principle in any kind of bar, *e.g*

3) A BAR OF $\frac{8}{8}$

a) *Regular divisions.*

Irregular divisions (unequal beats).

b) In 4 unequal beats.

c) In 3 unequal beats.

d) In 2 unequal beats.

f) *Rhythms.*

h) The same rhythm in $\frac{4}{4}$

i) The same rhythm in 3 unequal beats.

4) A BAR OF $\frac{9}{8}$

a) *Regular divisions* $\frac{9}{8}\left(\frac{3}{8}\cdot\right)$

b) *Irregular divisions (unequal beats)*

c) In 4 unequal beats.   d)

8

e) *In two unequal beats.*

f) *Rhythms.*

h) *In three unequal beats.*

5) A BAR OF $\frac{10}{8}$

A) *Regular divisions.*

B) *Irregular division.*

Rhythms.

6) A BAR OF $\frac{12}{8}$

A) *Regular division.*

B) *Irregular divisions (unequal beats)*

Rhythms.

7) A BAR IN $\frac{15}{8}$

A) *Regular divisions.*

B) *Rhythms with unequal beats*

8) CONTRASTS OF DIFFERENT SUBDIVISIONS OF LONG NOTE-VALUES IN SIMUL-
TANEOUS MELODIES.

EXAMPLE № 8.
1) MELODY IN ⅜ WITH UNEQUAL BEATS.

2) MELODY WITH UNEQUAL BARS.

3) MELODY WITH UNEQUAL BEATS.

4) SYNCOPATIONS OF UNEQUAL NOTE-VALUES.

EXAMPLE N⁰ 9.

CHANGING THE TEMPO BY TRANSFERRING THE BEAT TO A DIFFERENT NOTE VALUE.

♪ = ♪

♪ = ♪ of the preceding triplet.

♪ = ♪.

♪ = ♪

♪ = ♪ of the preceding duplet.

2)

3) Lento   *♪ = ♪ of the preceding quintolet.*

EXAMPLE N⁰ 10. Rests

a) *A rest on a strong beat is stronger than one on a weak beat.*

b) *The importance of a rest corresponds to the rôle played by the sound which it replaces in the musical phrase. A rest which lasts for a whole bar is more important than a rest which lasts for one beat only.*

*Notice the ₗₖₚ in this last rest.

c) *Crescendi, diminuendi, accelerandi and ritardandi continue during rests.*

d) *A rest replacing a rhythm anticipated* (dramatic effect).

Agitato.

e) *The length of a rest can vary.* (Extending and contracting metrical periods.)

f) *Rests gradually replacing the anacrusis of a rhythm.*

g) *Sudden exhaustion.*

h) *Gradual exhaustion.*

i) *Re-commencement.*

(The interpretation of the return of a theme after a silence varies accord_
.ing to the character of the preceding rhythm.)

j) *Force or accent can persist during a period of silence.*

k) *Fatigue can persist after a period of silence.*

l) *Gradually increasing during the silence up to the return of a theme.*

m) *Relaxing during silence.*

EXAMPLE.

SONATA Op.10. Nº 3. (Rondo)

BEETHOVEN

Allegro. *Rhythmic swing interrupted,*

See also:
Mozart, Sonata
for piano, in C minor.
(assai allegro.)

EXAMPLE Nº 11. HALVING THE VALUE OF A BEAT.

a)   *1) Without anacrusis*   *With anacrusis.*

        (Feminine rhythm.)   (Masculine rhythm.)

This halving of note-values is frequently met with in both classical and modern
works, but it is rare with an anacrusis.

2) Without anacrusis.   *With anacrusis.*

3) Without anacrusis.   *With anacrusis.*

b)   DOUBLING THE VALUE OF A BEAT.
      1) Without anacrusis.   *With anacrusis.*

2) Without anacrusis.   *With anacrusis*

etc.

c)   SUCCESSIONS OF AUGMENTATIONS AND DIMINUTIONS.
   (*Irregular circulation of the blood.*) The exact repetition of a rhythm twice
as fast or twice as slow produces unequal bars.

1.

2.

d) Syncopations twice as fast and twice as slow.
(Most of the following rhythms are found in Oriental music.)
  1) Without anacrusis.

  2) With anacrusis.

e) Melodies with augmentation and diminution.

f) A compound beat (ternary) three times as fast or slow.

(To find thrice the speed of a note, divide it into 3 parts and use only ⅓.)

g) QUADRUPLE RHYTHMS 3 TIMES AS FAST OR AS SLOW. (*Without altering length of bar.*)

1. Three times as fast.

Mathematical notation.

2. Three times as slow.

3. Rhythms.   or   or: Mathematical notation.

etc.

h) AN ISOLATED BEAT TWICE OR THREE TIMES AS FAST OR SLOW.

1.

2.

3.

i) AN ISOLATED SYNCOPATION TWICE OR THREE TIMES AS FAST OR AS SLOW.

1.

2.

3.

4.

Engraved & Printed by HENDERSON & SPALDING, Ltd , Sylvan Grove, London, S E 15

PRINTED IN ENGLAND BY
WILLIAM CLOWES AND SONS, LIMITED,
LONDON AND BECCLES

CPSIA information can be obtained
at www.ICGtesting.com
Printed in the USA
LVHW021117090423
743870LV00004B/184